RESCUING MALIA

GUARDIAN HOSTAGE RESCUE SPECIALITS: CHARLIE TEAM

Book 6

ELLIE MASTERS   MASTER OF ROMANTIC SUSPENSE

USA TODAY BEST-SELLING AUTHOR

JEM Publishing

Image/art disclaimer: Licensed material is being used for illustrative purposes only. Any person depicted in the licensed material is a model.

Editor: Erin Toland

Proofreader: Roxane Leblanc

Published in the United States of America

JEM Publishing

∿

Paperback ISBN: 978-1-964261-64-5

Dedication

This book is dedicated to my one and only—my amazing and wonderful husband.

Without your care and support, my writing would not have made it this far.

You pushed me when I needed to be pushed.

You supported me when I felt discouraged.

You believed in me when I didn't believe in myself.

If it weren't for you, this book never would have come to life.

Also by Ellie Masters

The LIGHTER SIDE

Ellie Masters is the lighter side of the Jet & Ellie Masters writing duo! You will find Contemporary Romance, Military Romance, Romantic Suspense, Billionaire Romance, and Rock Star Romance in Ellie's Works.

YOU CAN FIND ELLIE'S BOOKS HERE:

ELLIEMASTERS.COM/BOOKS

SUGGESTED READING ORDER

START HERE

Rockstar Romance

The Angel Fire Rock Romance Series

EACH BOOK IN THIS SERIES CAN BE READ AS A STANDALONE AND IS ABOUT A DIFFERENT COUPLE WITH AN HEA. IT IS RECOMMENDED THEY ARE READ IN ORDER.

Heart's Insanity

Ashes to New

Heart's Desire

Heart's Collide

Hearts Divided

Hearts Entwined

Forest's FALL

Hearts The Last Beat

Jenna's Protector

Rescuing Sophia

Rescuing Malia

Rescuing Ally

Delta Team (Coming Soon)

Rescuing Ember

Rescuing Aria

**STANDALONES IN THE GUARDIAN HOSTAGE RESCUE
SERIES YOU CAN READ ANYTIME**

Military Romance

Guardian Personal Protection Specialists

Sybil's Protector

Lyra's Protector

The One I Want Series

(Small Town, Military Heroes)

By Jet & Ellie Masters

EACH BOOK IN THIS SERIES CAN BE READ AS A STANDALONE AND IS ABOUT A
DIFFERENT COUPLE WITH AN HEA.

Saving Abby

Saving Ariel

Saving Brie

Saving Cate

Saving Dani

Saving Jen

The LaRouge Triplets

Asher

Brody

Cage

Billionaire Romance

Billionaire Boys Club

Hawke

Richard

Contemporary Romance

Cocky Captain

Romantic Suspense

EACH BOOK IS A STANDALONE NOVEL.

The Starling

The Swan

~AND~

Science Fiction

Ellie Masters writing as L.A. Warren
Vendel Rising: a Science Fiction Serialized Novel

**If you enjoyed this book by Ellie Masters, the LIGHTER SIDE
of the Jet & Ellie writing duo, and aren't afraid of edgier
writing, you might enjoy reading BDSM themed books
written by Jet, the DARKER SIDE of the Masters' Writing
Team.**

The DARKER SIDE

Jet Masters is the darker side of the Jet & Ellie writing duo!

Romantic Suspense

Changing Roles Series:

THIS SERIES MUST BE READ IN ORDER.

Command Me

Control Me

Collar Me

Embracing FATE

Seizing FATE

Accepting FATE

HOT READS

A STANDALONE NOVEL.

Down the Rabbit Hole

Light BDSM Romance

The Ties that Bind

EACH BOOK IN THIS SERIES CAN BE READ AS A STANDALONE AND IS ABOUT A DIFFERENT COUPLE WITH AN HEA.

Alexa

Penny

Michelle

Ivy

HOT READS

Becoming His Series

THIS SERIES MUST BE READ IN ORDER.

The Ballet

Learning to Breathe

Becoming His

Dark Captive Romance

A STANDALONE NOVEL.

She's MINE

ONE

Malia

DEAR DIARY,

SORRY, I haven't written in a while. Life's been crazy, like *cray-cray* crazy. Ever since Jenna was kidnapped, my life hasn't been the same. I thought she was lost to me. Little did I know she was rescued by real-life heroes.

The Guardians.

That's what they call themselves. Men who do anything to protect the ones they love.

And not just the ones they love.

I should amend that statement.

These modern-day superheroes risk their lives every day to rescue complete strangers. Not that Jenna was a stranger. She and Carter finally got over themselves and hooked up. About damn time. It was *soooo* painful watching the two of them dance around each other. I wanted to shove them in a closet and tell them not to come out until they fucked themselves silly.

Not that I ever get what I want.

The good news is that they figured it all out.

The bad news is that it took Jenna getting snatched off the street and kidnapped by some seriously bad dudes.

Like … *SERIOUSLY BAD.*

I didn't even know Jenna was gone until Walt got that call. Desperate after he found his loveable Max bleeding out on the sidewalk, Carter called Walt.

Ah, Max, I love that pup. Not really a pup. Max is a certified protector. He's the most loveable, fearsome, and loyal dog I've ever known. He nearly died protecting Jenna.

Boy, when that call came in …

Walt went from leaning in for a kiss—our first—to turning into something else entirely. I can't explain it better than that. Except to say, my date, the headliner of the dirtiest, filthiest sex dreams I've ever had, went from horndog into detached robot-killing mode the second Carter called.

Next I knew, Walt lifted me off my feet as he hauled me to his truck. We raced through the streets at breakneck speeds, with me screaming for him to tell me *What the fuck just happened?*

He ignored me. The guy was seriously *that* laser-focused.

I mean, he was *dialed in.*

When that switch flipped in Walt's head, he became another person entirely. Honestly, it was scary but also thrilling. He went into fierce, God-protector mode. If I didn't already have the hots for Walt, seeing him like that?

Whoa, all the girly-bits took notice.

Fucking hot on a stick.

I am *obsessed.*

Like, legitimately, obsessed.

But also pissed.

Pissed?

You're asking me why I'm pissed?

The fucking idiot was supposed to—you know—fuck me. He

doesn't know it, but he was supposed to take my cherry that night. Instead, he transformed into this laser-focused killing machine, leaving me on the sidelines. All hot and bothered with tons more material to use in my sex-fueled dreams.

Sex I didn't get to experience with Walt.

I'm still a virgin—and it's *his* fault.

Don't get me wrong. He didn't exactly ignore me. He put his hand on my thigh, just above my knee, and told me everything would be okay.

Everything?

Okay?

I didn't know *anything* was wrong.

Not until we pulled up beside a blood-soaked Carter as he knelt over Max, trying to save his dog's life. That's not the kind of thing you pull on a girl. I could've used a bit of advanced warning. Here I was, thinking I was finally going to get my cherry popped, and the guy I picked …

Well, you already know it didn't happen.

The whirlwind I was caught up in found me riding to the emergency vet with Carter and Max. Along the way, I discovered someone had taken Jenna. Walt didn't share that pertinent fact with me.

He thought I didn't need to know. Carter spilled that juicy bit while briefing Walt on what happened. After helping Carter load Max into the truck, we zoomed through the streets once more to the emergency vet, where I was left behind as Walt and Carter marched out of the vet's hellbent on doing whatever it took to get Jenna home.

Talk about a plot twist.

I don't know what happened over those next few days, except Walt stopped calling. Nobody would tell me shit. It was just me and Max chilling at the vet.

He did well, by the way—Max did.

I don't want anyone to think something terrible happened to Max. Rule number one of storytelling is don't kill the dog!

Max pulled through. He's fine. Better than fine.

But me?

I was forgotten in the hustle.

The Guardians saved Jenna. Whisked her away. Put her in protective custody. And still, no one told me shit.

Nobody.

Most notably, Walt.

And he can suck major donkey balls as a result because I don't play that game.

Which kind of makes the morning coffee rush at The Guardian Grind a bit—awkward.

Is that the right word?

Hell, I don't know what the right word might be, except I'm not speaking to Walt. I'm pissed with a capital *P* and a big ole *issed* kind of pissed.

He, of course, is oblivious. Like, he doesn't get why I'm all *"bristly"* when it comes to him. Can you believe that shit? He dares to call me *"bristly"* when he left me—clueless.

Is clueless the right word?

No, not clueless. He left me in the fucking Mojave Desert of Nothingness kind of clueless. I mean, he could've picked up the phone. He could've said something. He could've told me Jenna was rescued. He could've told me she was safe.

But no.

Nada.

I got nothing from him.

The only person who remembered I existed was Jenna. Now, she's a wealth of information and the bestest friend ever.

I'm going to make a long story short.

Turns out, the Guardians saved her. They saved her and

Sophia, along with the four missing girls Detective Carter was trying to find. It was a happily ever after for all involved.

Except me.

And … Yes!

I *am* being dramatic, but I get to be dramatic. This is my damn diary. This is where I lay it all out. The good. The bad. The ugly.

You, Dear Diary, get to hear all the shit.

"WHATCHA WRITING?" Jenna peeks over my shoulder.

I slam the cover closed on my diary.

"Nothing."

"Are you writing about Walt again? When are you going to stop playing games?"

"I'm not playing games."

"Come on." Jenna leans back, arms crossed over her chest, giving me the *mom* vibe, but I'm not taking it. Not today.

"Come on, what?"

"This has to stop."

"What?"

"You're not fooling me." She gives me another look. "You have to let this go."

"Let what go?"

"Your *I'm-not-speaking-to-Walt* thing." She uses air quotes for emphasis. She's constantly teasing me about how I'm staying mad at Walt for no good reason.

She doesn't get it.

Jenna's in domestic bliss with Carter. I'm in insufferable hell, treated daily to the man of my dreams who has no idea how much his actions hurt me. Like he's completely oblivious, with a capital *Oh-Bliv-Eeee-Ous.*

As for Jenna, she doesn't get it. She and Carter are shacking up in one of Guardian HRS's townhomes located on HQ grounds. She's in protective custody, the kind Guardian HRS provides. Which means she's a virtual prisoner and can't leave the premises.

Unlike me.

I can come and go as I please. Not that I do. There's tons to do on HQ grounds. I could spend a lifetime here and never get bored. What I can't stand, however, are the constant run-ins with Walt. I swear the guy stalks me.

He also loves coffee.

Which means he stops in at the Grind morning, noon, and night. Always with the same cheeky order. Always pretending as if I'm not pissed as hell at him.

I mean, he doesn't get it. He withheld pertinent info. The whole, *your bestie has been abducted* never once entered his mind as something I should know. He blathers on about *Mission need-to-know* bullshit while I—

"Earth to Malia." Jenna snaps her fingers in front of my face.

I blink, realizing I lost it, and focus on her.

"What?"

"We were talking …"

"No. I was writing, and you interrupted me." I run my fingers over the leather case of my laptop. It was a major splurge. Cost me a mint, but I'm a texture kind of girl. I explore the world by how it feels as much as I do by how it smells, and The Guardian Grind is my kind of heaven.

"Well, he's here. Demanding to speak with you."

"Who?"

"You know who." Jenna props her hands on her hips and gives me a look.

I roll my eyes.

"You can tell *Mr. You-know-who* that I am too busy doing

inventory to deal with him." It's not a total lie. Inventory doesn't do itself.

"I can do that. He's being obnoxious."

"Even more reason for me to stay exactly where I am."

"Fine, but you can't evade him forever."

"Watch me."

Jenna leaves and I glance at my computer, thinking of doing a bit more journaling about how obnoxious Walt is. He always comes in with some over-the-top coffee order, which slows things down. He does it deliberately to spend more time with me. Which is cute, but I'm not done being angry with him.

With a sigh, I put my computer aside and look at the shelves. Inventory doesn't take long, but I'm kind of obsessed at the moment.

Why?

Because this is where Sophia left all her clues. Forced to do the unthinkable by Malfor, she left clues behind that told the true story. I've been obsessed with that whole thing ever since.

Oh, you don't know about that?

The biggest infiltration in Guardian HQ history?

Sit back and buckle up because this one is a doozy.

Malfor used her to hack into Guardian systems. Walk right in through all their cyber protections like it was nothing. He used Sophia to do it, and he forced her to return to him when her task was done.

Talk about major upheaval. To say the shit hit the fan would be a massive understatement, but I still have questions.

Too many questions.

Evidently, Mitzy and her technical team were prepared for just such an attack. They implemented stuff to survive it. I say *stuff* because I'm not a tech girl. Me and computers are not friends.

But I have an inquisitive mind.

Sophia isn't the only one at Guardian HQ passing secrets to Malfor. Someone passed her at least two notes. One in her apron, and the other … Hmm, I don't remember all the details, but I'm going to figure it out.

I need to know.

My cellphone suddenly blares "The Ride of the Valkyries," and I grin.

My brother Malikai is checking in on me. He, of course, knows everything that happened and why I suddenly dropped off the face of the earth. When Jenna asked me to co-manage The Guardian Grind, there really was only one answer. Because of her protective custody and my inability to refuse her anything, I came on board and have basically self-isolated myself as a result.

But I'm heading out tonight.

"Hey, Bro." I answer the phone with a grin and a smile.

"Hey, Sissy." Malikai's cultured voice is as smooth as the creamiest latte.

I love our little nicknames. The *Hey, Bro* and *Hey, Sissy* is kind of our thing.

"What's up?"

"Just checking in to see if you're still free tonight."

"Of course. I've got it penciled in my calendar."

"What? No crayons?" He thinks my aversion to tech is funny, which is funny considering he lives and breathes in the quantum world.

Like seriously.

I'm not making that up.

Malikai is one of the pioneers in quantum mechanics and nuclear fusion. He's on the cusp of a real breakthrough in sustainable energy that's environmentally friendly. Meaning that he's a total nerd. Comes with the requisite horn-rimmed glasses and everything. Not that I'm sure what horn-rimmed glasses are supposed to be, but he wears the *fugliest* glasses with these thick, black rims.

Which is sad, considering Malikai is fucking hot. Like H-O-T.

He's a geek with the body of a god. Before you call me out on that, I don't have the *hots* for my brother. That's not what I'm saying, but I did grow up with him. Let's just say the girls glammed onto him the second he entered puberty when both his voice and balls dropped. He's got a physique that rivals some of the Guardians.

And we all know what *they* look like.

Maybe I should listen to Jenna and forgive Walt? He's the perfect guy to lose my virginity to, and I would.

Except I'm still pissed at him.

"Malia!" Malikai's voice shouts in my ear.

"What?"

"You were zoning again. Did you hear a word I said?"

"That depends."

"On what?"

"Whatever it is you said."

"Lord, you're hopeless."

I imagine him shaking his head. Not that it's my fault. My mind races a mile a minute, and that only gets worse after a couple of shots of espresso, and I may or may not have already had a few or more.

"I was telling you my schedule. My talk is over at four, and it takes an hour to get to you, so I wanted to make sure you'd be ready and if I had anything to worry about when it comes to the gate guards."

"You know, you could just text all of this." I may be hopeless with technology, but I know my way around my phone.

"A text you may or may not read?" He teases me. "Come on, Sissy, just answer the question."

"I told the guards you are coming. They want the make, model, and tag of your vehicle. Shouldn't be a problem getting in."

"And where am I picking you up? At the Grind or your apartment?"

"Technically, they call them the barracks, but I'm pulling an extra shift for Sophia, so come to the Grind."

"Got it." His deep, cultured voice takes on a softer tone. "I really miss you, Sissy. Can't wait to spend the weekend with you. I've got so much to tell you."

"Ditto right back." I glance at my watch. The lunch rush just ended, fortunately, with no intrusion from Walt. I should be able to finish inventory by five, which gives me time to figure out what to do with Malikai for an entire weekend.

TWO

Walt

____

THE MORNING SUN streams through Guardian's training facility, catching the rough surface of the hundred-foot rock wall that dominates the space. Charlie team gathers at the base, checking harnesses and ropes while Ethan outlines today's challenge.

"Listen up," Charlie-One commands, his voice echoing off the walls. "Today's about endurance and focus. We're running the Serpentine Route—full traverse across all three overhangs, then up the chimney section. I want clean transitions and perfect form."

I half-listen while checking my gear, my mind drifting to this morning's failed coffee run. Third time this week Malia's managed to be doing inventory right when I show up. Like she's got some sixth sense for avoiding me. The way she practically sprinted into the back room, that curtain of dark hair swinging behind her ...

"Walt!" Charlie-One's sharp voice snaps me back. "You got all that?"

"Yeah, yeah. Traverse, overhangs, chimney. Got it." I tug my harness straps tight, maybe a bit harder than necessary.

Blake raises an eyebrow as he walks up beside me. "You sure? Because that thousand-yard stare suggests otherwise."

"I'm fine," I growl, though *fine* is the last thing I am. Weeks of Malia's silent treatment is making me crazy. And not the good kind of crazy that usually leads to mind-blowing sex. The frustrated, can't-think-straight kind that's starting to affect my performance.

Gabe and Hank are already roped in, running their safety checks with the easy synchronization of longtime partners. Rigel takes the route to my left, leaving me with the center line—usually my favorite position, right where everyone can see exactly why I'm considered the best.

Today though? Today I'm off my game before we even start.

I swear, I'm going to wrap my hands around Malia's throat and throttle some sense into her. This silent treatment is the absolute worst, and I have no friggin' idea what the fuck I did wrong.

Thinking about choking her brings to mind images of tossing her over my knee and paddling that sweet little ass of hers. Tossing her over my knee brings images of putting her on her knees, and that brings other images to mind.

I'm hard again.

Reaching down, I make an adjustment and hope none of the guys notice. I swear, I spend the majority of my time hard as a rock thinking about Malia.

Thinking about fucking her.

Like ... All. The. Damn. Time.

And since the night Carter called and Jenna was taken, Malia went from *cute little hottie* to ...

I don't even know what to call it.

Indifferent?

No, I see the way she looks at me when she thinks I'm not

watching. She's hellfire wrapped up in the most demure and sexiest wrapping I can't stop thinking about tearing open.

Fuck.

And I mean that.

I think about fucking her all the time.

I think about fucking her, spanking her, forcing her to her knees, and feeding her my cock. God, I can just imagine the way that pert little mouth of hers will wrap around my cock. It's going to feel so damn good.

Especially after I redden her ass with a few well-placed swats.

She deserves that for keeping my cock hard and aching all damn day, all damn week. Fuck, it's been well over a month.

I'm cagey. Raw. And growing more obsessed by the day.

I need to fuck.

Has it really been over a month?

Talk about torture. I haven't experienced a dry spell like this ever, and I do mean ever. I lost my virginity at thirteen to a senior hotty. Talk about fucking like rabbits. That was probably one of the best years of my life, and she was a kinky bitch. Taught me all the things—the joy that comes with letting your freak flag fly, and I let mine fly freely.

And will again—once I can corner Malia and shove her against the wall, spin her around, turn that pretty ass of hers red, and fuck her like an animal.

Okay, the readjustment is doing absolutely nothing to ease my discomfort. I'm at the jerkoff stage. It's the only relief that can ease this ache. Not that it does shit for getting my mind off Malia. All my fantasies center on her.

And that's weird.

I've never been a one-woman man, and I've definitely never waited this long to fuck a woman I wanted. My dry spells last no longer than the length of the last mission because I love to fuck. I fuck before a mission, and I fuck as soon as we're back. It's the best way to cleanse my palate after a mission.

As far as that goes, finding women to fuck is easy. I'm a good fuck, and they love getting fucked by me.

That may make me sound a bit arrogant and cocky … Alright, I admit it's exceptionally arrogant and way beyond cocky, but something's changed in me.

Normally, I'd hit the bars and scratch that itch, except Malia did something to my head. From the day I met her, I haven't found another woman who interests me. Not that I haven't gone out with Gabe and Hank. We're the last bachelors of Charlie team. Gabe and Hank have no problem picking up a chick, fucking her in the bathroom, the alley, or even fucking them up against a wall.

Hank is into that. The shithead is an exhibitionist. And not that I'm judging, but Gabe gets off on it too. Not the exhibitionist thing, but the watching thing.

I've always wondered if there was more going on between them, but they're as straight as they come. They might share their women, but that's where things end.

I don't judge.

Or maybe that's where things begin with them? Maybe they haven't found the right woman who craves being dominated by two men.

Their kink is their kink, just as mine is mine.

Although, I have a feeling Gabe goes really dark with his, and Hank doesn't mind following into that darkness.

And just like that, my raging erection is gone.

There's nothing better than thinking about Gabe and Hank getting it on to lose a boner.

My dick deflates, and I snap back to attention as Ethan barks out another command.

Right. Training. Focus.

My mind's been drifting all morning, and I can practically feel my teammates rolling their eyes. The massive rock wall of Guardian's training facility looms before us, a hundred feet of sheer vertical challenge stretching the length of a football field.

"Walt! Get your head in the game!" Ethan's voice cuts through my thoughts from his position twenty feet above me.

I adjust my harness, muscle memory taking over as I search for the next hold. Usually, I set the pace, showing Blake and Rigel how these drills are done. But today? Today, I'm off my game, and everyone knows it.

"Watch your anchor point!" Hank calls out as my hand slips slightly.

Damn it. This isn't like me. I'm better than this—I'm the best, actually.

Just ask any of the women who've enjoyed my company. Well, anyone except Malia. She's the only one who seems immune to my considerable charms, and it's driving me absolutely crazy.

Sweat trickles down my neck as I push through the sequence. Below me, Gabe and Hank work in tandem, making the complex maneuvers look effortless. The familiar burn in my forearms is usually enough to keep my mind focused, but today, every handhold reminds me of curves I can't touch.

Charlie-One's whistle pierces the air. "Again! And this time, Walt, try to remember you're supposed to be an elite Guardian, not a lovesick teenager."

Rigel snorts from his position on the adjacent route. I shoot him my trademark grin, the one that usually has women falling all over themselves.

"Just giving you all a chance to catch up," I call back, forcing myself to lock it down. Time to show them why I'm considered the best.

I launch myself into a complex traverse, my body moving with the fluid grace that's made me one of Charlie team's top climbers. The rock face becomes a blur as I navigate the overhanging section, each movement precise despite my wandering thoughts. Fifty feet up, hanging by my fingertips, this is where I should feel most alive.

I can deal with Malia later. Right now, I've got a reputation to maintain and five teammates counting on me to keep my head in the game.

The next series of holds leads to a brutal overhang, which I usually dominate. My fingers find the familiar pockets in the synthetic rock, but my mind drifts to darker places. Well, darker hair, specifically. I can almost see Malia's long, dark tresses falling like a silk curtain, how it would feel wrapped around my fist … Yanking her head back while I fuck her from behind.

The image hits me like a physical blow, and suddenly, my grip isn't as sure as it should be. Hank shouts something—probably another warning—but it's lost in the rush of blood in my ears. All I can think about is how that hair would look splayed across my pillow or how it would feel brushing against my chest when she—

"WALT!"

My fingers slip at exactly the wrong moment. One second, I'm reaching for the next hold, muscles coiled for a power move I could normally do in my sleep, and the next, I'm falling. The world spins, my stomach lurches, and there's that sickening moment of pure freefall before my safety rope catches with a sharp jerk that knocks the wind out of me.

I dangle there like a rookie, spinning slowly forty feet above the padded floor while my teammates' voices echo off the walls.

"You okay, brother?" Ethan calls down, already rappelling toward my position.

"The only thing bruised is his ego," Gabe shouts from below, and I can hear the smirk in his voice.

The safety rope creaks as I hang there, my heart still

pounding from the fall—and, if I'm honest, from those thoughts about Malia.

"You're done for the day." Ethan's disappointed sigh carries across the entire facility.

"I'm fine," I protest, already planning my next attempt. "Just lost focus for a second."

"Exactly," he cuts in. "You lost focus on a hundred-foot wall. That's not like you, and we both know why. Hit the showers. Clear your head."

I rappel down slowly, my muscles protesting the sudden strain from the fall. The guys try not to stare, but I can feel their concern.

Walt doesn't fall.

Walt doesn't lose focus.

Except, apparently, when a certain dark-haired woman gets stuck in his head like a song he can't stop humming.

"Nice show of gravity there, hotshot," Rigel quips as my boots hit the floor.

"Bite me," I mutter, but there's no heat. He's right. We all know he's right. I'm losing my edge, and over what? A woman who won't give me the time of day?

The problem is, as I unclip my harness and head for the showers, I don't care. Because even now, with my pride bruised and my team's eyes on my back, all I can think about is that long, dark hair and what it would feel like running through my fingers.

I'm so screwed.

THREE

Walt

____

THE LOCKER ROOM IS QUIET, a sanctuary of sorts, as I make my way to the showers, my body still humming with adrenaline from the fall. The hot water calls to me, a siren's song promising temporary respite from the tension coiled tight within me.

I strip off my clothes, the fabric sticking to my sweat-slicked skin. The cool air is a harsh contrast, but it does nothing to diminish the heat coursing through my veins. I step under the spray, the water hitting my skin like a thousand tiny fingers, massaging the ache in my muscles. But it's not enough to ease the throb in my balls, the insistent pulse that's been my constant companion these past weeks.

I close my eyes, leaning my back against the cool tile. The steam rises, cocooning me in a hazy, surreal world where there's only me and the driving need within. I let my hand drift down, wrapping my fingers around my cock. It jerks in response, eager for the touch I've been denying it.

In my mind, Malia stands before me, her dark hair cascading over her shoulders, her eyes wide with anticipation. She's naked, her body bared to me, waiting for my command. My cock twitches at the thought, growing harder, thicker, in my hand.

I begin to stroke, my grip firm, the way I like it.

"Touch yourself," I tell her, my voice echoing in the empty shower. She complies, her hands cupping her breasts, her fingers rolling her nipples until they're hard and peaked. I stroke faster, my cock responding to the sight of her pleasuring herself at my command.

The pulse in my balls intensifies to a steady throb that grows more insistent with each stroke. My cock responds, hardening further, the sensation bordering on pain, but it's a sweet pain, one that promises pleasure beyond measure.

I can feel every vein, every ridge of my cock as I stroke, my hand moving faster, harder, in time with the thrusts I imagine feeding into her mouth. My grip tightens, and my imagination runs wild.

She's on her knees, her hands tied behind her back, completely at my mercy. Desire burning in her eyes with a hunger that matches my own.

"Open your mouth," I growl, and she does, her tongue darting out to wet her lips.

I can almost feel the warmth of her breath, the softness of her mouth as I thrust into her, my cock hitting the back of her throat. My balls tighten.

I reach down with my other hand, cupping my balls. The pressure sends a jolt of pure ecstasy through me. I roll my nuts in my palm, my fingers gently tugging as I continue to stroke my cock. The dual sensations are overwhelming, pushing me closer to the edge.

Malia's moans echo in my head, her body writhing as I fuck her mouth, my hands tangled in her hair, holding her still as I take what I want. Her surrender is like crack, sending me flying.

It drives me wild.

I stroke faster, my hips thrusting forward as I fuck my fist, the water cascading over me, heightening every sensation. My balls are tight, the ache almost unbearable, but I don't stop. I can't. I'm too far gone, lost in the fantasy, lost in the feel of my cock in my hand and the thought of Malia's mouth on me.

"That's it, baby," I groan, my voice harsh and guttural. "Take it all. Take every inch of me."

I can feel her swallowing around me, her throat convulsing as she takes me deep, and it's too much. With a roar, I come, my cock pulsing in my hand as I shoot hot and hard against the tile. My body shudders, the orgasm ripping through me, leaving me weak and breathless.

I lean against the wall, my chest heaving, the water cooling as it washes away the evidence of my release. My cock is still hard, still throbbing with need, but the edge has been taken off, the desperation eased.

But it's not enough. It's never enough. Not when it's my hand bringing me pleasure. Not when it's my fingers gripping my cock instead of hers. Not when it's my voice echoing in the shower instead of her cries of surrender.

I wash quickly, my movements efficient. The lingering haze of pleasure fades with each passing second. As I step out of the shower, toweling off, it's painfully clear this won't be the last time I find myself seeking relief in the quiet solitude of the locker room.

Not as long as Malia's in my head, her body a constant temptation, her submission a challenge I'm more than eager to take on.

Next time, I promise myself as I dress, pulling on my clothes with renewed determination. Next time, it won't be just my hand. Next time, it will be her. Her mouth, her body, her surrender. I won't stop until she's mine, completely and utterly, in every way that counts.

I leave the shower, the locker room's cool air hitting my skin, an abrupt change from the steamy warmth that still clings to me. My cock hangs thick and heavy between my legs, my erection spent but not entirely gone. The remnants of my desire still linger, a constant hum beneath my skin, a reminder of the need that's become a part of me.

I wrap a towel around my waist, tucking it in securely, but it does little to hide the evidence of what I've been up to. As I approach my locker, voices echo down the hall.

Fuck me.

I'm no longer alone. I grimace, bracing myself for the inevitable ribbing I'm about to receive.

The door to the locker room swings open and in file my teammates—Ethan, Gabe, Hank, Rigel, and Blake. They laugh and joke, but the moment they see me, their grins widen, and their laughs take on a knowing edge.

"Well, well, well," Ethan drawls, his eyes flicking to the bulge beneath my towel. "Looks like someone's been having a little 'alone time.'"

I shrug, trying to act nonchalant. "Just needed to relieve some tension." I open my locker and pull out my clothes.

Hank snorts. "Relieve tension? Is that what the kids are calling it these days?"

Gabe chimes in, a wicked gleam in his eyes. "You know, there are more interesting places to jerk off than the shower. Might want to explore your options."

I flip him off, pulling on my boxers and jeans. "Fuck off. Not all of us are exhibitionists like you."

"What can I say? Don't tell me you've never thought about putting on a show. There's something—intoxicating about having eyes on you while you're at your most raw." Gabe grins, unfazed. "I like an audience. There's something about a chick watching me while I stroke myself that gets me going. Besides, you know what they say … 'Picasso painted in public, so why not paint my masterpiece in a public place as well?'"

I shake my head, smirking. "You're fucked up. And Hank over here is just as bad, with his voyeuristic tendencies."

Hank chuckles, a low, suggestive sound. "Guilty as charged, but watching is just the warm-up. The real fun comes when I join in."

Gabe's grin widens, and he claps Hank on the back. "And that's when things get truly—entertaining. You should see how we can make a woman fall apart at the seams. It's a fucking masterpiece."

Hank nods in agreement. "It's a win-win situation. They get double the pleasure."

I raise an eyebrow, zipping up my jeans. "You two are something else. I prefer my conquests one-on-one."

"To each their own." Hank laughs, a deep, throaty sound. "Your loss. If you ever change your mind, just say the word. We'll introduce you to a world of pleasure you never knew existed."

Gabe nods, his eyes gleaming with mischief. "The ladies always leave with a smile on their faces. Every. Single. Time."

I chuckle, shaking my head as I finish getting dressed. "I'm sure they do, guys. But for now, I'll leave the group performances to you two. I've got enough on my plate with one woman."

Hank and Gabe exchange a look, grinning like the devils they are. "Suit yourself," Hank says. "You don't know what you're missing."

I smirk, pulling on my shirt. "I think I'll survive. Now, if you two are done corrupting the locker room …"

Rigel leans against the locker next to mine. His arms crossed over his chest. "Seriously, man, you've got it bad. Why don't you ask her out already?"

I slam my locker shut, the metallic clang echoing through the room. "It's not that simple."

Blake raises an eyebrow. "Sure it is. You ask, she says yes, you go out. It's called a date, Walt. You've done it before."

I glare at him. "Except the last time we tried to go on a date, it ended with a phone call about a dog getting shot and a kidnapping. Not exactly the romantic evening I had in mind."

Ethan claps a hand on my shoulder, squeezing it. "That was shitty timing, sure. But you can't let that stop you. You've got to get back on the horse, man."

Gabe smirks. "Or back on the girl, as the case may be."

I shove him, but there's no heat behind it. These guys are my brothers, my family. They might give me shit, but they also have my back, no matter what.

Hank steps forward, and his expression is serious for once. "Look, we all see the way you look at her. And we see how she looks at you when she thinks no one's watching. You two have something—you need to give it a chance."

Rigel nods in agreement. "Exactly. And if you don't ask her out soon, someone else might. You snooze, you lose, man."

The thought of Malia with someone else sends a surge of jealousy coursing through me, my hands clenching into fists at my sides.

"Over my dead body," I growl.

Ethan grins. "That's the spirit. Now go ask her out before you end up with carpal tunnel from all that 'tension relieving.'"

I laugh, the tension in the room broken. "Alright, alright. I'll ask her out, but if she says no, I swear to God, I'm blaming every single one of you assholes."

Gabe claps me on the back. "That's fair. But she won't say no. Not to you."

I hope he's right. As I leave the locker room, their laughter echoes behind me.

I want Malia, and it's time to do something about it. Time to take control and take what I want.

But first, I need to convince her to give me—give us—a chance. I pull out my phone, my thumbs flying over the screen as I type out a message.

Walt

AS I LEAVE Charlie team's bullpen, my boots echo against the tile floor. My phone is a heavy weight in my hand, but it's not the device—it's the choice. The next move. Gabe's words ring in my ears: *"She won't say no. Not to you."*

I wish I had that same certainty. Malia's been a puzzle, her every move calculated to keep me guessing, keep me at arm's length. But I'm done playing on her terms. It's time to change the game.

I pause near the exit, leaning against the wall, scrolling through our last texts. Each conversation feels like a dance, one step forward, two steps back. She laughs, she flirts, and then she pulls away like she's scared of what happens if she gets too close.

Maybe she is, but I'm not.

The weight in my chest grows heavier, but I push past it. Enough waiting, enough second-guessing. This isn't about patience anymore; it's about showing her I'm all in. I open a new message and type the words before I lose my nerve.

ME: **We never got to finish that date. Let me make it up to you. Dinner at my place. Tomorrow night.**

I HIT SEND BEFORE I can second-guess myself, my heart pounding in my chest as I wait for her reply. But this time, I'm not backing down. This time, I'm playing to win.

And Malia?

She's mine.

She just doesn't know it yet.

I stare at my phone, willing her to respond quickly, my heart thumping in my chest like a ticking clock. The screen stays frustratingly blank for what feels like an eternity before those three little dots appear, indicating she's typing a response. I grip the phone tighter, my palms sweating with anticipation.

MALIA: **Sorry, can't. Busy this weekend. My brother's coming into town.**

BUSY THIS WEEKEND. Her brother's coming into town.

She has a brother?

The words flash on my screen, taunting me. I scroll back to the message, reading it again, as if somehow the meaning will change. But it doesn't.

My jaw tightens as I shove the phone into my pocket, frustration coursing through me. She thinks she can keep me at a distance, that this game of avoidance will keep me from breaking through those walls she's built.

She's wrong.

I stop mid-step, my mind racing. Maybe I should let her have her space—be patient, play it cool, but then I shake my head. That's not me. That's not how I fight. And this?

This is a fight I'm not walking away from.

If Malia thinks she can brush me off with a simple text, she's got another thing coming.

When I push open the door to The Guardian Grind, it's bustling with the afternoon crowd. The rich aroma of coffee engulfs me, but I barely notice. I scan the room and zero in on Malia behind the counter. She's laughing with a customer, her dark hair swaying with the movement, her smile bright and genuine.

This only serves to stoke the fire within me.

I stride toward the counter. My gaze locked onto hers. As I approach, her laughter fades, her eyes widening slightly as she takes in my expression.

She knows I'm not here for coffee.

"Walt," she acknowledges, her voice steady despite the slight flush creeping up her cheeks. "What can I get for you?"

I lean against the counter, my voice low and intense. "You can start by explaining why you're brushing me off."

Her eyes flick to the side, checking if anyone's listening. She leans in slightly, her voice dropping to a near whisper. "I told you, I'm busy this weekend. My brother's coming into town."

"And?" I challenge, my eyes boring into hers. "You can't spare one evening for dinner? Or are you just afraid to be alone with me?"

"I'm not afraid of you." Her eyes flash with anger and something else—something that looks a lot like desire.

I lean in closer, my voice a low rumble. "Then prove it. Have dinner with me. One evening, that's all I'm asking."

She bites her lip, a sign of her indecision, and it takes every ounce of self-control not to reach out and tug that lip free with my thumb. Or my teeth.

I stare at Malia, her words echoing in my ears. My frustration is reaching a boiling point.

"I can't," she says, her voice firm with resolution. "I have plans with my brother. It's important."

Something inside me snaps. I slam my hand down on the counter, the sharp sound making her jump. Before she can react, I grab her wrist, pulling her toward me. She gasps, her eyes wide with shock and a hint of fear, but I don't stop.

I can't.

I've been pushed too far, and I'm done playing games.

"What are you—?" she starts, but I cut her off, my voice a low growl.

"You and I need to have a little chat."

I tug her toward the inventory room, her resistance is futile against my strength. Pushing open the door, I pull her inside and spin her around, pinning her against the wall. Her breath hitches as I press my body firmly against hers, one hand capturing her wrists, lifting and holding them above her head.

Her eyes blaze with defiance, but there's no mistaking the desire simmering beneath the surface. She wants this as much as I do, even if she won't admit it.

Leaning in, I claim her mouth with a wild, searing kiss. It's not gentle or tender; it's raw, primal, and filled with all the pent-up frustration and longing that's been building for weeks.

She struggles briefly, her body tense, but as my tongue demands entry, her resistance crumbles. She kisses me back, her body melding against mine, her lips parting to grant me deeper access.

The kiss turns into an erotic dance of tongues, lips, and teeth. I nip at her lower lip, eliciting a gasp from deep within her. My tongue plunges into her mouth, exploring every inch, tasting her sweetness. Her moans are muffled against my lips as our bodies grind together, the heat between us igniting into an inferno.

Her hands, still pinned above her head, flex and strain against my grip, but I don't let go. The sensation of her squirming only fuels the fire within me. I press harder against her, my hips grinding into hers, letting her feel the hardness of my cock—how much I want her. The kiss deepens, becoming more savage, more intense, as our bodies move in sync, driven by pure instinct and raw need.

When I finally pull away, her cheeks are flushed, her eyes glazed with desire. Her breath comes in ragged gasps, and I can feel the rapid rise and fall of her chest against mine. I take one of her hands and guide it to the bulge in my pants.

Her eyes widen as she feels the extent of my arousal.

"Feel that?" I growl, my voice low and husky. "That's what you do to me. I'm hard and aching for you every day, every hour, and every fucking minute. I'm tired of using my fist, tired of imagining what it would feel like to be inside you. You're mine, and it's time to show you what that means."

Her hand trembles slightly against my erection, but she doesn't pull away.

I lean in, my lips brushing against her ear as I whisper, "I want to feel your tight pussy wrapped around me. I want to hear you scream my name as I fuck you from one orgasm into the next. I want to mark you, claim you, make you mine in every possible way."

She gasps, her body trembling with shock and desire. I continue, my voice a low rumble filled with dirty promises.

"I want to redden your ass with my hand. I want to tie you up until you're helpless and completely at my mercy. I want to hear you beg for release as I tease your clit with my tongue, finger you until you scream, and cry out in pleasure as I drive my cock deep inside of you."

I pull back slightly, my eyes locked onto hers, burning with intensity. "I want to make you come so hard you see stars, and then I want to do it again and again until you're completely spent and utterly mine. I want to own every inch of your body, every gasp, every moan, every scream of pleasure."

Her breath hitches, and her eyes widen at my words. Fear flickers in her gaze, but it's quickly overshadowed by excitement. The thrill of the unknown reflects in her dilating pupils. The promise of pleasure beyond her wildest dreams makes her cheeks flush and her lips part in a silent gasp.

Her pulse races at the base of her neck, a rapid flutter that betrays her arousal. A shiver runs down her spine, a visible ripple beneath her clothes. Her thighs squeeze together as if trying to contain the heat building between them. She's imagining every-thing I promise to do to her, and her body responds in ways she can't control.

I keep going, my voice a dark, seductive whisper. "I want to push your boundaries. I want to show you what it feels like to surrender to desire. I want to make you feel things you've never felt before, things you never even imagined possible."

Her breathing grows more ragged, her body trembling violently as she listens to my words. Her nipples harden against the fabric of her shirt, two taut peaks that beg for my touch and ache for my tongue. Her hips rock toward me, seeking more contact, driven by an instinctive need for friction, for pressure, for release.

She's not just hearing my words—she's feeling them, deep within her core, stoking the fire burning inside her.

I lean in closer, my lips almost brushing against hers as I continue to paint a picture of the pleasure that awaits her. "I want to explore every inch of your body. I want to find all the spots that make you gasp, make you moan, make you scream in ecstasy. I want to drive you wild with desire until you're begging for release, until you're completely and utterly at my mercy. Until you're mine."

Her eyes are glazed with desire, her body aching with need.

A battle rages within her—the part of her that wants to give in, to surrender to the promise of pleasure, and the part that's still clinging to control.

I know which side will win.

She pushes against my chest, trying to put some space between us.

"You can't claim me like some caveman. It doesn't work like that." Her voice rises in defiance.

"Wrong, sweetheart." I tighten my grip on her wrists, my body pressing firmly against hers. A dark chuckle escapes my lips, sending a shiver down her spine. "You can deny it all you want, but you crave the caveman within me. You crave the primal, raw, unyielding power that makes me who I am."

"That's not true."

"Isn't it?" My voice drips with raw desire. "You want to feel the power of my body against yours, the strength of my hands holding you down, the force of my passion driving into you. You want to be fucked by a man who knows how to handle a woman like you."

I lean close, my breath hot against her ear, my voice a low rumble. "You want a man who can pin you against the wall, who can hold you in place while he ravishes your mouth, your body. You want a man who can make you feel protected and desired all at once, who can take control and make you surrender to his touch."

Her eyes widen, and her pupils dilate with excitement and anticipation. Her breath hitches, and her body tenses against mine. I see the truth in her eyes. Her body already responds to the promise of my strength against her softness.

"I'm going to make you feel every inch of my cock and fill

you with every ounce of my desire until you're screaming my name and begging for more."

She wants this, even if she won't admit it.

"You belong to me. You've belonged to me since I laid eyes on you, and now that I've tasted you, I'm not letting you go."

I pull back slightly, my eyes locked onto hers, burning with intensity. "And that's exactly what I'm going to give you. Have dinner with your brother, but make no mistake—I'll be waiting. When you're done, I'm taking you to bed."

Her eyes widen, and her pupils dilate with fear and excitement. Her heart races, beating so hard that I feel it against my chest.

My voice becomes a dark whisper filled with sinful promises. "I'm going to make you scream, make you beg, make you come so hard that you see stars. When I'm done, you'll never want to be anywhere else but in my arms."

I step back to give her some space but keep my eyes locked on hers. The promise of what's to come hangs heavily in the air.

"This is happening. You and me. Tonight. So be ready because I'm not taking no for an answer."

With that, I turn and walk out of the inventory room, leaving her breathless and flushed, her body humming with the promise of what's to come.

I march out of the Grind, the bell above the door jingling merrily in stark contrast to the storm raging within me.

She thinks she can resist me, resist this thing between us, but I know better. I see the desire in her eyes, the way her body responds to mine. She wants me just as much as I want her.

Worked into a frenzy, I head straight for the rock wall, my body humming with restless energy. I need to climb and push myself physically since I can't have the release I crave.

Not yet. But soon.

I strap on my harness, the familiar routine grounding me,

focusing my thoughts. As I ascend, my muscles strain with the effort, but it's a welcome distraction.

Each handhold brings me closer to the top, closer to my goal. One step at a time. One hold at a time. I won't stop until I reach the summit. Malia will be mine tonight, and neither of us will ever be the same again.

FIVE

Malia

MY LEGS TREMBLE BENEATH ME, refusing to move from the spot where Walt pinned me. The rough texture of the inventory room wall bites into my back, a reminder of his power, his control.

His holy-hell-fire-that-was-hot!

His scent lingers—spice, sweat, raw masculinity—making my head spin. The thundering of my heart drowns out the distant hum of coffee grinders and customer chatter from the front of the shop.

The shelves of coffee beans blur before my eyes. Everything seems sharper, more vivid. The warmth between my thighs pulses in time with my racing pulse. My lips tingle, bruised from his savage kiss. A whimper escapes my throat as I press my thighs together, trying to ease the unfamiliar ache.

Dear God.

That wasn't a kiss.

It was a claiming.

A promise.

A threat.

My fingers drift to my wrists, still burning from his grip. The ghost of his touch sends shivers racing down my spine. The air feels too thick, too heavy. Each breath carries the lingering taste of him—coffee and mint and pure, unleashed male.

Heat floods my cheeks as his words echo in my mind: *"You're mine."*

Simple. Direct.

Brooking no argument. The raw possession in his voice makes my knees weak all over again. Never in my life has anyone spoken to me like that, touched me like that, made me feel like— that.

The door handle rattles and I jump, my heart leaping into my throat, but it's just the ventilation system kicking on. It sends a rush of cool air across my overheated skin. I close my eyes, trying to steady my breathing, but that only makes it worse. Behind my eyelids, I see Walt's intense gaze, the flex of his muscles as he held me, the bulge of his …

Oh God.

It's big.

The throb between my legs intensifies, and I squeeze my thighs tighter. What's happening to me? How can one kiss, one touch, leave me so completely undone?

His words replay in an endless loop, each one stoking the fire in my belly higher. *"I want to redden your ass with my hand."* Images flash through my head—me, bent over his knee, his palm coming down hard on my bare flesh. A rush of heat floods my core, my body clenching around nothing.

What's wrong with me?

I should be outraged and offended.

Instead, I tremble with need, imagining the sting of his hand, the bite of his teeth, the stretch of his …

Stop it.

My brother's coming. I need to focus on inventory. On

anything but how Walt's body felt pressed against mine, hard and demanding. The way his cock felt against my stomach, thick and ready. The promises he made about what he'd do to me, how he'd make me scream …

The pencil in my hand snaps, bringing me back to reality. Broken pieces scatter across the floor as I gather my scattered thoughts.

But it's useless. Every movement reminds me of his touch, his taste, his overwhelming presence.

His last words haunt me: *"This is happening. You and me. Tonight."*

Oh, my diary is going to have a steamy entry later tonight!

A shudder runs through me—fear? Anticipation? Both? I've never felt so out of control, so desperate for something I can barely name. The warmth between my legs has become an insistent throb, demanding attention I don't know how to give.

The inventory sheet before me might as well be written in Sanskrit. The numbers swim before my eyes as memories assault me—his growled commands, his iron grip, the predatory gleam in his eyes when he promised to claim every inch of me.

What have I gotten myself into?

My phone vibrates against my hip, the buzz amplified by the metal shelving. A shiver runs through me—not from the vibration, but from the lingering sensation of Walt's hands on my body. The screen blurs, then focuses. Malikai's smiling face fills the display, grounding me in reality.

"Hey, Sissy." His cultured voice fills my ear, familiar and safe. So different from Walt's growled promises. "Still good for dinner?"

"Yeah, of course." My voice sounds strange and breathy. Walt's words echo: *"I'm going to make you scream."* Heat floods my cheeks.

"Great, I've made reservations at Salvatore's for seven."

Papers rustle in the background. "They've got that carbonara you love."

The phone slides against my sweaty palm. Salvatore's. Fancy. Which means I need to wear a dress. The thought triggers another memory of Walt: *"I want to feel your tight pussy wrapped around me."* My thighs clench involuntarily.

"You okay? You sound distracted." Concern colors Malikai's tone.

"Fine." I clear my throat, trying to sound normal. Except for the throbbing between my legs and Walt's promise: *"I want to tie you up until you're helpless."*

Images flood my mind—Walt's hands pinning my wrists, his body pressing me against the wall. His breath hot on my neck. The hard length of him grinding against me.

"Everything's fine."

"If you say so." A pause. "You're being weird."

"Just busy doing inventory." The lie tastes bitter on my tongue, mixing with the lingering taste of Walt's kiss. "Text me when you're heading over?"

"Will do, Sissy." The nickname makes me flinch. How can I sit across from my protective big brother tonight with Walt's marks burning on my skin? "Love you."

"Love you too." I end the call, letting my head thunk back against the metal shelving. The cool metal does nothing to ease the fire under my skin.

I return to the job at hand with effort, but the inventory sheet mocks me. Numbers swim before my eyes. I've counted the same row of coffee beans six times, each attempt derailed by memories of Walt's assault on my senses.

"I want to redden your ass with my hand."

My inner muscles clench. The pencil creaks in my grip as I imagine being bent over his knee, completely at his mercy. The hard ridge of his cock pressed against my stomach, promising exactly what he'd do to me after.

"I want to hear you beg for release."

Coffee beans scatter across the floor as I bump the shelf. The rich aroma fills the air, but all I can smell is him—spice, sweat, and raw male need. My nipples tighten against my bra, sending sparks of pleasure through my body.

"I want to own every inch of your body."

The paper crumples under my white-knuckled grip. Every shift reminds me of how he felt pressed against me, hard and demanding. His strength, his control, the way he took what he wanted …

I squeeze my thighs together, trying to ease the persistent ache. What's wrong with me? I'm supposed to be angry. He manhandled me, threatened me, promised to-to …

"I want to make you come so hard you see stars."

A whimper escapes my throat. Heat pools between my legs, my body responding to memories of his touch, his taste, the dark promises in his voice.

"I want to push your boundaries."

The inventory sheet floats to the floor, forgotten. My hands shake as I brace myself against the shelving. I've never felt like this— out of control, desperate, aching for something I can barely name.

"Holy shit, what happened to you?"

I whirl around, nearly knocking over a display of specialty blends. Jenna stands in the doorway, her eyes wide as she takes in my disheveled state. Heat floods my cheeks as I try to smooth my hair and straighten my clothes.

"Nothing." My voice cracks. "Why?"

"Maybe because Walt just stormed out of here looking like he wanted to murder someone or fuck them senseless." She steps closer, studying my face. Her eyes narrow at whatever she sees there. "Since you look like you've been thoroughly kissed, I'm going with fucking over murder." She pauses, gaze dropping to my neck. "Is that a hickey?"

"What?" My hand flies to my throat, finding the tender spot where his mouth branded me. "He marked me?"

"Something did happen!" Triumph lights her face as she closes the door behind her. The lock clicks with finality. "Spill. Now. And don't you dare leave out a single detail."

"I …" Words fail me as fresh heat floods my cheeks. How can I explain what happened when I barely understand it myself?

"That good, huh?" Jenna's grin turns wicked. "Your face is the color of our Valentine's Day hearts. What exactly did Mr. Tall-Dark-and-Deliciously-Dominant do to get you so flustered?"

The memory of his growled commands makes me shiver. "He … We … I mean …" I sink onto a box of coffee filters, my legs too shaky to hold me. "He kissed me."

"Kissed you?" She arches an eyebrow. "That's what has you looking like you just starred in your own personal porn movie?"

If possible, my face burns hotter. "It wasn't just a kiss. It was …" I gesture helplessly, unable to find the words.

"A claiming?" Jenna supplies, her smile knowing. "Welcome to the dark side, sweetie. Looks like Walt finally decided to show you exactly what you've been missing."

"This is going to sound crazy." I twist my hands in my lap, unable to meet Jenna's eyes. The inventory room suddenly feels too small, too warm. "But when Walt pinned me against the wall—"

"You liked it." Jenna perches on a nearby box, her expression softening.

I nod, cheeks burning. "Is that—normal? Because he wasn't gentle. He was demanding and forceful and …" My voice trails off.

"And that turned you on?" She keeps her tone neutral and encouraging.

I've never talked to anyone about sex, but I feel safe with Jenna. She understands and won't make fun of me.

"Yes." The word comes out as barely a whisper. "He said things too. Things that should horrify me. Things that probably make me sound like some kind of …"

"Some kind of, what?"

"Pervert." The word tastes bitter.

"Pervert? Why would you say that?"

"Because normal girls don't get excited when a guy threatens to spank them, right?"

"Oh, sweetie, you have no idea how normal that is." Jenna's laugh is gentle and understanding. "Trust me, there's nothing wrong with you. Men like Walt know how to spice things up, and as long as you're okay with it, there's nothing to feel bad about." There's no judgment on her face.

"He said he wanted to tie me up." Heat floods my core at the memory. "And I wanted him to. God, I still want him to." My thighs clench at the memory. I can't stop thinking about it.

"That's nothing to be ashamed of." Warmth fills her voice. "And it's not crazy at all."

"No?" I bite my lip. "Because it feels—intense. Like maybe I'm in over my head."

"Walt knows what he's doing." Jenna chooses her words carefully. "He won't do anything without your consent."

"But that's just it." I wrap my arms around myself. "He didn't ask. He just—took control. Demanded."

"Oh, honey. Walt will never force anything on you. He'll test your limits and respect them."

"No?" I dare to glance up. "Because he didn't just stop there. He said he wanted to …" I swallow hard. "… and instead of being scared or angry, I just felt—"

"Hot? Excited? Like your whole body was on fire?"

"God, yes." Relief floods through me. "Is that wrong? I mean, I'm getting turned on by the idea of him—controlling me like that."

"Hey." Jenna touches my arm. "There's no reason to feel bad about how he makes you feel. It's normal to find it exciting."

"You sure?"

"Yes. The way he looks at you? That's everything."

"He said I'm his." My voice trembles. "That after tonight …"

"Are you ready for that?"

The question hangs in the air. Am I? The ache between my legs screams yes, but my inexperience makes me hesitate. How can I tell her I've never … That I don't know how …

Nope. That's one secret I'm not ready to share. Because I'm in my twenties, everyone assumes I've had sex. That I know what I'm doing. I'm more afraid to tell Jenna I'm still a virgin than I am talking to her about Walt tying me up and spanking me.

I can't face another minute surrounded by coffee beans and memories of Walt's hands.

I chew on my bottom lip as I search for an escape from this conversation. My pulse is still racing, my body betraying me with the memory of Walt's hands, his voice, his promise.

I glance at Jenna, feeling the weight of her gaze. How she looks at me—like she's waiting for me to spill every secret tangled in my chest. It makes my skin prickle.

I shift on my feet, suddenly hyperaware of the snug fit of my apron and the oppressive warmth of the shop.

"I—uh … Switch of topic." My voice wobbles, and I fake a laugh, brushing my hands on my apron as if there's something on them. "My brother's in town for dinner." I fidget with my apron strings. "I know I said I'd work Sophia's shift, but is there any chance I can duck out early?"

It's a clumsy pivot, but it works. At least, I hope it does.

"Of course." Jenna's eyes sparkle with mischief. "Gives you time to process—everything." She leaves me with a smile on her lips. The door clicks behind her, leaving me blessedly alone. I lean against the metal shelving. The cool surface feels good against my overheated skin. Then, I remember this is the same spot where Walt pinned me.

My body remembers every second. His strength replays in my muscles, how he effortlessly controlled my body and lifted my wrists above my head. How I let him. The unyielding press of his thighs against mine. His lips on my mouth.

Power radiates from him, even in memory. The way he took control, brooking no argument was beyond hot. His muscled body trapped me, leaving no room for escape. Not that I wanted to escape. The hard ridge of his cock grinding against my stomach sent electricity shooting through my core. And the size? Dear Lord, how is it ever going to fit—down there?

His growled promises replay in vivid detail: *"I'm going to make you scream."* The deep timbre of his voice, the dark promise in each word. My nipples tighten, and I press my thighs together, trying to ease the persistent ache.

How can one kiss—one moment—change everything?

Transform me from a confident businesswoman to this trembling mess? As another memory hits, my phone slips from my suddenly clammy palm—his teeth grazing my neck, marking me.

Time slips away as I stand frozen, lost in the sensory assault. The rich coffee aroma fades beneath the phantom scent of his skin—spice, sweat, and pure male. The sounds of the café dim against the echo of his words: *"When I'm done, you'll never want to be anywhere else but in my arms."*

Shit. I'm going to be late.

I need to get ready. I need to somehow face my brother across a dinner table while my body thrums with unfulfilled desires. I need to do that while Walt's marks burn on my skin.

One advantage to living and working at Guardian HQ is it doesn't take long to get from one place to another. I take one of the ever-ready free-roaming golf carts and speed to my barracks.

My apartment feels foreign, charged with new energy. Everything I touch reminds me of Walt's promises. The doorknob—his grip on my wrists. The kitchen counter—his threat to bend me over and spank me. The couch—God, the things he could do to me there.

I stumble into my bedroom, pulse racing. The ceiling fan stirs the air, raising goosebumps on my heated skin.

My closet holds no answers. Sundresses mock me with their sweet patterns. Jeans feel too restrictive for my sensitized skin. Professional wear seems laughably prim after Walt's filthy promises. My favorite blue wrap dress that usually says *"Professional"* now whispers, *"Unwrap me."* I can't wear the red cocktail dress. It screams, *"Fuck me."*

Clothes litter my bed—rejected outfits that suddenly seem too innocent, too naive. Too virginal.

What does someone wear when meeting their brother for dinner but can't stop thinking about another man's promise to spank them?

My hands shake as I push hangers aside. Nothing feels right. Everything feels charged with new meaning. Even my cotton panties feel too restrictive, too warm against my heated flesh.

Walt's words echo: *"I want to own every inch of your body."*

I grip the closet door, steadying myself. How am I supposed to sit through dinner knowing what's coming after? Knowing Walt's out there, waiting, planning to claim every part of me?

The black dress catches my eye. Simple. Elegant. But the way it hugs my curves ... The neckline dips low enough to hint at cleavage but still remains modest. The hem hits mid-thigh, showing enough leg to make a man wonder but not too much to be indecent.

Would Walt approve?

The thought shoots straight to my core. Since when do I care about his approval?

Since he pinned you against that wall and promised to own you.

Yeah, me and my diary are going to have a long, hard talk after tonight.

My hands shake as I slip the dress from its hanger. The silk whispers against my skin as I hold it up. I could be the woman Walt sees in this dress—sexy, desirable, ready for his touch.

But first, dinner with my brother. Sweet, protective Malikai has no idea his little sister is about to …

Heat floods my cheeks. How can I sit across from him, knowing what Walt plans to do to me later? Knowing that under this sophisticated dress, I'm wet and aching for a man's touch?

The dress pools on my bed as I sink down beside it. What am I doing? This isn't me. I don't dress for men. I don't tremble at the thought of being spanked. I don't …

Walt's voice echoes in my head: *"You're mine."*

My body clenches in response. Maybe this is me—just a version I've never dared to explore before.

I reach for the dress again, and a decision is made—time to find out.

SIX

Malia

MY PHONE BUZZES against the vanity, nearly lost among scattered makeup products. The screen lights up with a simple message from Walt.

Walt: After dinner. My place.

His words set my body on fire. The mascara wand trembles in my grip, leaving a black smudge beneath my eye.

My fingers tangle in the blow dryer cord, nearly yanking it from the wall. Hot air blasts my face as I desperately try to tame my mane. The long, dark waves refuse to cooperate, falling in a tumbled mess around my shoulders where they spill down my back. Like they've been gripped by strong hands, twisted around forceful fingers …

The thought sends heat pooling low in my belly. I switch off the dryer, letting the sudden silence fill the bathroom. Steam clings to the mirror, but as I wipe it clean, I pause. The woman staring back at me looks—different. Changed.

My eyes are darker somehow, heavy with secrets. My lips, still tender from Walt's savage kiss, seem fuller. More sensual. The mark on my neck stands out against my flushed skin—a badge of possession I can't quite hide.

My phone vibrates against the counter. Another message from Walt.

Walt: Wear a dress. No panties. You won't be needing them.

The phone slips from my fingers, clattering against the marble countertop. The sound echoes off the bathroom tiles, matching the thundering of my heart.

Heat floods my core, my inner muscles clenching at his commanding tone. Even through text, his dominance makes me weak. I grip the edge of the vanity, cool stone anchoring me as memories of his touch ghost across my skin.

"Focus," I whisper to my reflection. The makeup wipe shakes in my hand as I clean up the mascara smudge. I've never been this unsteady putting on makeup before. Never felt this electric anticipation humming through my veins.

I stumble to my dresser, yanking open the drawer containing my most intimate things. The cotton briefs I usually wear suddenly seem childish. Without conscious thought, my fingers seek out the black silk and lace I bought on a whim but never dared to wear.

The delicate fabric slides up my trembling legs. Defiance and desire war in my chest—I'm not bold enough not to wear panties, but the whisper of silk against my sensitized flesh feels decadent.

Forbidden.

My phone rings—Malikai's ringtone breaking through the tension.

"Hey, Bro."

"Hey, Sissy, I'm early. Traffic was lighter than expected." Papers rustle in the background. "I'm going to swing by and pick you up. Which building are you in again?"

Ice floods my veins. "The east barracks." My voice sounds strange and breathy. "But you don't need to——"

"Nonsense. I'm already at the gate. Security waved me through." Car doors slam in the background. "Be there in five."

The line goes dead before I can protest.

Five minutes.

My hands shake as I fumble with the lipstick, nearly dropping it into the sink. The woman in the mirror looks panicked now—half made-up, hair still damp from a rushed shower.

The contents of my makeup bag scatter across the counter as I search for concealer. There's no time to cover the mark Walt left on my neck. No time to calm my racing pulse or cool my flushed skin.

Malikai will take one look at me and know something's wrong. My analytical, genius brother reads people like quantum equations and will see right through me.

The dormitory buzzer sounds, echoing through my apartment like a warning bell.

My badges jingle as I snatch them from the hook, the metal biting into my palm. One last glance in the hallway mirror shows a woman on the edge—caught between innocence and awakening. Between the good girl I've always been and the woman Walt sees when he looks at me.

The buzzer buzzes again, more insistent this time. Malikai waiting impatiently, unaware his little sister is about to step into a world of dark pleasure and savage claiming after a quiet dinner with him.

I reach for the door handle, my pulse thundering in my ears. The cool metal grounds me, but only for a moment. My hand freezes, phone heavy in my other palm. Should I text Walt back? Let him know I'm disobeying his command about the panties? My inner muscles clench at the thought of his punishment.

No. Focus.

This is dinner with Malikai. I can always ditch the panties after dinner.

Walt and his dark promises can wait.

I square my shoulders, adjusting the drape of my dress. The silk whispers against my skin as I step out of the barracks and into the humid evening air.

My heart stops because two men stand in the parking lot.

Malikai, looking professorial in his blazer and horn-rimmed glasses, gestures animatedly. And beside him—tall, dark, and radiating lethal grace—Walt stands with a cocky nonchalance.

The smirk curling his lips says he knows exactly what his texts did to me. His eyes rake over my body, lingering on the hem of my dress as if he can see straight through the silk to the lace panties that lie beneath. Heat floods my cheeks.

"There's my girl!" Malikai wraps me in a bear hug. "Though I'm hurt you didn't tell me about your boyfriend."

"Boyfriend?" My mouth goes dry. The word echoes as I pull back from Malikai's embrace. "I …" The protest dies on my lips as Walt steps forward, his presence overwhelming my senses.

"That's my fault." Walt's voice holds a hint of amusement. "I didn't know your brother was in town. When I stopped by to surprise you for dinner, he invited me to join you."

"But …" The word catches in my throat as Walt's gaze locks with mine. Dark heat burns in his eyes, a look that makes my knees weak and my core clench.

Walt's hand settles on my lower back, fingers splaying possessively against the silk. His touch brands me through the thin fabric, sending sparks of electricity racing up my spine.

"Salvatore's is perfect." His thumb traces small circles against my back. "I've heard great things about their wine selection."

My brother launches into a discussion about Italian wines, but I can't focus on his words—not with Walt's fingers dancing along my spine and the memory of his texts burning in my mind.

His lips brush my ear, his breath warm against my skin. "Did you get my texts?"

I manage a small nod, my pulse racing at his proximity.

"And did you do what I asked?" His voice drops lower, rougher, as his fingers trail down my spine to rest just above the curve of my ass.

The silk and lace beneath my dress suddenly feel like the most dangerous secret I've ever kept. My breath catches as his fingers drift lower, a silent question that demands an answer.

SEVEN

Walt

THE TENSION in the car is as thick as the low hum of the engine. Malikai maneuvers the rental out of the parking lot. Malia sits stiffly in the passenger seat, her arms crossed and her gaze fixed out the window, her lips pressed into a thin line.

She's been quiet since we left, but the shallow rise and fall of her chest betrays the storm brewing beneath her calm exterior.

From the backseat, I can't help but smirk. Her fingers clamp around the edge of her seat, knuckles blanching against the dark fabric. The sharp set of her jaw and the barely contained tension in her shoulders scream frustration.

She's furious—every rigid line of her posture makes it clear—but I don't regret tagging along, even if it's earned me her wrath.

Not for a second.

The soft ping of a text interrupts the silence. Her phone lights up in her lap, and she darts a glance down.

I know exactly what the text says.

LOVE THE DRESS. Did you follow my other instructions?

I LEAN AGAINST THE SEAT, watching her squirm. My text is playing havoc with her thoughts. She doesn't say anything, but from the way her shoulders tense, and how her fingers twitch, she tells me I've already taken up residence in her head, just like I want.

"Everything okay?" Malikai breaks the silence as he glances between the two of us.

Malia clears her throat, her voice tighter than usual. "Fine."

It's a lie, of course, but I don't call her out on it.

Not yet.

As the car pulls into the restaurant parking lot, her shoulders tense, and her foot taps against the floor. She lets out a sharp breath; her frustration evident.

I step out, smoothing down my shirt, and catch her eye as she climbs out of the car. Her glare is sharp, but I grin.

This is too much fun.

The hostess greets us at the door, her welcoming smile bright. She leads us through Salvatore's dimly lit interior, past white-clothed tables and the gentle clink of fine china. Malikai's charm takes over instantly. His warm baritone fills the space as he chats with the waitress about the restaurant's wine list.

I let them walk ahead, slipping a hand to the small of Malia's back, guiding her with a subtle touch. She flinches at first, but I keep my hand steady, letting it linger just enough to remind her who's in control.

"You're stunning." I lean in close, just enough so Malia can hear me. I keep my voice low and deliberate. "Though I can't help but wonder …" I pause, letting the words hang between us like a challenge. "Did you follow my instructions—or will I have to check for myself?"

Her step falters, her hand gripping her purse strap a little tighter. The prettiest pink flush colors her cheeks as she shoots me a glare that's all fire and fury, but the way she avoids my gaze says more than her words ever could.

I bite back a grin.

The game is on.

"Corner booth," I murmur to the hostess before she can seat us at a standard table. A quick smile and slight nod toward Malikai. "More private for conversation."

I gesture for Malia to slide in first, then smoothly take my place beside her before Malikai can suggest any other arrangement.

The strategic position leaves her bracketed between the wall and my solid presence. Her brother sits opposite, oblivious to how she shifts slightly away from me.

"This is perfect," Malikai says, accepting the wine list. "Excellent choice on the booth. The acoustics in the main dining room can be challenging for conversation."

I lean back, letting my arm rest along the booth behind Malia's shoulders. My fingertips lightly bounce on her bare shoulder, a playful touch meant to tease.

Her head tilts slightly to let me know she feels it, but she doesn't pull away. Her pulse flutters visibly in her throat as she picks up her water glass. The slight tremor in her hand doesn't escape my notice.

The leather menu crackles as I open it, deliberately leaning against her shoulder. She stiffens but doesn't pull away.

Small victories.

The wine list is extensive, but I know exactly what I want.

"The 2015 *Brunello di Montalcino*," I tell the hovering sommelier, not bothering to consult the menu further. "And let's start with the burrata."

Malikai's eyebrows rise with interest. "You know your Italian wines."

"I spent some time in Tuscany." I let my thumb graze the bare skin of Malia's shoulder, feeling her subtle shiver. "The Sangiovese grape is particularly fascinating. The way it changes character is based on elevation and soil composition."

My free hand traces the rim of my water glass as I describe the region's specific characteristics. Each gesture is calculated, drawing Malikai's attention. Subsequently, beneath the table, my thigh presses firmly against Malia's leg. She tries to shift away, but the booth's design works in my favor.

"Most people don't realize," I continue smoothly, "that the same grape grown just a few hundred meters apart can produce entirely different flavors." I pause as the sommelier returns, presenting the bottle with practiced grace.

The ritual of wine service gives me the perfect excuse to lean closer to Malia, ostensibly to examine the cork. Her scent surrounds me—vanilla, coffee, and something uniquely her. I approve the wine and watch as ruby liquid splashes into crystal.

"To new connections," I propose once our glasses are full, holding Malikai's gaze as we touch glasses. Malia's hand trembles as she lifts her glass, the wine rippling with her movement.

"So, Walt," Malikai sets down his glass, his expression curious, "were you a SEAL before joining the Guardians?"

"No. I was Air Force Special Operations." I keep my tone neutral, though my hand tightens fractionally on the stem of my wine glass. "Special Tactics Pararescue Squadron."

"That must have been intense." He leans forward, genuinely interested. "What made you transition to the private sector?"

The question is loaded—testing me, though Malikai probably doesn't realize how transparent his protective instincts are. I respect it. The kind of brother who flies across the country to check on his sister deserves my honesty.

"Guardian HRS offered something the military couldn't." I'm hyperaware of Malia's tension beside me. "The chance to make a real difference without political constraints. To protect people directly."

As if on cue, Malia shifts, her silky thigh brushing against my leg. The movement draws my focus like a laser, but I maintain eye contact with her brother.

"The team here … They're family. We look out for our own."

The double meaning isn't lost on Malia. Her breath catches slightly, but her brother just nods.

"Family is everything," he agrees, raising his glass again.

I join the toast, letting my fingers brush Malia's wrist as she reaches for her glass. Her pulse races under my touch—a silent confirmation that despite her outward composure, she feels every point of contact between us just as intensely as I do.

Malikai, on the other hand, is anything but subtle. His gaze sharpens as he watches the exchange, his protective instincts kicking into high gear. He sets his glass down carefully, leaning back against the bench with a calculated ease that doesn't fool me.

"How long were you in?"

"Ten years." I keep my tone neutral, though my grip on the stem of my wine glass tightens just enough to betray the weight of those years.

Malikai's gaze sharpens, his brow drawing tight as his fingers tap a slow rhythm against the table. The gears in his head are turning—ten years in the Air Force, a few years with the Guardians. His eyes dart to Malia, then back to me, the unspoken calculation heavy in the air.

I hold back a grin, keeping my expression neutral. He's sizing me up, weighing the age gap between me and his little sister while trying to decide whether he should trust me.

His lips twitch, but the calculating look doesn't leave his face.

Malia shifts beside me, clearly uncomfortable with the exchange, but I stay where I am, my expression calm. Let him do the math. Let him analyze.

I'm not going anywhere.

"That's a long time, and thank you for your service." Malikai hums thoughtfully, his fingers tapping a slow rhythm against the tablecloth.

"Didn't feel that way some days," I reply with a faint smile, deflecting just enough to keep the details vague. "Felt like it was the blink of an eye."

Malia shifts slightly beside me, her discomfort obvious as she glances between us.

"Malikai, seriously," she interjects, trying to steer the conversation back to safer waters. "Stop."

I don't mind the scrutiny. Let him dig.

"Stop, what?" He turns his attention to his sister.

"Stop grilling him."

"Just asking questions, which I wouldn't have to do if my sister told me she was dating someone, and a Guardian at that." His eyes light up with interest.

Malia shifts beside me, her silky thigh brushing against me. The contact sends heat coursing through my veins, but I maintain steady eye contact with her brother.

"The success comes from specialized training and precise execution." I trace a thin scar along my forearm, drawing both siblings' attention. "Take a mission in Myanmar. Two hostiles had a civilian trapped in a market stall. Traditional military response would have meant a full tactical team, high risk of collateral damage. We were surgical—precise."

"How do you train for situations like that?" Malikai adjusts his glasses, leaning in. "The variables must be astronomical."

"Every situation is fluid." My thumb absently strokes the scar, aware of Malia's gaze on the movement. "You learn to read micro-expressions and predict movement patterns. The human body telegraphs intent if you know what to watch for."

"Like quantum variables," Malikai muses, swirling his wine. "Each action creates ripples of possibility."

"Exactly." I catch Malia's subtle shift closer to me and the barely perceptible increase in her breathing. "I noted a slight muscle twitch in the primary target's forearm. Told me exactly when he'd reach for his weapon."

"And the civilian?" Malia's voice comes soft, concerned. She's barely spoken since the wine arrived.

"Walked away without a scratch." I turn toward her, letting my thigh press more firmly against hers under the table. I let my voice drop lower, more intimate. "Protection is always the priority. Whether it's a stranger in a foreign market or someone closer."

"I take it Guardian HRS recruits heavily from the military?" Malikai asks.

"Guardian's recruitment process is what sets us apart," I explain, my voice steady, my thumb tracing slow, deliberate circles against Malia's knee beneath the table. "But yes. We mostly come out of the military."

Malia's breath catches just slightly—a sound so faint I doubt Malikai notices, but I hear it loud and clear.

The conversation flows naturally from there, giving me ample opportunity to tease Malia.

Under the table, I place my hand just above her knee. Her muscles jump beneath my palm, but she maintains her composure, though a slight flush creeps up her neck.

"We look beyond military background, beyond physical capabilities. It's about instinct, adaptability, and ..." I pause, increasing the pressure of my touch, feeling her pulse quicken under my thumb, "... knowing how to read people. Knowing what they need."

My words are directed at Malikai, but the way Malia shifts in her seat, the slight tremor in her posture, tells me she knows exactly who I'm really talking to.

"The psychological component must be fascinating," Malikai says, oblivious, as he picks up the wine bottle and refills our glasses with practiced ease. "How do you quantify something as intangible as instinct?"

I let my hand glide a fraction higher along Malia's thigh. My movements are slow enough to appear casual but deliberate enough that her thigh tenses beneath my touch.

"You don't quantify it." I keep my tone even. My gaze flicks briefly to her before landing on Malikai again. "You watch, listen, pay attention to the details most people overlook. It's about understanding someone's needs before they can articulate them themselves."

Malia swallows hard, her fingers tightening around the stem of her wine glass. Her composure is slipping. She knows exactly what I'm talking about.

"It takes practice, doesn't it?" Malikai leans back in his chair, studying me, his curiosity still rooted in professionalism. "Knowing how to read someone like that."

I shrug, my thumb grazing the sensitive skin above Malia's knee. "Practice. And patience. You learn to notice the little things ... Like when someone's holding back or waiting for permission to let go."

Malia's breath hitches, and I slowly sip my wine, letting the silence between my words hang heavy. I slide my hand up another inch, feeling Malia's sharp intake of breath.

"It takes careful observation." The silk of her dress is cool beneath my palm, a stark contrast to the heat of her skin. "You can train someone to shoot, to fight, but that sixth sense that warns you when something's off? That's innate."

My fingers curve around the soft skin of her inner thigh, sliding higher. I keep my movements deliberate and slow.

Her fork clatters against fine china, the sound sharp in the intimate murmur of the restaurant. Malia stiffens, her breath catching. Her knuckles turn white as she clutches her napkin.

Malikai glances up, his brow furrowing slightly in concern. "You okay?" he asks, his gaze flicking between us.

Malia forces a tight smile. Her voice strained but steady enough to pass. "Just fine."

I let my thumb graze closer to where she's hyperaware of every point of contact. Her pulse hammers beneath her skin, a silent confession she can't control.

Malikai, oblivious, resumes his conversation. I sit back, sipping my wine, letting a faint smile play at the corner of my lips. This game is far from over.

"Sorry," Malia breathes, her voice slightly unsteady. "Just— clumsy."

"No harm done." I squeeze gently, a silent warning against further disruptions. "As I was saying, it's about reading situations." My thumb resumes its lazy circles. "Knowing when to advance and when to hold."

I maintain eye contact with him while my hand slides a fraction higher, feeling the tremor that runs through Malia's body. My fingers curve around her inner thigh. One more inch and I'll know whether she followed my instructions about not wearing panties.

"That's pretty cool." Malikai's enthusiasm is genuine, and his scientific mind is engaged.

The waiter approaches with our appetizer, and I reluctantly withdraw my hand from beneath the table, keeping my thigh firmly pressed against Malia's. Her breathing has quickened, and her chest rises and falls in short, controlled bursts. I hide my smile behind my wine glass, knowing she's fighting to maintain her composure.

This dance of control and restraint, of pushing boundaries while maintaining the appearance of propriety—is its own kind of mission. And, like every mission, timing is everything. I reach for the burrata, already planning my next move.

"The burrata here is exceptional." I pierce the creamy center, watching it spill across the plate. White against red, like secrets bleeding into the open. My hand returns to Malia's thigh as I offer the first bite to her. "You should try it."

Beneath the table, my fingers drift upward, slow and deliberate, tracing the edge of her thigh. Malia stiffens beside me, her breath hitching so softly only I can hear it.

Her fork hovers mid-air, her knuckles tight around the handle as she tries to maintain her composure. Her shoulders shift, a subtle attempt to steady herself, but her thighs clench tighter around my hand, trapping me in place. I don't move—don't need to. The warmth of her skin and the shallow rise and fall of her chest tell me everything I need to know.

The waiter arrives to take our dinner orders, providing a momentary distraction. Malia's relief is palpable as I withdraw my hand to gesture at the menu.

"The veal saltimbocca is their specialty." I maintain my composure as Malia shifts restlessly beside me.

"The wine would pair perfectly with that," Malikai notes, oblivious to his sister's growing distress. "The Brunello's tannins ..."

While he orders, my hand heads back under the table, where it slides further up Malia's thigh. There, I encounter the whisper of silk and lace.

So she didn't follow my instructions about the panties? My

fingers flex against her skin—a promise of consequences to come.

Malia reaches for her water glass, nearly knocking it over. I steady her hand, using the moment of contact to lean close. "Careful," I whisper against her ear, my breath stirring her hair. "We wouldn't want to make a scene."

The flush creeping up her neck tells me she understands the double meaning. Under the table, my fingers continue their torturous exploration, mapping the boundary between silk and skin. Each touch reminds me of my earlier promises and what awaits her after dinner.

The real question is: how long can she maintain her composure under my relentless assault?

"Enough about me. Your background in quantum mechanics is fascinating," I redirect the conversation, letting Malikai's enthusiasm for his work distract from his sister's heightened state. "I'd love to hear more about your work."

My hand returns to a more respectable position on Malia's knee as our entrees arrive. The rich aroma of herbs and wine sauce fills the air, providing a welcome shift in focus. I notice how her fingers tremble slightly as she arranges her napkin.

"I love the parallels between our work." Malikai leans forward, glasses glinting in the candlelight.

"How so?"

"Well, you mentioned it yourself. In both fields, the mere presence of an operative—or observer—fundamentally changes the dynamics of a situation. I find that fascinating."

I set my knife down deliberately. "I suppose so. Success requires absolute focus, unwavering commitment, and …" I meet Malia's eyes briefly, "complete dedication to the objective."

I maintain perfect composure as I cut into my veal, though my awareness of Malia never wavers. Her breathing has steadied somewhat, but the tension in her shoulders tells me she's far from relaxed.

Good.

Hot and bothered is exactly where I want her.

I catch every flicker of her micro-expressions, every subtle hint of the war she's waging within herself. Tonight's dinner is its own tactical operation, and so far, I'm dominating the battlefield.

"Malia mentioned you get to work with some of the best tech?"

"The latest advancements in tactical gear have revolutionized our approach to hostage extraction." I keep my tone steady as Malia's fork freezes halfway to her lips. My hand rests lightly on her thigh, unmoving, but the tension in her body is a silent, charged undercurrent. "The technology allows us to protect our teams while minimizing civilian casualties."

"The applications must be extensive," Malikai says, leaning forward, his wineglass forgotten. "Especially in urban environments where traditional tactical gear might be too conspicuous."

He's doing it again—redirecting the focus back to me. His curiosity is too sharp, slicing through the conversation with questions too precise to be casual. He hasn't mentioned his work once for someone with a background in quantum engineering and fusion reactions.

Instead, he keeps circling back—probing the Guardians, the scope of our operations. His words pull at loose threads, always leading back to what I do. But there's another omission, glaring now that I notice it.

What about Malia? Not one word about her work at The Guardian Grind, no interest in how she's carved out her place there.

A low hum of conversation fills the restaurant, the occasional clink of silverware against plates punctuating the air. A faint aroma of garlic and charred meat lingers, mingling with the sharper tang of Malikai's wine as he swirls it, his movements almost too deliberate.

"Is that all you do?" His voice is casual, but his eyes stay locked on mine, the kind of focus that isn't just polite. It's calculated.

"What do you mean?"

"Rescue hostages? Does Guardian HRS ever provide security work?" His question hangs, laced with just enough curiosity to mask whatever's driving this line of questioning.

I lean back slightly, letting the faint creak of the booth accompany my deliberate calm. Across from me, Malikai's jaw tightens ever so slightly, his polished exterior showing its first real crack. I glance at Malia—she's quiet, her fingers curled around her fork, but her chest's quick rise and fall tells me she's not as unaffected as she appears.

I keep my expression neutral, letting the weight of his question settle before I respond. "As a matter of fact, we do." My voice is steady, even as my thoughts churn. "Is that something you're interested in?"

Malikai's lips press into a thin line before relaxing into a faint, polite smile. His shoulders shift, the movement too casual to be unintentional. He leans back, resting one arm on the booth, swirling his wine again. The soft slosh of liquid against glass feels louder in the momentary pause.

"Let's just say my work isn't without its challenges." His words are carefully chosen, each one measured. He glances at Malia, a fleeting look that gives nothing away before his gaze settles back on me. "Security is always a concern."

His tone is light, his expression calm, but his fingers tighten slightly on the stem of his glass. A subtle tell, but enough to set my instincts on edge. Whatever he's fishing for, it goes deeper than curiosity—and Malia's silence only deepens the unease clawing at my gut.

My grip on her thigh tightens slightly, more out of instinct than intent. She shifts, her body stiffening under my touch, but she doesn't pull away.

"Security's a universal concern," I say, matching his measured tone. "But you seem particularly interested in the overlap between my work and your—challenges. Is there something I should know?"

Malikai offers a tight smile, but his eyes betray him. "No. No. Nothing pressing. Just professional curiosity."

His words might say one thing, but the unease beneath them tells another story entirely. I'm starting to wonder how far this curiosity extends—and what it might cost Malia.

The cream sauce on my veal is growing cold as I process what Malikai isn't saying. His questions about Guardian security services nag at my instincts, but his phone buzzes before I can probe further.

"Excuse me." He glances at the screen, a flicker of tension crossing his face. "I need to take this. Work never sleeps."

Malia rounds on me the moment he steps away, her voice low but sharp. "What the hell do you think you're doing?"

"Enjoying dinner with my girlfriend and getting to know her brother." I take a deliberate sip of wine, savoring her indignation.

"I am not your girlfriend," she hisses, though the flush creeping up her neck betrays her. "And you need to stop ..."

"Stop, what?" I lean closer, letting my breath stir the hair by her ear. "Stop noticing how you shiver every time I touch you? Stop watching your pulse race when I get too close?"

"This isn't funny, Walt." Her fingers clench around her napkin. "My brother is right there."

"Your brother is conveniently occupied." My hand finds her knee again. "Which gives us time to discuss your—disobedience."

Her eyes widen. "My what?"

"I believe my instructions about tonight's attire were quite clear." I let my thumb trace slow circles on her skin. "Yet here you are, wearing panties. We'll have to address that later."

"You're impossible." But there's a tremor in her voice that has nothing to do with anger.

Through the restaurant's front windows, Malikai paces on the sidewalk, one hand pressed to his ear. His gestures are agitated, shoulders tight with tension. Something about that call has him rattled.

"He's been acting strange all evening," Malia murmurs, following my gaze. The fight drains from her posture, replaced by concern.

"I noticed." My tactical mind kicks in, cataloging details—his pointed questions about Guardian security, his reluctance to discuss his work, and now this call. "Has he mentioned any problems at work?"

"No, but …" She bites her lip, uncertain.

I catch movement at the door. "We'll finish this discussion later." My voice drops lower. "And believe me, we have a lot to discuss."

Malikai returns, his polished demeanor slightly cracked. A bead of sweat traces his temple despite the restaurant's cool air.

"Everything alright?" Malia asks.

"Just a minor lab issue." He forces a smile that doesn't reach his eyes. "Nothing to worry about." But as he reaches for his wine, his hand trembles ever so slightly.

My instincts, honed by years of reading subtle tells, ring alarm bells. Whatever that call was about, it isn't a minor lab issue. What kind of trouble has Malia's brilliant brother gotten himself into?

EIGHT

Walt

———

MALIKAI CLEARS HIS THROAT, straightening his silverware with precise movements. "I've been terribly rude, haven't I?" He looks at Malia with genuine regret. "Here I am, interrogating Walt about Guardian operations when I haven't asked my own sister a thing about her new business venture."

The change in topic visibly brightens Malia's expression. The tension in her shoulders eases as she leans forward, and I find myself completely captivated by the transformation.

Gone is the woman fighting for composure under my touch. In her place sits someone enthusiastically radiant.

"The Guardian Grind is amazing," she says, her eyes sparkling. "Though I still can't believe Jenna offered me a partnership. I mean, I was just her employee before …"

"Before everything went sideways," Malikai finishes, his expression darkening slightly. He glances around the restaurant, lowering his voice. "Speaking of which, are you sure it's safe? Working there? Given Jenna's—situation?"

I notice the subtle shift in his posture—how his shoulders tense and his eyes scan the room. It's the same heightened awareness I've observed in him all evening, but now it's directed at his sister's safety.

"Guardian HQ is the safest place she could be," I interject smoothly, my hand moving from Malia's thigh to rest protectively against her lower back. Not to tease now, but to reassure. "The entire compound is secure."

Malia shoots me a grateful look before turning back to her brother. "Seriously, Kai, it's fine. And the Grind? It's become this amazing hub for the whole compound. You should see it in the morning when the Guardian teams come in after training …"

I lean back, letting my hand drop away as she launches into animated descriptions of her daily routine. The way her face lights up as she describes experimenting with new coffee blends, the pride in her voice when she talks about their customer base—it's mesmerizing.

"… and we've started doing these specialty drinks named after different teams," she continues, gesturing expressively. "The Alpha Ambition is pure adrenaline in a cup," Malia explains, her hands animating her words. "Four shots of espresso with caramel and vanilla, topped with cinnamon-dusted foam. Alpha team runs hot and fast, so their drink matches their energy."

"Four shots?" Malikai's eyebrows shoot up. "That's practically rocket fuel."

"You should see them in the morning," I add, grinning. "They order doubles like it's going out of season. Malia is not just the best barista at HQ; she's a caffeinated chemical genius."

Malia looks at me with genuine pride and keeps rolling. "There's the Bravo Boldness." Her enthusiasm is infectious. "It's this amazing cold brew that we age in bourbon barrels. It's not alcoholic, of course, but it picks up these incredible notes of oak and vanilla. We serve it over coffee ice cubes with a splash of cream and maple syrup."

"Coffee ice cubes?" Malikai leans forward, intrigued.

"So it doesn't get watered down," she explains. "Bravo team hates anything diluted. They're all about intensity."

"And Charlie team?" Malikai glances at me with a knowing smile. "What's your poison?"

"The Charlie Challenge." Malia's eyes dance as she looks my way. "Dark chocolate mocha with a hint of ghost pepper and sea salt. Smooth at first, then it hits you with an unexpected kick."

Just like you. I love watching her describe my team's signature drink perfectly.

"Then there's Delta Darkness. It's an incredible dark roast with hints of chocolate and cayenne that took forever to get the balance right, but now it's one of our best sellers."

"Sounds amazing."

"But my favorite to make is the Tech Tempest," she adds, and Malikai perks up at the mention of the technical division. "It's for all the brainiacs at HQ—you know, your kind of people, Kai. We do this incredible fusion of matcha and espresso layered with honey and lavender. It's precise, complex, and totally unexpected, just like them."

"The tech division must be fascinating," Malikai says, his earlier tension momentarily forgotten. "All those brilliant minds working on cutting-edge systems …"

"Oh my God, you should hear them when they get going." Malia laughs. "They turn the Grind into their personal think tank some afternoons. All these incredible discussions about quantum computing and artificial intelligence go completely over my head. You'd love it. It's like a coffee-fueled genius convention."

Malikai's eyes light up at this, his fingers tapping thoughtfully against his wine glass. "Sounds like my kind of crowd." The tension from earlier seems to fade.

"They're definitely your kind of people," Malia agrees.

"Total science nerds, but in the best way. They make me feel like I'm serving coffee in the future."

The pride in her voice as she describes her creation makes something warm unfurl in my chest. She's built more than just a coffee shop—she's created a nexus point for the entire organization, understanding each group's personality so well that she can capture it in a cup.

"You always did have a knack for flavors," Malikai says fondly. "Remember that summer you insisted on making your own tea blends?"

"Oh God." Malia laughs, the sound pure and unrestrained. "Those were terrible! But hey, failure is the best teacher, right?"

I find myself smiling, caught up in her enthusiasm. I haven't seen this side of Malia before—passionate, creative, and completely in her element. Her talk about coffee like it's an art form, her eyes dancing as she describes the perfect crema on an espresso shot—it's intoxicating in a completely different way from our earlier tension.

"The best part," she says, "is watching people connect over coffee. We've got these beautiful reclaimed wood tables that Jenna found, and sometimes, I'll look out from behind the counter and see operators from different teams sharing ideas or tech specialists brainstorming over lattes. It's become this amazing community space."

"You've always had a gift for creating welcoming environments," Malikai observes. "Even as a kid, your treehouse was the neighborhood gathering spot."

"The Fort of Perpetual Snacks." Malia giggles, and the sound does something to my chest. "I forgot about that!"

I watch her laugh, really watch her—the way her nose crinkles slightly, how her whole face lights up with joy. My earlier plans of domination and control seem suddenly out of place. Yes, I want her body, but watching her now, I want so much more.

I want to know every story behind that laugh, every memory that shaped her into this vibrant woman who can turn a simple coffee shop into a sanctuary.

"What about you, Walt?" Her question pulls me from my thoughts. "Any favorite Guardian Grind creations?"

"Besides watching you work?" The words slip out before I can stop them, softer and more honest than intended. Her cheeks flush, but it's different from her earlier embarrassment—warmer, sweeter somehow. "I love how focused you get when challenged."

"Like the Charlie Challenge," she admits, meeting my eyes with a hint of shyness. She turns to her brother, animated and excited again. "I worked on that one for weeks, trying to perfect it. Had to capture that whole 'dangerous but sophisticated' vibe."

I remember those weeks, watching her experiment behind the counter. The cute way she scrunched her nose when a blend wasn't quite right, her triumphant grin when she finally nailed it. I'll never admit it, but I purposely started arriving early for my morning coffee just to catch those moments. To see her lost in concentration, hair twisted up in a messy bun, completely absorbed in her craft.

"The ghost pepper was inspired," I say, and her whole face lights up at the compliment.

It hits me then—I could spend hours watching her like this. Her hands dance through the air as she talks, and her eyes sparkle when she's excited about something.

In the inventory room, I thought I knew what I wanted from her. I thought it was all about claiming her body and marking her as mine.

But this? This vibrant, incredible woman who puts so much thought and care into everything she creates? Who knows that Charlie team needs that extra kick of heat to match our intensity?

She's gotten under my skin in ways that have nothing to do with physical desire.

Something shifts in my chest as I watch her describe her dreams for the Grind's future. The raw desire is still there, burning hot and insistent, but it's joined by something deeper—something that makes me want to protect not just her body but also her passion, this ability to create warmth and connection in even the most unlikely places.

God help me. I'm not falling for Malia; I'm already in deep. So deep there's no climbing out.

Watching how her whole being lights up when she talks about her passion, I realize I passed the point of no return weeks ago.

This isn't desire or possession or even falling in love. I'm already there. Already completely, irrevocably in love with every facet of her—from her creative spirit to her fierce independence, even that stubborn defiance that drives me crazy.

I want it all. Want to be the one who makes her eyes light up like that, want to protect her dreams as fiercely as I want to protect her body.

I want to wake up every morning to her experimenting with coffee blends, be the first to taste her latest creations, and hear every story and memory that crosses her mind.

The realization should terrify me. I've never wanted anyone like this—wholly, completely, with a depth far beyond the physical.

But as I watch her laugh at something Malikai says, all I feel is certainty. She's it for me. The beginning and end of everything I never knew I was looking for.

NINE

Malia

THE FAMILIAR CADENCE of Kai's voice washes over me as he asks about our specialty roasts. It's so easy falling back into our rhythm, that special shorthand that only siblings who grew up finishing each other's sentences have.

God, I've missed him. Video calls and texts aren't the same as having him here, seeing his eyes light up behind those ridiculous glasses as he geeks out over our brewing methods.

"You're using precision temperature control for the pour-overs?" He leans forward, genuinely fascinated. "That's brilliant. The molecular composition of the beans would react differently at varying heat levels ..."

"Oh no." I laugh, the sound warm and natural. "No quantum coffee lectures allowed at dinner. But yes, we invested in some seriously high-tech equipment. The tech team especially appreciates the precision."

"Of course they do." His grin is infectious. "They're my people."

Watching him now, relaxed and animated, it's hard to believe he seemed so agitated earlier. That phone call must have rattled him, but looking at him across the table, all I see is my big brother—the same guy who used to help me with science projects and chase away playground bullies.

His hands are steady as he gestures, no sign of the earlier tremors. Maybe I imagined his distress, reading too much into things after Walt's words about Kai's strange questions.

"Remember when you tried to teach me about electron configurations?" I ask, smiling at the memory. "Using coffee beans as atoms?"

"And you kept eating my electron shells." His laugh echoes across the table. "Worst teaching assistant ever."

"Hey, I was seven! And hungry!"

The conversation flows effortlessly, years of inside jokes and shared memories making everything comfortable and right.

Almost everything.

Because while my mind is fully engaged with Kai, my body remains traitorously aware of Walt beside me. Every slight shift reminds me of his earlier touches, his fingers skating up my thigh, the way he …

Heat floods my cheeks and I reach for my water glass, trying to cool down. The silk of my panties is uncomfortably damp, a constant reminder of Walt's effect on me. Of all the filthy promises he whispered in my ear at the coffee shop. Of how badly I want him to fulfill every single one.

"Remember that summer you decided to become a scientist?" Kai asks, pulling me back from dangerous thoughts. "You set up that 'lab' in the garage?"

"Using Mom's kitchen supplies." I grin. "She was so mad when she found her measuring cups full of dirt and leaves."

"*But, Mom, I'm doing science!*" Kai mimics my childhood voice perfectly.

"God, I miss this," I say softly. "Miss you. Video calls aren't the same."

His expression softens. "I know, Sissy. I miss you too. Maybe I could come out more often? The quantum lab's expanding our research sites. Might be able to coordinate some work on the west coast."

The hope in my chest blooms, but Walt shifts beside me, his thigh pressing against mine, and suddenly, all I can think about is his hands, his mouth, his promises. My body thrums with awareness, the silk between my legs growing damper by the second.

"You okay, Sissy?" Kai's voice breaks through my thoughts. "You look flushed."

"Just warm," I manage, though Walt's soft chuckle beside me says he knows exactly why I'm overheated.

I focus on my brother, on our conversation about the Grind's future plans, but my body has other ideas.

The pressure in my bladder is becoming impossible to ignore, compounded by all the wine and water I've been nervously drinking. Every shift reminds me of my growing need and the slick evidence of Walt's effect on me.

"Speaking of the Grind," Kai continues, "have you thought about expanding? Maybe a second location?"

I try to focus on his question, but Walt's presence beside me is overwhelming. The heat of his body, the lingering ghost of his touch on my thigh—it's all too much.

"Excuse me," I murmur, starting to rise. "I need to …"

"I'll walk you." Walt's voice is low but commanding, brooking no argument.

I start to protest—I'm perfectly capable of finding the restroom on my own—but the look he gives me stops the words in my throat. His eyes are dark with promise, reminding me of every touch, every whispered threat of punishment for my disobedience.

My mouth goes dry as he stands, offering his hand with gentlemanly courtesy that feels anything but gentlemanly.

"I can find my way to the ladies' room by myself," I murmur as we weave between tables, keeping my voice low enough that only Walt can hear.

The soft clink of silverware and murmured conversations create a gentle backdrop, the rich aroma of garlic and wine filling the air.

"That's where you're wrong, princess." His hand settles at the small of my back, warm and possessive through the silk of my dress. "Escorting you is exactly my job. Making sure you're safe …" His voice drops lower, sending shivers down my spine. "And ensuring you follow instructions."

A waiter passes with a tray of desserts, the sweet scent of vanilla and caramel momentarily distracting me.

"What do you mean?"

Walt guides me past a table of business diners, their laughter covering his next words.

"Those panties you're wearing? The ones I specifically told you not to wear?" His thumb traces small circles against my back. "They're mine now. You'll remove them and hand them over when you're finished."

I nearly stumble, catching myself on his arm.

"What?" The word comes out as a shocked whisper. Around us, the restaurant continues its elegant dinner service, completely oblivious to how my world has just tilted on its axis.

"You heard me." His smile is perfectly pleasant to any observer, but his eyes burn with dark promise. "Consider it the first consequence of your disobedience."

"But …" I glance around at the other diners and the bustling waitstaff. "What am I supposed to do with them?"

His soft laugh sends heat pooling low in my belly. "Hand them to me, of course. They belong to me now." He leans closer, ostensibly steadying me as we pause to let a couple pass. "Just like you do."

The words should outrage me. Should make me pull away in indignation. Instead, warmth floods through me, my pulse quickening.

How does he do this? Turn my world upside down with just a few words and make me crave things I never knew I wanted?

We reach the hallway leading to the restrooms, the ambient noise of the restaurant fading slightly. The lighting here is softer and more intimate. Walt turns me to face him, his body effectively shielding me from view.

"Don't make me wait too long." His voice is velvet over steel. "Your brother might wonder what's keeping us. If I'm ravishing his little sister in the bathroom."

"You wouldn't?"

He doesn't answer. Instead, he reaches over my head and pushes the ladies' room door open.

My cheeks burn as his soft chuckle follows me inside. My heart thunders in my chest, my body humming with a mixture of embarrassment and arousal.

What's happening to me? When did I become this woman who gets excited by such outrageous demands? But even as I question it, I know I'll do exactly what he asked.

Because God help me, I want to.

The restroom is one of those elegant spaces built for one—all marble and soft lighting, with fresh flowers by the sink and plush hand towels monogrammed with the restaurant's logo. No multiple stalls. The lock clicks behind me with surprising finality.

My reflection stares back at me, cheeks flushed, eyes bright. I look different somehow, changed, like Walt's commands have awakened something in me I didn't know existed.

After using the facilities, I almost pull my panties back up out of habit. Then I remember his words: *They belong to me now.*

My hands tremble slightly as I step out of the black lace,

hardly believing I'm actually doing this. The silk is still damp—evidence of his effect on me that I'll have to hand over.

"This is insane," I whisper to my reflection as I ball the delicate fabric in my fist. But even as I say it, heat pools low in my belly. The thought of walking back to the table like this, with nothing between my skin and the silk of my dress …

I wash my hands, trying to steady my breathing. The marble counter is cool beneath my palms as I lean forward, giving myself one last chance to back out. To be sensible. To be the good girl I've always been.

Instead, I straighten my dress and grip my panties in a fist.

When I open the door, Walt is waiting exactly where I left him. His eyes drop immediately to my clenched hand, catching a glimpse of black lace between my fingers. Something dark and hungry flashes across his face.

He moves forward before I can step out, forcing me back into the restroom. The door closes behind him with a soft click, and suddenly, the spacious bathroom feels very small.

"Walt?" My voice comes out breathy, uncertain.

The wicked gleam in his eyes makes my knees weak.

His hand extends, palm up, an unspoken command.

When I place the delicate lace in his hand, his fingers curl around mine for just a moment, trapping me there. The air between us thickens, charged with possibility. My heart hammers against my ribs, so loud I'm sure he must hear it.

Walt lifts the silk to his face, inhaling deeply, his eyes never leaving mine, and my brain short-circuits. A whimper escapes my throat at the blatant gesture.

He's sniffing my panties.

Like, really sniffing them. I always thought that was just some weird urban legend, something guys joked about but didn't actually do. But Walt's eyes drift closed as he inhales deeply, his nostrils flaring slightly, and there's nothing joking about his expression.

I should be mortified. Should be grabbing my panties back and running from the bathroom. Instead, I'm frozen in place, watching his eyes open again, darker than before, hungry in a way that makes my knees weak.

The raw masculinity of the gesture, the way he doesn't even try to hide how much he's affected by my scent—it's the most erotic thing I've ever seen.

A whimper escapes my throat before I can stop it. His lips curve into a knowing smirk as he folds the lace deliberately, almost reverently, before tucking it into his suit pocket. Heat floods my body as I realize he'll have that intimate piece of me with him for the rest of dinner.

How is it possible that something I would have found creepy from anyone else becomes unbearably sexy when Walt does it? Maybe because he doesn't try to hide his desire, doesn't apologize for wanting every part of me, even the parts I've been taught to be embarrassed about.

"Good girl," he murmurs, and something inside me melts at the praise.

He steps forward, and I instinctively retreat, my pulse thundering in my ears.

There's something primal about the way he moves—smooth, controlled, predatory like a lion stalking its prey. The comparison should frighten me, but instead, it sends shivers of anticipation racing down my spine.

Another step.

My breath catches as he mirrors my movement.

The air feels electric between us, charged with possibilities. I've never felt like this before, never been the focus of such intense, male-focused desire.

It's terrifying and thrilling all at once.

He takes another step.

I take a retreating step back.

The cool marble of the sink presses against my lower back, startling a gasp from my lips.

Still, he advances, each deliberate movement closing the distance between us. My body responds to his proximity in ways I never knew it could—skin tingling, breasts feeling heavy and sensitive, an ache building low in my belly.

His size overwhelms me as he cages me in.

I've always known Walt was big, but now, trapped between his body and the sink, I feel deliciously small. His broad shoulders block out the rest of the room, his arms bracketing me as his hands grip the counter on either side of my hips.

The position leaves me nowhere to go and nowhere to hide from the heat in his eyes.

My heart races so fast that I feel lightheaded. Every breath brings his scent—cologne and something uniquely Walt—flooding my senses. The warmth radiating from his body seeps into mine, though he's not quite touching me.

Not yet.

The anticipation of that first contact has me trembling.

I should feel trapped. Cornered. Instead, I feel—protected.

Desired.

Safe, even as my body hums with a dangerous kind of excitement. The contradictions make my head spin—how can I feel both vulnerable and completely secure?

Both prey and precious?

His breath fans across my face, and I realize just how close he is. Close enough that I can see the flecks of gold in his dark eyes, count each of his eyelashes, and notice the slight stubble darkening his jaw.

Close enough that the slightest movement would bring our bodies together.

The thought makes me shiver. Or maybe it's the way he's looking at me—like he wants to devour me whole, like I'm everything he's ever hungered for.

I've never felt so aware of my own body. Of the rapid rise and fall of my chest, the way my fingers grip the counter's edge, and the heat pooling between my thighs. Even the silk of my dress feels too rough against my sensitized skin.

Without my panties, I feel exposed, vulnerable—wanton.

His presence surrounds me completely—sight, smell, the promise of touch. He makes my head spin with all the possibilities—not just of sex, but of everything he's promised.

The way he commanded me earlier, how naturally I responded to his orders … It awakens something primal inside me. A need I never knew existed.

I should be scandalized by the things he's whispered he wants to do to me. Should be horrified by how casually he talks about spanking me, controlling me, making me beg. Instead, each dark promise sends heat flooding through my body. The thought of being bent over his knee, of feeling his palm coming down hard while he tells me exactly why I'm being punished …

The rest of the world fades away until there's nothing but this moment, this man, this electric tension building between us.

My mind races with possibilities, with wants and fears tumbling together in a dizzying rush.

His cologne surrounds me—spice and cedar and pure masculine essence. My hands grip the counter's edge as he towers over me, his body radiating heat and control. His eyes drop to my parted lips, darkening with hunger.

Oh God.

This is really happening.

My thighs press together, trying to ease the ache building between them. What's happening to me? When did I become this woman who craves not just physical intimacy but submission?

Who gets wet at the thought of following commands and being completely at his mercy?

His earlier words echo my thoughts: *"I want to push your boundaries."*

And I do want that. Want him to take control, to show me all these dark desires I never knew I had. Want to kneel for him, to please him, to surrender everything to his experienced hands.

His eyes darken as if he can read my thoughts and see the depraved directions they're taking. Instead of feeling ashamed, I feel—powerful. Sexy. Like my submission would be a gift he'd treasure as much as my virginity.

Heat floods my cheeks at the realization. I want it all—the tenderness and the roughness, the pleasure and the pain, the praise and the punishment. I want to explore every filthy promise he's made, discover every dark desire he awakens in me.

But not here.

My first time can't be here, in a restaurant bathroom with my brother waiting at our table.

Can it?

The thought sends conflicting waves of excitement and uncertainty through me. I want Walt—I have wanted him for so long my body aches.

But not like this.

Not rushed and secret between courses of dinner in a public restroom. I want time to explore this properly, to let him guide me into these uncharted waters slowly, thoroughly, and completely.

"Walt ..." His name comes out as a breathless plea, torn between desire and hesitation. I want him to kiss and touch me, but I also want—more.

I want it to be special.

He braces one hand on the counter beside me, the other rising to cup my jaw. His thumb traces my bottom lip, and I shiver at the intensity of his gaze. Everything in me wants to surrender to this moment, to let him claim me right here.

"Mine," he growls softly, leaning down.

"Wait," I whisper, pressing my palms against his chest. His heart thunders under my touch, matching my own frantic rhythm. "I want this; want you. So much it scares me." The confession tumbles out, raw and honest. "But I've never … I mean, I haven't …"

Understanding softens his expression, though the hunger in his eyes remains. "Never?"

I shake my head, heat flooding my cheeks. "I was saving it. Waiting for …" The right moment? The right person? "For someone who mattered."

His other hand frames my face, forcing me to meet his gaze. "And do I matter?"

"Yes." The word comes without hesitation, surprising me with its certainty. "But I don't want my first time to be here. Like this. Quick and rushed in a bathroom." My voice drops to barely a whisper. "I want to be able to take my time. Want to explore everything you promised me earlier." My voice catches on *"every-thing,"* my eyes dropping to his mouth before meeting his gaze again, hoping he understands what I can't quite say.

That I'm not just talking about sex. That when he threatened to spank me, to tie me up, to make me beg … Those promises made me ache in ways I never knew possible.

I bite my lip, gathering courage.

"I want all of it," I whisper, my cheeks burning as my body thrums with need. "Everything you said. Everything you promised."

My fingers twist in his shirt, not pulling him closer, not pushing him away, just holding on as I try to convey without words how much I want to submit to him. How ready I am to explore these dark desires he's awakened in me.

His sharp intake of breath tells me he understands exactly what I'm trying to say. His eyes darken further, and his grip on the counter tightens until his knuckles whiten.

"Say it again," he commands softly, and his tone—that mix of authority and hunger—makes me shiver. "What is it you want from me?"

"Everything," I breathe, letting all my newfound cravings color that single word. Hoping he hears in it my willingness to kneel, to obey, to surrender completely to whatever filthy desires he has planned for me.

For a moment, I fear he'll be angry. That my rejection will break whatever spell has been building between us. Instead, his thumb strokes my cheek with surprising tenderness.

"When you're ready," he promises, his voice rough with restraint. "I'm going to spend hours with you. Learn every inch of your body. Make you come apart in ways you've never imagined." His forehead rests against mine. "But you're right. Your first time shouldn't be here."

"You're not mad?" Relief and disappointment war in my chest.

His soft laugh stirs my hair. "Mad? Baby, knowing I'll be your first?" His hands tighten possessively. "That makes me want you even more. Makes me want to do this right."

The tension shifts, not dissipating but transforming into something sweeter, full of promise rather than urgency. His control and his willingness to wait only make me want him more.

TEN

Walt

—————

THROUGH THE SOFT ambient lighting of the hallway, I guide Malia back toward the dining room, my hand steady at the small of her back. The silk of her dress whispers beneath my palm, but my thoughts linger on the delicate lace tucked in my pocket—still warm from her skin, still damp with evidence of how I affect her.

As we emerge from the restroom, the restaurant's sounds wash over us: the gentle clink of silverware, murmured conversations, and wine glasses meeting in distant toasts.

But all my senses focus on Malia—the subtle tremor in her breathing, the way she carefully measures each step as if hyper-aware of the air against her now-bare skin.

My fingers brush the lace in my pocket, and I remember how it felt to inhale her scent—sweet, musky, and uniquely hers. The knowledge that she's walking beside me without panties, that she surrendered them at my command despite her innocence—or perhaps because of it—makes my blood run hot.

"You're doing so well," I murmur, low enough that only she can hear. Her step falters slightly, and I steady her, fighting back a smirk as her brother comes into view at our table.

I guide her into the booth first, deliberately brushing against her as she slides in. Her sharp intake of breath is barely audible over the restaurant's ambient noise. I settle beside her, casually draping my arm along the booth behind her shoulders.

"Everything okay?" Malikai asks, adjusting his glasses. He's the picture of brotherly concern, utterly unaware that his sister's panties are currently pressed against my thigh in my pocket.

"Perfect," I respond smoothly, reaching for my wine glass with my free hand. My other hand dips into my pocket, fingering the delicate lace while maintaining eye contact with him.

Your sister just gave me her panties and confessed she's saving her virginity for me.

She wants me to teach her about submission and pleasure.

The irony of the situation—sitting across from her protective older brother while possessing such an intimate token—adds an edge of danger that only heightens my awareness of her.

Every shift of her body beside me, every carefully controlled breath, reminds me of her confession in the bathroom.

A virgin.

And not just any virgin—one who craves the darker pleasures I plan to introduce her to. The responsibility and privilege of being her first sends heat coursing through my veins.

The waiter appears to clear our plates, and I take advantage of the moment to lean close to her ear, ostensibly to be heard over the noise.

"I can smell how wet you are," I whisper, delighting in her sharp inhale. "Such a good girl, sitting here so properly while I hold your pretty panties."

Her wine glass trembles slightly as she raises it to her lips. Malikai launches into a story about their childhood, oblivious to how his sister squirms beside me, how her thighs press together under the table.

I finger the lace in my pocket again, remembering her breathy confession: *"I want everything you promised."*

The words replay in my mind as I catch her eye across the rim of my wine glass. Her cheeks flush prettily as I raise an eyebrow, a silent reminder of exactly what *"everything"* entails.

Soon, I think, watching her nibble her lower lip. Soon I'll teach her exactly what submission means. But for now, I savor the anticipation, the sweet torture of waiting, as we sit across from her brother, sharing a secret that makes every moment electric with possibility.

Malikai deflects another question about his research, smoothly steering the conversation back to Guardian HRS operations.

This is the third time tonight that he has dodged discussing his quantum work. For someone Malia describes as obsessed with his research, his reluctance is interesting.

"The tiramisu here is exceptional," I interrupt his questions about our Protectors, personal security experts, gesturing to the waiter. "You have to try it."

The dessert arrives—layers of coffee-soaked ladyfingers and mascarpone cream dusted with rich cocoa powder. Malia's eyes widen slightly as I gather a small portion with my fingers rather than using the delicate dessert fork provided.

"Open," I command softly, holding the morsel to her lips.

Her hesitation lasts only a heartbeat before she complies, her lips parting. The intimacy of feeding her, of watching her accept what I offer, sends heat coursing through my veins.

Her tongue darts out to catch a drop of cream, and I have to suppress a groan. When she releases my fingers, I deliberately lick them clean, maintaining eye contact. The flush creeping up her neck tells me she remembers exactly what else I plan to taste.

Malikai's phone buzzes against the table. The same ringtone as earlier—the one that made him tense and check his watch repeatedly. He glances at the screen, and I catch a flash of something like fear before he masks it.

"Excuse me," he says, already standing. "I need to take this."

As he strides away, his fingers flex, curling into tight fists before relaxing—a restless, unconscious motion. His right hand twitches, just once, as though resisting the urge to grip something—or someone. The subtle tremor ripples through his fingertips before he shoves his hand into his pockets, his shoulders rigid with control he's struggling to maintain.

Something's off.

"Walt?" Malia's voice pulls me back to her. In the soft lighting, she looks vulnerable and uncertain. "About what I said earlier—about …" She can't say it.

I turn toward her, letting my arm drop from the booth to curl around her shoulders. The silk of her dress is cool beneath my fingers, but her skin burns hot.

"Are you disappointed?" she whispers. "That I've never—"

"Listen to me carefully," I interrupt, turning her face toward mine. "You being a virgin doesn't disappoint me. It makes me want you more." My thumb traces her bottom lip, remembering how she trembled in the bathroom. "Knowing I'll be your first …" I let my voice drop lower, rougher. "And your last …"

Her breath catches.

"You heard me." I brush my nose along her jaw, inhaling the sweet scent of her perfume mixed with arousal. "Once I have you, once I show you everything I promised? You'll never want anyone else."

The lace in my pocket burns against my thigh, reminding me of exactly how wet she got from my earlier promises. How readily she responded to commands.

"But what if …" She bites her lip, and I have to force myself not to claim her mouth right here. "What if I'm not good at it? At any of it?"

"Baby," I chuckle darkly, "you're already perfect. The way you respond to my touch and how eager you are to please …" My hand slides to her neck, and I feel her pulse race. "We're going to have so much fun exploring exactly what you can take."

Malikai's voice carries from the hallway—sharp and agitated, not the measured tones of an academic discussing research.

"Is he always like this?" I ask, nodding toward where her brother paces. "The mysterious calls, the evasive answers?"

Malia frowns, worry creasing her brow. "No, actually. He's usually so focused, so steady. Almost robotic sometimes with how precise he is." She watches him gesture sharply into his phone. "I've never seen him this—scattered."

I file that away, adding it to the growing list of inconsistencies. A quantum physicist who won't discuss his work. Who asks pointed questions about security protocols. Who gets mysterious calls that leave him shaking.

"He's probably just stressed," Malia says, but she doesn't sound convinced. "His research is at a critical stage—"

"What exactly is his research?" I keep my tone casual, even as I catalog every detail of Malikai's agitated movements. "You mentioned fusion reactions?"

"Honestly? I don't understand it. Something about quantum tunneling effects in plasma containment?" She shrugs. "He usually loves explaining it, but lately …"

Malikai returns before she can finish, his tie slightly loosened, glasses askew. His fingers drum an erratic pattern on the table as he signals for the check.

"Everything okay?" I ask mildly, noting how his eyes dart between exits.

"Fine, fine." He forces a smile that doesn't reach his eyes. "Just a small issue at the lab. Nothing to worry about."

But as I help Malia from the booth, I catch him checking his phone again, his hands still trembling slightly. Whatever's going on with Malikai, it's not just lab trouble.

As someone responsible for his sister's safety, I intend to find out what he's hiding.

Evening shadows stretch long across the pavement as we exit Salvatore's, the warm glow from inside spilling out behind us. A light breeze carries a mix of aromatic scents from the kitchen vents, mingling with the crisp scent of approaching rain.

My hand settles naturally at the small of Malia's back as we pause under the awning.

Things feel different between us.

Inevitable.

Malikai's fingers drum against his thigh—a nervous gesture I cataloged throughout the evening. "We should get going. It's getting late."

Something in my gut tightens—that sixth sense that's kept me alive through countless missions. The parking lot is too quiet, too still. Even the crickets have gone silent.

I scan our surroundings, muscle memory taking over. The parking lot sprawls before us, half-empty at this hour. Standard layout—rows of vehicles creating channels of shadow between security lights. Four vehicles stand between us and Malikai's rental.

Two lamp posts out—creating shadows perfect for concealment. The restaurant's exterior lighting casts long shadows across the asphalt.

Two security lights are dark.

The lot is too quiet.

No other patrons leaving.

No staff on smoke breaks.

"No rush." I carefully note how Malikai's eyes dart between shadows. "The tiramisu was worth lingering over." I scan the perimeter as I speak, professional habits kicking in despite the civilian setting.

Malikai's behavior sets off every alarm in my head. His movements are erratic—head swiveling too quickly, hands shaking as he fumbles with his keys.

My years of experience kick in.

Four exits.

Two cameras.

Both dark.

Loading dock to the east.

Tree line beyond offering cover.

Malikai checks his phone again—the fourth time in ten minutes. His hand trembles slightly, causing the screen's blue light to dance across his features. The gesture reminds me of soldiers before an ambush, that desperate last check for intel or orders.

"Kai?" Malia's voice holds concern. "What's wrong? You've been jumpy all evening."

"Nothing." The word comes too quick, too sharp. "Just—lab stuff. You know how it is."

But I've seen this before. In hostages who knew their captors were coming. In targets who felt the noose tightening. This isn't the distraction of an academic.

This is prey sensing the hunter is close.

"The car's right over there," he says, gesturing to his rental—a non-descript sedan parked under one of the dead lights. His other hand keeps touching his breast pocket, an unconscious tell suggesting something valuable hidden there.

We start across the lot, our shoes clicking against the asphalt. Each sound makes Malikai flinch. He's scanning constantly now, not even trying to hide his paranoia. The confident scientist from dinner has vanished, replaced by someone who expects violence at any moment.

A car door slams in the distance. Malikai stumbles, nearly dropping his keys.

"Here, let me," I offer, reaching for them. The movement puts me between him and the darkest section of the lot.

Two men by the dumpster, suits too nice for trash duty.

A van idling just beyond the property line, its position offering clear sight lines.

The security camera above the entrance is dark—recently disabled.

My hand instinctively moves to the small of my back where my Glock should be, but I'm unarmed. Dinner with the girlfriend's brother didn't seem to warrant tactical gear.

Rookie mistake.

The weight of my absent Glock is an uncomfortable void against my back.

The click of dress shoes on the pavement draws my attention. The men by the dumpster are moving, their casual poses shifting to something more purposeful.

Professional.

Military.

"Kai?" Malia's voice carries concern. "Are you okay?"

Her brother's glasses catch the light as his head jerks toward a sound I can't hear. "Fine. Just … Let's get to the car quickly.

The screech of tires on asphalt splits the night. A black SUV barrels into the lot, headlights off, engine growling like a predator. No plates. Reinforced bumper. Tactical modification package.

These aren't amateurs.

Time crystallizes into perfect clarity as adrenaline floods my system. Malikai's reaction tells me he knew they were coming.

"Move!" I grab Malia's arm, already calculating trajectories and cover options. The SUV's approach angle cuts off access to Malikai's car. The restaurant's entrance is too far. That leaves …

"Down!" I shove them behind a concrete planter as the

SUV's tires squeal. The acrid smell of burning rubber fills the air. My body moves on pure instinct, muscle memory from countless missions taking over.

Time slows, fragments into tactical segments:

The SUV's approach vector—professional, designed to cut off escape routes.

The way Malikai's face drains of color—he expected this. His hand lifts and hovers over his breast pocket.

Malia's rapid breathing beside me—civilian, priority protect.

The click of car doors opening—multiple hostiles deploying.

I need a weapon. Need to get them to cover. Need to figure out what the hell Malikai has gotten his sister involved in.

But first, I need to keep them alive.

The SUV's engine roars closer. Malia's fingers dig into my arm. Her brother mutters something like equations under his breath, numbers tumbling out in a desperate stream.

This isn't a random attack.

They're here for someone.

And I know exactly who.

Malikai's fingers scrabble at his breast pocket, frantic movements that set off every combat instinct I possess. He yanks something free—small and metallic, glinting in the parking lot lights.

"Take it!" he hisses, trying to shove it into my hands. "You have to—"

Pure tactical reflex takes over. Unknown object, potential threat—I bat it away without conscious thought. The object skitters across the pavement, scraping against asphalt before disappearing under a concrete planter.

Malikai makes a strangled sound of despair. "No! You don't understand—"

I hook his elbow, trying to drag him toward cover, but he

resists. His body goes rigid as he stares at where the object vanished, his face a mask of pure terror.

"We have to get it!" He tries to pull away, but I tighten my grip. "You don't understand what they'll do—"

Movement catches my eye—the suits by the dumpster advance …

Shit.

"Get down!" I push backward, trying to keep both siblings shielded. The SUV's brakes squeal. Doors burst open. Three more hostiles emerge—combat stance, tactical gear.

Professional hitters. We're outnumbered. No weapon. No backup.

Think. Move. Survive.

Something's off about his tension—not fear. Calculation.

"Walt!" Malia's scream pierces the night as two men drag her brother toward the van.

The suits open fire.

White-hot pain explodes in my shoulder. Another round tears through my chest.

I stagger but stay upright, forcing my body between Malia and the approaching men. Blood soaks my shirt, turning silk to crimson. Each breath burns, but I reach back for her, trying to keep her safe.

One of the suited men speaks into a radio, his voice clipped and professional. "Primary target secured."

A crackled response. Words I can't make out.

"Target's sister is present." The man's eyes fix on Malia.

More static. A single word cuts through: "Insurance."

"Understood." His expression shifts, cold calculation replacing professional detachment. "Grab the girl."

"No!" The word rips from my throat, copper-tinged and desperate. I try to push her further behind me, but my legs betray me, blood loss making every movement sluggish.

"Nothing personal," the man says, gesturing to his team. "But your brother's been very uncooperative. Maybe you'll help him remember his priorities."

Strong hands grab her. She fights—God, she fights—kicking, scratching, screaming my name. The sound of her terror cuts deeper than any bullet as they drag her toward the van.

"Walt!" Her voice breaks on my name. "Please!"

"No!" The word rips from my throat.

I lunge forward, my body refusing to obey as blood pumps from my wounds. One of the men slams his rifle butt into my solar plexus, dropping me to my knees. He follows it with a kick to my gut, and I collapse on the ground.

They force Malia into the van. Her dark hair wild and her eyes wide with fear and something worse—betrayal.

Not of me, but of Malikai, who won't even look at her.

"Your brother made his choice," one man tells her as they slam the door. "Now you get to live with it."

Doors slam. Tires squeal. The van accelerates, taking my whole world with it.

I lurch forward, legs going numb. Blood drips onto the asphalt as the van disappears.

They took her to force his cooperation. Made her collateral damage in whatever game her brother's playing.

The thought burns hotter than my wounds as consciousness fades.

They took her.

And her brother let them do it.

The thought pounds through me with each fading heartbeat as I collapse.

They took her.

Darkness creeps in at the edges of my vision. In the distance, sirens wail.

They took Malia.

Cold seeps into my bones as I press my face against the rough pavement. The coppery taste of blood fills my mouth.

They took her.

And I failed to protect her.

Consciousness slips away as red and blue lights paint the night.

Find her, I think into the darkness.

Whatever it takes.

Find her.

ELEVEN

Malia

"NO!" Walt's shout echoes across the parking lot as strong hands drag me backward. I fight—kicking, clawing, desperate to reach him as he staggers, blood blooming across his white shirt.

The bullets hit him because of me.

Because he tried to protect me.

"Walt!" I scream his name as he crumples to his knees. His eyes lock with mine, filled with a fury I've never seen before. Even bleeding, even falling, he tries to reach for me.

"Enough." The word comes cold and precise as rough hands grab my arms. I thrash against their grip, but these men are professionals. My struggles might as well be a child's for all the good they do.

"Please," I beg as they drag me toward the waiting SUV. "He needs help. You can't just leave him—"

A rifle butt slams into Walt's stomach. He doubles over and hits the pavement hard. One of the men kicks him, and my scream splits the night.

"Stop! Please stop!"

They shove me into the SUV's back row, two suits sliding in

to bracket me. Through the windshield, I can still see Walt. Still see him trying to push himself up, blood pooling beneath him on the asphalt. His lips move—my name, I think—before another blow sends him sprawling.

Malikai is forced into the middle row ahead of me, two more suits caging him in. He won't look at me. Won't look at anything except his hands twisting in his lap.

The doors slam shut with military precision. The engine roars. As we accelerate away, I press my hands against the tinted window, watching Walt's body grow smaller until darkness swallows him completely.

The SUV hurls us through the night, every turn slamming me between the two operatives bracketing me in the third-row seat. Their shoulders form an immovable wall on either side, expensive suits unable to hide the military muscle beneath.

I can't stop shaking. Can't stop seeing Walt fall, his shirt blooming red as the bullets punched into him. The way he tried to reach for me even as his legs gave out.

The SUV's leather seat still holds that new car smell, but all I can smell is copper—Walt's blood on my hands, my dress, smeared across my skin where I tried to reach him. My stomach heaves. The operative on my right shifts slightly, creating an inch more space, but it's not kindness. Just practicality. They don't want me getting sick in their vehicle.

"Walt!" The name tears from my throat before I can stop it.

The operative on my left—older, with steel-gray hair and a face like carved granite—squeezes my arm in silent warning.

"Quiet." The command comes from the man to my right—suit pristine despite the violence, his face expressionless as marble. Professional. Cold.

Malikai sits rigidly on the center bench, his head bowed, his glasses reflecting the passing streetlights.

Two more suits bracket him, just like me. He hasn't looked at me once since they forced us into the SUV. He rocks back and forth, likely counting prime numbers the way he always does when he's stressed.

But this isn't normal academic pressure. This is something much darker.

The driver takes another corner too fast, and my shoulder slams into the man on my right. He doesn't budge, solid as a brick wall. I'm caged, trapped in the back row between living barriers while we speed further from the only man who might be able to help us.

If he's still alive.

The image of him falling flashes again—the way his body jerked as the bullets tore into his flesh, the terrible finality of him sprawled on the pavement. How much blood can someone lose and still survive?

"He's going to die." The words come out raw, broken. "You shot him. You left him there to die."

Another suit speaks from the passenger seat, his tone clipped and efficient. "Your boyfriend's fate is no longer your concern."

Boyfriend. The word catches in my chest. We never even got the chance to …

"Malikai." I lean forward, trying to see him better between the seats. "What's happening? Who are these people?"

"I'm sorry." The words barely carry over the engine's growl. "I'm so sorry, Sissy. I never meant … They weren't supposed to …"

"Enough." The suit beside me yanks me back against the seat. "You know the rules, Professor. No talking."

These men know exactly who my brother is—what he does. This isn't random.

I force myself to breathe, to think past the panic clawing at my throat. Walt taught me to observe and gather intel; right now, it's the only way I can honor him.

Six men total. Two with me in the back row, two with Malikai in the center, and two up front. Expensive suits that can't hide their military bearing.

Earpieces.

Weapons holstered.

These aren't random thugs—they're professionals.

"Your brother's been remarkably uncooperative." The suit in the passenger seat studies me through the rearview mirror with clinical interest.

"Leave her alone." Malikai's voice cracks.

"I don't understand." But even as I say this, pieces start clicking into place: Malikai's strange behavior at dinner, his evasive answers about his research, and the mysterious phone calls. "What do you want from him?"

"Motivation to complete his work without—complications." The man shifts his attention to my brother. "Your presence will help him focus on what matters."

I look at Malikai again, really look at him. In the dim light, his skin holds a sickly, ashen hue, the faint undertone of exhaustion etched into every sharp line of his face. His clothes hang loose—he's lost weight since I last saw him. This isn't new. Whatever's happening has been building for weeks, maybe months.

"Kai?" I keep my voice soft, the way I did when we were kids, and he'd get lost in his equations. "Talk to me. Please."

He shakes his head frantically, still rocking between his guards. "I can't. They'll hurt you if I … I can't."

"We're merely ensuring cooperation." The passenger suit's voice holds no emotion. "Your safety depends entirely on your brother's choices."

The casual threat sends ice through my veins. These men will hurt me—kill me—without hesitation if Malikai steps out of line. And my brother knows it.

Malikai stares out the dark window, his reflection showing a haunted expression I've never seen before. His hands twist in his lap, and I catch fragments of whispered numbers—prime numbers, his way of trying to impose order on chaos.

"You should have cooperated from the beginning." The suit beside Malikai speaks for the first time, his voice oddly gentle. "Family makes things—complicated. Messy. But often necessary."

Malikai slumps in his seat, defeated. His lips move silently—more equations, trying to make sense of a world that's stopped following logical patterns.

"How much farther?" The driver's question carries.

"Twenty minutes." The passenger suit checks his watch. "Right on schedule."

I close my eyes, trying to remember every detail of the route. Three right turns after leaving the restaurant. Highway entrance heading east. Now trees and darkness stretch endlessly ahead.

Walt would track these details automatically. Walt would know what to do.

Walt might be dead.

The thought hits like a physical blow. I press my fist against my mouth, fighting back a sob. I can't think about that now. Can't let myself remember how still he looked, sprawled on the pavement as they dragged me away.

Focus. Observe. Plan.

The suits are armed but professional—they won't shoot without orders. They need Malikai alive and cooperative. Need me alive as leverage. That gives us some protection, however small.

My brother's work—whatever it is—matters enough to kidnap and kill.

And Walt …

I squeeze my eyes shut, remembering his strength, his protection, and his promises. He survived special forces. Survived war zones. He has to survive this.

He has to.

Because if—when—I get out of this, I'm going to need him to help me understand why my brother let these men take me.

The SUV turns onto gravel, and the change in surface sends vibrations through the metal floor.

We're nearing our destination.

Trees press closer, blocking the moonlight and erasing any reference points that might help me track our location.

"Almost there." The driver's voice carries no emotion. He's not speaking to whoever is in the van. He's talking to someone through the earpiece tucked into his ear.

The clinical detachment in their voices terrifies me more than anger would. These men see us as objects—things to be moved, stored, and used as needed.

I glance at Malikai again, studying his defeated posture. My brilliant, confident brother has been reduced to this trembling shell. What have they done to him? What are they going to do to me?

The SUV slows, gravel crunching under the tires. Metal groans—a gate opening. We pass through, and I count the seconds until it clangs shut behind us.

"Staging point reached," the passenger suit reports into his earpiece as we emerge into a massive clearing. Floodlights pierce the darkness, illuminating a temporary military staging area.

The distinctive *whump-whump-whump* of helicopter blades splits the night.

My heart stops as a helicopter descends onto a lit landing pad, its rotors throwing grass and debris in violent circles. This isn't just a pickup point. This is the first leg of something much worse.

"No." The word comes out broken as I understand. "Please—"

"Move." They drag me from the SUV, efficient and impersonal.

The rotor wash whips my hair, stinging my eyes as they force us toward the waiting helicopter. Malikai stumbles ahead of me, his shoulders hunched in defeat.

He knows where we're going.

Has known all along.

The flight is mercifully short—twenty minutes that feel like forever, trapped in the thundering cabin with men who won't even look at me.

Through the window, I watch civilization slowly return: distant lights, roads, and then, finally, the bright sprawl of a commercial airport.

But they don't take us to the main terminal. The helicopter touches down near a private hangar, where a sleek, white jet waits. Its engines are already spooling up. The plane gleams under the floodlights, with no markings or registration numbers visible.

"Final transport ready," one suit reports as they hustle us across the tarmac. The jet's stairs descend with expensive precision, leading to a cabin that steals my breath despite everything —honey-colored wood panels, cream leather, and soft lighting that probably costs more than my car.

But all this luxury makes it worse. Like putting a pretty frame around a nightmare.

"First leg is seven hours to Honolulu," a suit informs us as they secure us in the leather seats. "Fuel stop, then another eight to our destination."

Fifteen hours. They're taking us across the Pacific. Thousands of miles from where Walt lies bleeding on that parking lot pavement. The distance hits me like a physical blow.

Malikai sits across the table from me, but he might as well be on another planet. He stares out the oval window as we taxi, his lips moving in silent equations.

Trying to calculate a way out of this?

Or just retreating into the numbers where none of this is real?

The jet lifts off smoothly, banking west into darkness. Walt's blood has dried on my dress, stiff and brown now. How long ago did they shoot him? Two hours? Three? The night stretches endless around us as we climb higher, each minute carrying us farther from any hope of rescue.

I close my eyes but can't stop seeing him fall. Can't stop hearing his voice calling my name as they dragged me away. Even if he survives—please God, let him survive—how will he ever find me on the other side of an ocean?

The suit beside me offers a cashmere blanket, the gesture almost kind if not for the gun visible under his jacket. "Long flight ahead. You should try to sleep."

Sleep. Right. As if I could sleep in this beautiful prison, watching the black ocean slip beneath us while my brother pretends I don't exist. The cabin lights dim to a soft amber glow, making the wood paneling gleam. A flight attendant appears—because, of course, they have a flight attendant—offering drinks in crystal glasses.

I refuse everything, staying rigid in my seat as we chase the darkness west. Seven hours to Hawaii. Another eight beyond that. Each mile takes me farther from Walt.

TWELVE

Walt

____

RED and blue lights strobe across my vision as my cheek presses against the cold asphalt. Each heartbeat sends another wave of warmth spreading beneath me, my blood painting abstract patterns on the pavement.

They took Malia.

The thought pounds through me with each pulse of pain. I try to push myself up, but my arms refuse to cooperate. The world tilts and spins as shock sets in.

Images flash through my mind—the terror in her eyes, the way she fought as they dragged her away.

Her scream echoing my name.

I should have seen it coming.

All evening, Malikai dodged questions about his research. Changed the subject whenever quantum mechanics came up. His hands shaking. The mysterious phone calls. Every sign was there, and I missed them all because I was too focused on playing games with Malia under the table.

Now, she's paying the price for my distraction.

"Sir, don't move!" A voice cuts through the haze. Hands press down on my shoulders, trying to keep me still. "GSW to the chest and shoulder. Significant blood loss. BP dropping …"

The EMT's voice fades in and out as they work. I focus on breathing through the burning in my chest. Each inhale sends daggers of pain through me, but I welcome it.

Pain means I'm alive.

And I need to stay alive to find her.

Professional hit team.

Military training, but not American forces.

Their movements were too rigid, too formal. Eastern European, maybe, or former Soviet bloc. The kind of men who do wet work for the highest bidder.

But why Malikai? What's a quantum physicist working on that's worth sending a tactical team to grab him?

And Malia … My sweet, innocent Malia, caught up in whatever game her brother's playing. A quantum physicist who won't talk about his work, who jumps at phone calls, who brought his sister to dinner knowing trouble was coming.

The questions pile up with each throb of pain. What kind of research attracts a professional hit team? Why was Malikai so afraid to discuss his work? And most importantly—why bring Malia anywhere near this if he knew he was being hunted?

"Sir, can you tell me your name?" A penlight flashes across my eyes, making me wince.

"Walt," I grit out. "Need to contact my team …" The words come automatically, years of training kicking in.

"Stay with us, Walt. We're going to get you stabilized." The EMT's face swims into focus—young, competent, already moving as he cuts away my blood-soaked shirt. "Multiple entry wounds. No exit wounds visible. We need to move fast."

I grab his wrist, ignoring how the movement sends fresh agony ripping through me. "Phone. Need my phone."

The rage builds with each throb of pain. Malikai knew they

were coming. The way he kept checking his phone, his nervous glances. He knew, and he still brought his sister to dinner. Put her in harm's way.

His own sister.

What kind of man does that?

"BP 90 over 60 and dropping. Give another bolus of LR." The voices above me blur together as they work. "Ready for transport in three …"

My vision grays at the edges as they lift me onto the gurney. The movement sends fresh waves of agony through my chest, but I welcome it. Pain keeps me focused.

Keeps me present.

Keeps me remembering every detail I'll need to hunt these bastards down.

"Malia," I mumble through numb lips. "Have to find …"

Her face floats in my mind—not the terror of tonight, but earlier in the storage room. The way she trembled under my touch. Her confession about being a virgin. Trusting me to be her first. To show her pleasure and submission and everything in between.

Now, she's in the hands of men who view her as nothing but leverage against her brother.

The ambulance doors slam shut. Sirens scream to life above me. The vehicle lurches into motion, each bump in the road sending fresh spikes of agony through my body.

I stare up at the ambulance's ceiling, forcing myself to focus through the pain and blood loss. To remember every detail that might help track them.

The SUV reinforced bumper. The way they moved with military precision but didn't use standard US tactical formations. The leader's slight accent.

But most of all, Malia's scream as they dragged her away.

The terror in her eyes. The way her brother wouldn't even look at her.

Whatever Malikai's involved in, it's big. The kind of big that gets people killed. And he dragged his sister into it without a second thought.

"BP still dropping," one EMT calls out.

That sounds bad.

The cold rush of fluids enters my veins, but it does nothing to quell the fire building inside me. They thought shooting me would stop me from coming after them.

They have no idea what I'm capable of.

What I'll do to anyone who hurts her.

"Almost there," someone says above me. "Hang on."

I bare my teeth in what might be a smile. Oh, I'll hang on. I'll survive these wounds. I'll heal. And then I'll hunt down every single person involved in taking her.

Starting with her brother. He's got answers I need, and once I find him, he's going to talk.

The ambulance screams to a stop. Doors burst open. More hands grab the gurney, rushing me into fluorescent-lit halls that blur past overhead.

"Multiple GSWs, significant blood loss, BP unstable …"

I tune out their voices, focusing instead on burning every detail of the attack into my memory. The way they moved. Their tactics. Every piece of intel I can use to track them down.

"Sir, we need to prep you for surgery." A doctor's face appears above me, all business. "The bullets need to come out."

I grab his sleeve, ignoring how the movement sends fresh fire through my shoulder. "Phone," I rasp. "Need to make a call first."

"After surg—"

"Now." I pour every ounce of command presence I have into the word.

Something in my eyes must convince him. He nods to a nurse, who pulls my phone from the bag of personal effects.

I dial with shaking fingers, leaving bloody prints on the screen. It rings once before Ethan's voice answers.

"What's up?" he barks.

"Code Black." I grit out. "Malia's been taken. Her brother too."

"Details. Now."

"Professional team. Six men. Military training, possible Eastern European. Black SUV, tactical package." The words come in short bursts between waves of pain.

"Weapons?"

"Soviet-bloc standard issue. Suppressed."

"Targets?"

"Primary target was Malikai. Took Malia as …" My voice breaks. "As leverage."

"What's the brother involved in?"

"Quantum research. Fusion. Something big enough to send a wet team."

"We'll dig into his work. Find out who wants it bad enough to grab him." Ethan's voice turns hard. "How bad are you hit?"

"Shoulder. One in the chest. Still breathing."

"We're mobilizing everything we have." Ethan's voice cuts through the growing fog. "I'm contacting Doc Summers. We'll get you the best care."

I don't tell him I'm seconds away from going under the knife. I don't have enough breath in me.

"If they hurt her …" The phone slips from my numb fingers as consciousness fades. The surgical team moves in, masks and gloves ready.

Whatever it takes, I'm coming for you, Malia.

I'm going to find you.

And God help anyone who stands in my way.

Darkness takes me, but I hold onto that vow like an anchor. They think shooting me will stop me from coming after them?

They have no idea what they've awakened.

Because they didn't take a woman I want.

They took the woman I love.

And I'm going to tear the world apart to get her back.

THIRTEEN

Walt

THE STEADY BEEP of monitors pulls me from the darkness. My chest feels like it's been crushed in a vise, each breath a careful negotiation with pain. The sharp, antiseptic smell of the hospital permeates everything, mixing with the metallic scent of blood that still lingers in my nose. My tongue tastes copper and chemicals—remnants of surgery and intubation.

There are multiple people in the room—familiar breathing patterns of my team.

Someone's drinking coffee—the rich aroma pushes back the sterile hospital air. It smells like Guardian Grind's special roast. One of Malia's signature drinks.

My heart clenches, remembering Malia behind the counter, the way she smiled as she brewed my ridiculous custom orders.

My eyes crack open to the fluorescent glare. Through the haze, I make out Doc Summers' petite form beside my bed. Her dark hair is pulled back in its usual neat braid, her presence radiating that quiet strength I've always admired. Beyond her towers Forest, his massive frame nearly brushing the doorframe. The fluorescent lights catch his shock-white hair, those ice-blue eyes intent as he studies me.

"Welcome back," Doc says softly, her gentle tone belying the steel I know lies beneath. Her small hand feels cool against my wrist as she checks my pulse. "How's the pain?"

"Like I got shot," I manage, trying for humor, but my voice comes out raw.

My throat feels like sandpaper. Ice chips appear in a small cup—Hank's doing, always anticipating needs. The cold soothes my throat but does nothing for the burning in my chest.

"Twice," she corrects, adjusting something in my IV. The cold rush of medication dulls the edges of the agony. "The shoulder wound was relatively clean. The chest shot ..." She pauses, her dark eyes serious. "You were lucky. Half an inch to the left, and we wouldn't be having this conversation."

Lucky isn't the word I'd use. Lucky would have been spotting the threat before they took her. Lucky would have been noticing how Malikai's hands shook every time his phone buzzed. Lucky would have been protecting her like I promised her I would.

My teammates spread out around the room in defensive positions—old habits die hard. Ethan stands near the window, his posture alert despite hours of waiting. Blake and Rigel flank the door while Hank and Gabe occupy opposite corners. The usual playful energy between those two is gone, replaced by cold professionalism.

Memory slams back like a physical blow. Malikai trying to hand me something. Metal glinting in the parking lot lights before skittering away under the planter. The terror in his eyes when it fell.

"Wait!" I try to push myself up, ignoring the explosion of pain in my chest. The monitors shriek in protest as my heart rate spikes. "The parking lot—there's something ... Malikai tried to give me something right before they came. Small, metal. It fell under the planter. We have to——"

"Easy," Forest's deep voice rumbles as his massive hand gently but firmly pushes me back down. The man's like a mountain—immovable when he chooses to be. "You're not going anywhere with those wounds."

"You don't understand," I grit out, fighting against both his grip and the darkness threatening to pull me under. Sweat breaks out on my forehead from the effort. "No one knows about it. Whatever it was, he was terrified they'd get it. I have to go back …"

I catch the look Doc and Forest exchange. Something in their expressions sets off every alarm in my head. I've seen that look before—when they uncovered Townsend's trafficking ring that took Jenna. One of nine pillars of evil, each headed by a Sentinel, all orchestrated by the phantom who's haunted Guardian HRS since its inception: Malfor.

We took down Townsend, but he was just one head of the hydra. Eight Sentinels remain, each controlling their criminal empires. The thought churns my gut worse than the bullet wounds.

"What aren't you telling me?" I look between them, noting how my teammates have gone still around the room's perimeter. Even Hank and Gabe drop their usual swagger, their expressions grim. "You know something about why they took him."

Rigel pushes off from the door. "Been running scenarios since your call. The targeting bears similarities to what happened with Mia." His jaw tightens—we all remember how she was hunted after she uncovered deuterium thefts. How close we came to losing her."

"Yeah, but how's that related?" My mind's still muddled with the aftereffects of anesthesia.

"Mitzy's been digging while you were in surgery," Doc

Summers adds, pulling up data on her tablet. "She found a pattern we missed before. The Third Sentinel isn't dealing in nuclear materials anymore. He's systematically targeting quantum physicists."

That catches my attention. "Malikai's field of expertise."

"Precisely." Forest's ice-blue eyes narrow. "According to Mitzy's analysis, three research facilities have been hit in the past month. Each time, their lead physicist disappeared. In two of those cases," he pauses, his expression grim, "family members were taken as leverage."

My hands clench in the sheets. "Like Malia."

"Seems the Third Sentinel's evolved his game," Rigel adds. "From stealing materials to acquiring the minds that could weaponize them."

"Mitzy's still investigating Malikai's research," Doc continues, "but preliminary analysis shows he made some kind of break-through in quantum tunneling effects three months ago."

Three months.

When Malia said he changed. When he stopped talking about his work and started jumping at shadows.

"What kind of breakthrough?" I ask, though my gut churns with the probable answer.

"The kind that could revolutionize particle containment fields," Forest says. "Or destabilize them. Mitzy's working on the technical details, but if she's right …"

"It's exactly what the Third Sentinel would want," I finish. The pieces click into place with sickening clarity. "Malikai refused to cooperate, so they took his sister."

The monitors spike again as rage floods my system. The Third Sentinel. The same monster who hunted Mia, who's now branching into something potentially even more devastating.

The monitors register my spike in heart rate, but I barely notice. All I can see is Malia's face as they dragged her away.

Another piece in Malfor's grand design, executed through his Sentinels.

We've been hunting these bastards since they first surfaced. Nine pillars of organized crime, each specialized, each deadly. Townsend's human trafficking operation was just one piece. The Third Sentinel's nuclear ambitions are another. And still, Malfor stays hidden, orchestrating it all from the shadows.

What kind of man brings his sister to dinner knowing killers are hunting him?

"Are you thinking what I'm thinking?" Doc Summers turns to Forest."

"This isn't about the abduction of a quantum physicist anymore." Forest's pale eyes turn serious.

"That's what I'm thinking too," she says. "Ever since Mia exposed Sentinel's deuterium operation, the Third Sentinel shifted focus. He or she isn't collecting nuclear materials anymore —they're collecting the minds that can weaponize them."

"And Malfor's letting it happen," Forest adds grimly. "The timing's too perfect. Right after we shut down the Third Sentinel's heavy water operation, they pivot to quantum fusion research. Fucking frustrating. It's like Malfor is always three moves ahead."

"What's the endgame?" I ask, frustration making my voice rough. "First deuterium stockpiles, now quantum physicists?"

"Global destabilization," she says quietly. "That's what Mia suggested. But destabilization through controlled fusion? That's a whole new level of threat." Her voice carries quiet authority she wields like a blade. "What did this object look like?"

I force myself to focus past the pain, past the fury and guilt churning inside me. "Small. Metallic. Maybe a thumb drive or data chip? He was desperate to give it to me, kept reaching for his breast pocket all night ..." The memory sharpens. "He checked that pocket every time his phone buzzed. Like he was making sure it was still there. I need to get back to that parking lot." I start pulling at the IV in my arm, ignoring how the movement sends fire through my chest. "Whatever Malikai tried to give me, it's important enough that he risked his sister's life. Important enough that a Sentinel sent a hit team."

"Walt." Ethan steps forward, his expression grim. I've never seen him look so concerned. "You can barely sit up."

"Then find me a wheelchair," I growl. "I'm going back to that lot. Now."

"You've lost too much blood," Doc Summers interjects, her small hand surprisingly strong as she stops me from yanking out the IV. "The bullet in your chest barely missed your heart. You need time to heal."

"Malia doesn't have time!" The words tear from my throat, raw with desperation. "They're using her to control him. You know what people like that do to their leverage when they're done with it."

A heavy silence falls. They all know exactly what happens to leverage that's outlived its usefulness. I've seen too many missions end that way.

"I promised to protect her," I continue, my voice dropping to a harsh whisper. "Whatever Malikai was working on, whatever he tried to give me—it might be our only lead to finding her."

Forest and Doc Summers exchange another look, having one of their silent conversations. Despite not being blood-related, they read each other like family. Finally, Forest nods.

"I'll take a team back to the restaurant," he rumbles. "We'll tear that parking lot apart if we have to."

"Mitzy's already digging into Malikai's research," Doc adds, already typing on her tablet. "See what would interest a Sentinel enough to risk such a public grab."

"Not good enough." I force myself to sit despite the protestations of my body. Black spots dance at the edges of my vision. "I need to be there. I saw exactly where it fell."

"You'll tear your stitches," Doc Summers warns, but there's resignation in her voice. She knows me well enough to know I won't stay put. Not with Malia's life on the line.

"Then you better come with us," Forest says to his sister with a hint of approval in his ice-blue eyes. "Because he's going whether we help him or not. We're going to need someone to stop the bleeding when he pops those stitches."

Ethan steps forward, already issuing orders to the team. Within minutes, they've procured a wheelchair and are helping me into it, careful of the tubes and wires. Each movement sends daggers of pain through my chest, but I welcome it.

I've said it before, and I'll say it again, pain means I'm alive. I'll never stop hunting for her as long as I'm alive.

FOURTEEN

Walt

MY WHEELCHAIR SCRAPES against broken asphalt as Forest pushes me across the restaurant parking lot. Every tiny bump sends shockwaves of agony through my chest, but I welcome the pain.

The lot looks different in the harsh glare of police floodlights —alien and wrong, like seeing a familiar face distorted in a funhouse mirror.

Just hours ago, Malia walked through here on my arm, her silk dress whispering against my skin, her body warm and trusting against mine.

Now, crime scene tape flutters in the pre-dawn breeze, yellow plastic stark against the bloodstained pavement where I fell.

My blood stains the pavement black under the artificial lights, a grotesque Rorschach that spreads wider than seems possible.

Did I really lose that much blood?

The thought swims through my head, made fuzzy by whatever cocktail of painkillers Doc Summers pumped into me before allowing this excursion.

I hate how the drugs blur my edges and dampen my reactions. I need to be sharp. Need to remember every detail of where that drive fell. Need to focus past the way the world keeps tilting sideways when I move too quickly.

"Take it slow," Forest rumbles from behind me, his massive hands steady on the wheelchair's handles. "Skye's already planning how to lecture you when those stitches tear."

I grunt in acknowledgment, but my attention fixes on the massive concrete planter looming ahead.

Memory assaults me—hits like a physical blow: Malia's scream as they dragged her toward the van. The terror in her eyes. The way she fought them even as they forced her inside. Her brother's defeated slump as he watched it happen.

My hands clench on the wheelchair's arms, ignoring how the movement pulls at my wounds. The IV line in my arm tugs uncomfortably, the portable drip stand rattling as Forest navigates another uneven patch of pavement. More drugs. More things dulling my edge when I need to be razor-sharp.

"Hard right," I grit out as we near the planter. "It fell somewhere along this side. I remember—"

The world suddenly tilts sideways, darkness creeping in at the edges of my vision. My grip on consciousness feels tenuous, like trying to hold smoke.

When did it get so hard to breathe?

"That's enough." Doc Summers materializes beside me, her small frame radiating authority despite barely reaching my shoulder. "O2 sats are dropping. I need to check those bandages before you end up back in surgery."

"I'm fine." The lie comes automatically, but she's already pulling supplies from her medical bag.

Her movements are precise and efficient—the same way she's patched up countless Guardian operators over the years.

"You took two rounds to the chest less than six hours ago," she reminds me, her voice carrying that blend of steel and compassion I've never heard from anyone else. "The only reason you're here and not still in ICU is because I know you'd try to leave AMA if we didn't help. So you're going to let me check these bandages, and you're going to tell me if you feel light-headed or short of breath."

"We don't have time—"

"Make time." She cuts me off with a look that could freeze hell. "Because if you pass out from blood loss or respiratory distress, you're no good to Malia."

Malia's name hits like another bullet. Six hours. They've had her for six hours while I lay unconscious in surgery. For six hours, she's been in the hands of men who see her as nothing but leverage against her brother.

My resistance crumbles as Doc Summers eases my shirt aside, her gloved fingers gentle despite her stern expression. The bandages are already showing spots of red—not major bleeding, but enough to concern her, judging by the tight line of her mouth.

"You're going to need another chest X-ray after this …"

I tune out her medical litany, focusing instead on the planter. Trying to reconstruct those frantic moments through the haze of blood loss and fading adrenaline.

The metallic glint as Malikai tried to press something into my hands. The soft scrape as it skittered across the pavement. The raw terror in his eyes when it disappeared beneath the concrete monster looming before us.

Whatever's on that drive, it was worth sending a professional hit team to retrieve. Worth taking Malia as collateral. The thought sends fresh fire through my veins, burning away some of the drug-induced fog.

Worth him handing it to me, a virtual stranger.

"Pain level?" Doc Summers asks, intruding on my thoughts.

"Manageable." Another lie, but she lets it slide. She knows

me too well—knows I'll push through anything to find Malia. To undo my failure to protect her.

"You're a horrible liar." Doc Summers gives me a look that could slice through solid granite, but she doesn't force me to stop.

She knows I won't listen.

The rich aroma of coffee drifts from the restaurant's kitchen vents. The combination turns my stomach, reminding me of Malia's smile as she crafted my ridiculous custom drinks. The way her eyes lit up when she talked about her coffee creations. The softness in her voice when she confessed she was saving herself for someone who mattered.

For me.

And I let them take her.

"Walt." Doc Summers' voice carries warning as she finishes checking my bandages. "I know that look. Whatever you're planning—"

"Just get me closer to that planter." I cut her off, unable to handle her concern right now. "Please."

She studies me for a long moment, her dark eyes seeing too much. Finally, she nods to Forest. "Ten minutes. That's all I'm giving you before these bandages need changing. And if you try to get out of that chair—"

"You'll sedate me into next week." I manage a ghost of a smile. "I remember the speech."

"Good." She starts repacking her medical bag, every movement precise and controlled. "Because I mean every word. The only reason you're alive is pure dumb luck. That chest round barely missed your heart. The shoulder shot nicked your subclavian artery. You shouldn't even be conscious right now, let alone—"

"Doc." My voice comes out rougher than intended. "I know. But I have to find that drive. Have to find her." The words catch in my throat. "I promised to protect her."

Her expression softens slightly. "I know you did, but you can't protect her if you're dead." She shoulders her medical bag, gloved fingers leaving bloody prints on the strap. "So let us help. Let us be your strength until you get yours back."

The words hit harder than I expect, cracking something in my chest that has nothing to do with bullet wounds. I manage a short nod, not trusting my voice.

Doc takes position beside my wheelchair, medical supplies at the ready, silent support radiating from her small frame. She's seen me through worse—patched me up after missions gone sideways, put me back together when the job tried to tear me apart.

But this isn't just a mission gone wrong.

It's Malia.

And nothing—not bullets, not blood loss, not even the Doc's threats of sedation—will stop me from finding her.

The same images flash in my mind.

The glint of metal as Malikai tried to press something into my hands.

The soft scrape as it skittered across pavement.

The raw terror in his eyes when it disappeared beneath the planter.

"Here." My voice comes rough, barely recognizable. "It went under here."

I grip the wheelchair's arms, ready to stand, but Forest's massive hand clamps down on my shoulder.

"Not yet." His ice-blue eyes scan the scene with tactical precision.

Being Guardian operatives comes with certain advantages— we're also deputized as federal marshals, our badges giving us access to crime scenes that would normally be off-limits to a private security firm. "Ethan—deal with the cops. Blake, Rigel— clear the perimeter. Hank, Gabe—get ready to move this thing. Skye—"

"Already prepped for when he rips those stitches," she cuts in, medical bag at her feet. "Which he will, because he's an idiot."

"An idiot who's going to find that drive." I push against Forest's restraining hand. Fire rips through my chest, but I grit my teeth against it. "Whatever Malikai tried to give me, it was worth killing for. Worth taking his sister over."

Worth taking Malia.

Her name burns in my throat. *Six hours since they took her. Six hours she's been in the hands of men who view her as nothing but leverage.*

"Ethan?" Forest calls.

"On it." Our team leader strides toward the approaching police, badge already out to buy us time and give us a chance to find whatever Malikai risked his sister's life to protect.

Forest positions my wheelchair near the planter, his movements precise despite his bulk.

I force myself up despite Forest's growl of protest. The world tilts dangerously, but I lock my knees. I won't fail her again. Won't collapse until we find what we need to track her down.

Hank and Gabe position themselves around the planter, a massive concrete structure with thick, weathered sides.

The base rests on short, sturdy feet, creating a narrow gap beneath it—just wide enough for a flash drive to slip through but far too small for a hand to reach under.

"Ready?" Gabe asks, hands braced against the concrete.

"Always with the heavy lifting." Hank's complaint carries no real heat as he and Gabe take position. "We had plans tonight, you know. Leggy brunette, sexy lips, very—"

"Flexible," Gabe finishes with a grin. "Don't forget flexible."

My legs wobble, and my knees threaten to give out as the edges of my vision blur. The concrete feels uneven beneath my boots, though I know it's not—the weakness is in me.

Blood loss and whatever the hell they pumped into my system earlier are dragging me down, making every step feel like wading through quicksand. I fight a battle to stay upright.

I've never understood their dynamic—two straight men sharing women, threesomes, whatever they're into.

The thought of sharing a woman doesn't sit right with me. I wouldn't. Couldn't. But hey, to each their own. Some guys find camaraderie in the weirdest places.

"Less talking, more lifting," Forest rumbles, his voice steady as granite. His hand clamps down on my shoulder, the grip firm enough to root me in place. "More sitting for you," he adds, his tone leaving no room for argument.

I tense, ready to argue anyway, but the sudden pressure pushes me backward. Before I can react, Forest forces me back into the wheelchair. The chair creaks under my reluctant weight, and I glare at him, but he's already moving, his broad shoulders lowering as he drops to his hands and knees.

"Let's do this." Shaking his head, Forest mutters under his breath.

Doc Summers drops to her knees beside him, her braid swinging over her shoulder as she pushes aside a handful of loose gravel.

"Skye." Forest's voice carries warning as she examines the tiny gap beneath the planter. "Don't even think about—"

"About what?" She doesn't look up. She looks under the planter, pulling out her phone to shine a light under the concrete monster. Her nimble fingers already probe the edges of the narrow space. "Using my small, surgically-trained hands to retrieve something without having to move this entire concrete monster? Because that seems a lot smarter than letting these two meatheads try to lift it."

"Hey!" Hank protests. "We're very coordinated meatheads."

"When we want to be," Gabe adds with a wink.

"Skye." Forest drops to one knee beside her, his bulk shadowing her smaller frame. "Your hands—"

"Are exactly what we need right now." She cuts him off,

shifting to get a better angle. "Unless you think those bear paws of yours will fit under there?"

"If anything happens to those surgeon hands—"

"Nothing will happen except me retrieving this drive." Her voice softens slightly. "I know what I'm doing, big brother. Let me work."

Forest grumbles something under his breath, his jaw tightening as his focus shifts upward. His piercing glare fixes on Hank and Gabe, who are braced on either side of the planter.

"They're getting impatient," Ethan warns through comms.

"Stall them." Forest shifts his attention to Gabe and Hank. "You two," he warns, his voice low and dangerous, "if you so much as twitch wrong and this thing comes down on my sister, your lives won't be worth a damn."

Gabe snorts, his hands curling tighter under the planter. "Relax, big guy. We've got it."

"Yeah, we're not dumb enough to drop this on Doc," Hank adds, though there's a flicker of tension in his jaw as he glances at the planter's edge.

Forest doesn't look convinced. His gaze lingers on them for a beat longer, sharp and assessing, before he returns his focus to the ground.

"Just remember," he growls, "I'm close enough to make good on my promise."

"You're always so dramatic, Forest." Skye shakes her head as she shifts a small pile of gravel aside.

"Yeah? And you're reckless." Forest nudges her aside with his shoulder, his larger hands taking over the space she's clearing.

"If you're so worried, why don't you help Hank and Gabe?"

"I would, but there's no room—"

"Then stop bitching and let's do this," she cuts him off. "I've got this."

Forest mutters a string of curses under his breath, clearly torn between pulling her back and letting her do her thing.

He glances up at Gabe and Hank. "If you drop it—"

"Yeah, yeah," Gabe interrupts, his voice strained from holding the weight. "We're dead men walking. We got it, Forest. Chill."

Gabe and Hank position themselves on either side of the planter. "On three," Gabe says, fingers curling under the edge.

"Two," Hank grunts, his muscles bunching in preparation.

The planter groans as they lift, its weight making the strain on their faces evident.

Doc Summers reaches beneath the planter, her hands moving with surgical precision, brushing aside loose gravel and dirt.

"Nothing," she reports as Hank and Walt expose the ground beneath the planter. "Just dirt and cigarette butts."

"It's here." The words come out harsher than intended. "I saw it fall. Right at the edge, near the base—"

"Walt." Forest's voice carries warning as I stand.

Fresh blood seeps through my bandages. "You need to sit down before you fall down."

I ignore him, stumbling forward. The movement sends daggers through my chest, but I barely notice. All I can see is Malia's face as they dragged her away. The terror in her eyes. The way she screamed my name.

I drop to my knees, ignoring Doc's curse and Forest's aborted grab for my arm. Fire explodes through my chest as stitches tear, but I don't care. My fingers scrabble at the crack, brushing metal. Blood drips onto concrete—mine, again—but I barely notice.

"There!" Metal glints from a crack where the planter meets the pavement. Small. Barely visible. Easy to miss if you weren't looking for exactly the right thing.

"Got it." The words come out triumphant as my fingers close around a small metallic object—a quantum storage drive that looks military-grade. "What the hell was Malikai doing with hardware like this?" My voice is steady as I lift a small, dark device.

It's cracked, but functional—I hope.

Voices carry from the entrance—Ethan smooth-talking local law enforcement won't last long. They want their crime scene back and don't understand what's at stake.

"Dammit, Walt." Doc Summers springs to her feet. With the help of Forest, they lift me back into the wheelchair.

Gabe and Hank lower the planter, their faces flushed with the exertion of lifting the heavy structure.

Doc Summers fusses over me. "What did I say about not bleeding out?" Doc demands, already pressing fresh gauze against my chest.

I barely hear her.

I clutch the drive tight as they wheel me toward our waiting vehicle, letting Doc fuss over my bleeding bandages. Hank and Gabe fall into flanking positions while Rigel and Blake converge from the perimeter.

My phone's already in my hand, Mitzy's number dialing before we reach the car.

"Need you to crack this drive," I rasp as Forest helps load me into the vehicle. "Whatever's on it—"

"Is worth killing for," she finishes. "Worth taking Malia over. I know. Get it to me fast. And, Walt?" Her voice softens with rare emotion. "We'll find her."

Suddenly, the drive hums to life in my palm, cracked but functional.

"Um, is this normal?"

"What?" Mitzy asks.

I change to a video call and show her the drive. A single line of text scrolls across its surface: *Protocol Echo. If compromised, destroy immediately. Authorization: Lazarus*

"No. That's not normal."

I let them load me back into the vehicle, the drive clutched tight in my bloody fingers.

I stare at the cracked drive as we pull away, police lights reflecting off its surface. Whatever secrets Malikai tried to protect, whatever made him risk his sister's life—it better be worth it.

FIFTEEN

Malia

ENDLESS DARKNESS STRETCHES beyond the oval window, broken only by the rhythmic flash of the light on the jet's wingtip.

Red. Dark. Red. Dark.

Walt's blood pulsing onto the asphalt.

I press my forehead against the cool glass, letting the subtle vibration of engines rattle through my skull. Anything to drown out Malikai's quiet breathing across the polished wood table. Anything to block the image of Walt falling, of blood spreading beneath him like spilled wine.

The thought brings bile rising in my throat. I swallow hard, focusing on the steady drone of engines that cocoons us at thirty-five thousand feet. The sound should be soothing, like white noise masking the universe's chaos. Instead, it reminds me of distance —every minute carrying me further from Walt and any hope of rescue.

Has it really only been hours since dinner at Salvatore's? Since Walt's hands teased me under the table, since his dark promises made me ache? My body still tingles with phantom sensations—his fingers sliding up my thigh, his breath hot against my ear, the weight of his presence overwhelming my senses.

Now, all I feel is numb.

The silk of my dress has gone stiff where Walt's blood dried. I couldn't bring myself to accept the fresh clothes they offered. These bloodstains are all I have left of him.

"Sissy …" Malikai's voice breaks the artificial quiet.

I squeeze my eyes shut, pressing harder against the window. The glass fogs with my breath, creating a halo around the distant wingtip light.

Red. Dark. Red. Dark.

Like a dying heartbeat.

Is that what Walt's heart looked like, struggling to keep beating as his blood painted the pavement? Did someone find him in time? Or did he bleed out alone in that parking lot, reaching for where they dragged me away?

"Please." Kai's voice cracks on the word. "Talk to me."

I curl tighter in the wide leather seat, knees drawn to my chest despite the designer dress. My bare feet—they took my heels during the security search—press against the soft leather. The position feels defensive, childish maybe, but I can't bring myself to care.

What is there to say? That I trusted him?

That I never imagined my brilliant, gentle brother could be involved in something that would get a man shot? That would get me kidnapped?

The guard on my right shifts slightly, his expensive suit rustling. They move like soldiers despite their civilized appearance. Every motion is precise, controlled, and lethal. Just like the casual way they gunned Walt down.

Tears burn behind my eyes, but I refuse to let them fall. Won't give these men the satisfaction of seeing me cry. Won't let Malikai see how deeply his betrayal cuts.

The endless Pacific stretches below, invisible in the darkness but felt in the vastness pressing against the window. Thirty-five thousand feet of empty air between me and the waves. Between me and any chance of escape.

How many hours since takeoff? Two? Three? Time blurs in this pressurized cocoon of leather and polished wood. In the window's reflection, I catch glimpses of the cabin behind me—the guards bracketing Malikai, their faces impassive as marble.

The fresh scent of coffee drifts through the cabin—rich and familiar enough to make my throat tight. How many mornings did I craft the perfect roast at The Guardian Grind? How many times did Walt come in to flirt over ridiculous drink orders?

The memory hits like a physical blow: Walt's smile as he leaned against my counter, the way his eyes darkened when I bent to retrieve fresh beans, how he found any excuse to linger ...

"Miss?" A voice intrudes, cultured and professional. "Would you like a beverage?"

The flight attendant moves gracefully through the cabin as if this were just another charter flight for wealthy executives. Her uniform is crisp, navy with gold accents, and her makeup is perfect despite the late hour. She could be serving champagne to CEOs instead of coffee to kidnappers.

I ignore her just like I ignore my brother. Let the silence stretch until she moves away.

Red light flashes against the window again. Like an emergency beacon. Like the strobes of police cars arriving too late. Like Walt's blood ...

I press my fingers against the cool glass, watching my prints fade into ghostly shapes. How many miles now? How much ocean between me and the man I love?

The thought catches me off guard.

Love?

When did that happen? Somewhere between his cocky smiles

and gentle hands? Between his dark promises and desperate protection?

Now, I may never get to tell him.

A single tear escapes, sliding down my cheek. I wipe it away before anyone notices, but Malikai makes a soft sound—part pain, part guilt. I curl tighter into myself, refusing to acknowledge him.

The darkness beyond the window offers no answers. Only the endless flash of the red light marking time like a metronome. Like a heartbeat growing fainter with each mile.

I turn my attention inward, away from the inescapable blackness outside.

The private jet's cabin gleams with obscene luxury. Honey-colored wood panels line the walls, polished to a mirror shine that reflects the soft amber lighting. Twelve oversized leather captain's chairs, arranged in pairs around polished tables, probably cost more than my yearly salary at The Guardian Grind.

Everything speaks of money and power—from the hand-stitched leather to the crystal glasses arranged on the sideboard. The kind of wealth that makes kidnapping look civilized. That turns abduction into a first-class experience.

I hate how comfortable the chair is, how the leather cradles my body like a lover's embrace. Hate the way wealth tries to mask violence with elegance.

A plush cream-colored sofa curves along the back wall. The sight of it sends an unexpected pang through my chest—remembering Walt's promises about what he'd do to me on my couch. How he claimed me against the inventory room wall just hours ago.

Has it been just hours?

It feels like years.

The memory feels distant, dreamlike: his hands pinning my wrists, his body pressing me against rough concrete, his voice growling dark promises in my ear. Now, those promises might never be fulfilled.

The cabin pressure changes slightly, making my ears pop. One of the guards shifts in response, his movement drawing my attention to the holster visible beneath his jacket. These men wear their weapons like accessories—deadly fashion statements to complement their thousand-dollar suits.

"More coffee, sir?" The flight attendant materializes beside Malikai, her crisp uniform and professional smile bizarre in their normalcy.

Kai shakes his head, his hands trembling slightly as he grips the armrests. His glasses catch the ambient lighting, hiding his eyes. But I know my brother—know the tension in his jaw, the way his fingers tap silent equations when he's afraid.

What kind of research is worth all this? Worth getting Walt shot? Worth trading his sister's freedom?

The guard on my right adjusts his position, leather creaking beneath him. His shoulder brushes mine—a reminder of my captivity wrapped in expensive fabric.

A crystal decanter of amber liquid catches the light, sending honey-colored reflections dancing across the polished table. The flight attendant's heels click against the floor as she moves through the cabin, maintaining the illusion of normal flight service.

"Perhaps some wine?" She gestures to a bottle of what's probably obscenely expensive red. "We have an excellent Bordeaux ..."

Her voice trails off as both guards shake their heads. No alcohol. Of course not. Can't have their prisoners—sorry, passengers—getting drunk at thirty-five thousand feet.

The entire scene feels surreal, like a twisted parody of luxury travel. The flight attendant's perfect makeup and practiced smile. The guards' expensive suits and casual violence. The beautiful cage hurtling us toward whatever fate awaits across the Pacific.

Fresh tears threaten, but I blink them back. Focus instead on cataloging details like Walt taught me. Notice everything. Miss nothing. Knowledge is power, even when you feel powerless.

Six men total. Two with me in the back row, two with Malikai in the center row's captain's chairs, and two up front. All wearing identical dark suits, but their weapons vary. Shoulder holsters for the four guards in the back. The two up front favor ankle holsters, visible when they shift.

Two emergency exits—one over each wing. A bathroom at the rear.

Would they shoot me if I tried to run?

Where would I run to?

There's nothing but ocean and sky for thousands of miles in every direction.

The thought sends claustrophobia clawing at my throat. I press my palm against the cool window, trying to ground myself in sensation. The glass vibrates slightly with the engines' steady drone that should be soothing but instead reminds me of distance —every second carrying me further from home, from Walt, from any hope of rescue.

"Are you sure I can't get you anything?" The flight attendant is back. Her smile never wavers as she hovers near my seat. "We have an excellent selection of—"

"She's fine." The guard to my right cuts her off, his voice carrying the same emotionless tone I'm learning to hate. These men speak like machines, their humanity stripped away by whatever training made them into weapons.

I study them through lowered lashes, noting how they maintain perfect posture despite the hour. No slouching, no casual adjustments. Their vigilance never wavers.

"The galley is always open." The flight attendant's voice

carries that particular tone of high-end service—helpful without being pushy. "Just let me know if you change your mind."

Her heels click softly as she moves away, the sound oddly normal in this abnormal situation. She reaches the forward galley and begins preparing something. The domestic sounds of coffee brewing and china clinking floats back to us.

The flight attendant returns, pushing a cart laden with fine china and crystal. "Dinner service will begin shortly." She maintains that perfect flight attendant smile. "We have a five-course meal prepared by our onboard chef."

Of course, they do. Because why serve prisoner rations when you can maintain the illusion of civilized behavior?

"I'm not hungry." The words come out sharper than intended.

"You should eat." The older guard's voice carries no emotion. "It's a long flight."

A threat? A warning? Or just practical advice from men who view me as cargo to be delivered intact?

The flight attendant begins setting out linens and silverware. Real silver. Real crystal.

"The chef has prepared a lovely, seared ahi tuna with wasabi cream for the first course." She recites the menu like this is a Michelin-starred restaurant instead of a prison at thirty-five thousand feet. "Followed by—"

I tune out her words, focusing instead on the guards' positions. Their perfect stillness. The way they watch everything while appearing to watch nothing.

Four hours down. Eleven to go before we reach wherever they're taking us. Eleven hours trapped in this beautiful cage with men who kill as casually as they adjust their silk ties.

The flight attendant places a glass of water near my hand, condensation beading on crystal. Such a normal gesture in such an abnormal situation.

"Just let me know if you need anything." Her smile never reaches her eyes as she moves to serve the others. Professional to the end, even when serving kidnappers and killers.

The guard on my right straightens imperceptibly as she passes. Always alert, always watching. These men don't rest, don't relax, don't show any sign of human weakness.

I wonder if they were born this way or if someone trained the humanity out of them. Stripped away everything until only the weapon remained, wrapped in expensive suits and casual violence.

The flight attendant disappears behind the galley curtain, leaving us in that artificial quiet unique to private jets. Just the steady drone of engines and the soft clink of crystal as she prepares dinner service.

My voice breaks the artificial silence, startling even me. Kai's head snaps up, hope flashing across his features before guilt shadows them again.

"What did you do?"

"Sissy, I—"

"No." I cut him off, leaning forward. "No pet names. No deflections. What did you do that was worth getting Walt shot?"

One of the guards shifts, a subtle warning. "Miss—"

"She deserves to know." Kai's voice cracks. He starts to reach across the table but stops when I flinch back; he retreats. "I never meant ... God, Malia, I never thought they'd find me so fast. I thought I'd have time to say goodbye."

"That's not an answer." My hands clench in my lap. "What kind of research gets a quantum physicist kidnapped? Gets his sister taken as collateral?"

"That's enough." The older guard's voice carries steel. "His work is classified."

"Classified?" I laugh, the sound brittle. "Is that what we're calling this? A classified flight to God-knows-where while Walt bleeds out on American soil?"

"Malia, please." Kai's fingers drum equations on the armrest—his tell when he's struggling to find words. "I can't … There are things I'm not allowed to explain. But I need you to understand—I tried to protect you. I thought dinner would be safe. Public. I thought—"

"You thought wrong." The words come out raw. "You knew they were coming. That's why you kept checking your phone."

"Miss," the younger guard cuts in. "No more questions."

The flight attendant chooses that moment to appear with the first course. "Seared ahi tuna with wasabi cream," she announces, as if this were just another dinner service. "Chef's specialty."

"I told you, I'm not—" My protest dies as Kai's eyes meet mine across perfectly arranged plates.

"Please eat something." His voice softens to the tone he used when I was sick as a kid. "You need your strength."

"How do I know it's not poisoned?" I stare at the artfully presented food, my stomach churning with equal parts hunger and nausea.

"No one's going to poison you." Kai picks up his fork with trembling fingers. "They're professionals, not monsters."

"No, they shoot people and kidnap their families." But I lift my fork anyway; the silver cool against my palm. If I can't fight, can't run, I can at least keep my strength up.

The tuna melts on my tongue, perfectly prepared. I hate how good it tastes.

"I really liked him, you know." Kai's words come soft, meant just for me. "Walt. I could see why you chose him. The way he looked at you …"

"Stop." My voice cracks on the word.

"He's alive." Kai sets down his fork. "Men like that—they don't die easily."

"Men like, what?" The words come out sharper than intended. "You don't even know him."

"I know enough." Kai's eyes meet mine, steady for the first time since takeoff. "I watched him trying to protect you even after they shot him. He would've kept fighting if they hadn't …" He swallows hard. "If they hadn't used you to stop him."

"Sir." The warning in the guard's voice could cut steel. "That's enough." His hand shifts toward his weapon.

The tension within me finally snaps, a coil wound too tightly for too long. I push back from the table, the silverware clattering as I glare at the guard.

"Why?" My voice cuts through the stale hum of the cabin. "Why are you even reaching for your weapon? What are you going to do? If that thing goes off, we all go down. The plane, you, me, your boss—everyone."

The guard's hand freezes, his expression unreadable, but the warning in his posture remains stiff and unyielding. He doesn't speak, doesn't dare.

"That's what I thought." My heart pounds as I drop back into my seat, the cushion squeaking beneath me. Crossing my arms tightly over my chest, I lean back, staring daggers at the guard until he shifts his gaze away.

Kai watches me, his eyes wide with worry, but he doesn't say a word. The plane feels impossibly small, the recycled air choking as I settle deeper into the seat, my pulse still hammering. I refuse to let the guard—or anyone else—see the trembling in my fingers as I clench my hands into fists.

"I'm sorry." Kai's voice breaks on the words. "God, Malia, I'm so sorry. For all of it. For Walt. For dragging you into this. I never thought … I should have known they'd use you. Should have protected you better."

"You should have told me what was happening." Tears blur my vision, but I refuse to let them fall.

"I couldn't. Not without putting you at risk." His fingers tap out another equation—probably calculating odds of survival or escape trajectories. "I'm sorry."

The flight attendant appears to clear our plates, her movements precise and practiced. For a moment, the only sounds are the clink of fine china and the steady thrum of engines carrying us farther from home.

Kai's eyes meet mine across the table, and for a moment I see my big brother again—the one who taught me quantum mechanics using coffee beans, who chased away playground bullies, and explained the mysteries of the universe.

"Well, seeing as we're here …" I gesture vaguely around the cabin. "I deserve an explanation."

"They're collecting us." Kai's voice drops low as the flight attendant retreats with dessert dishes.

"What?" I lean closer, keeping my voice barely above a whisper. "They? Who's they?"

"Theoretical physicists. Fusion specialists." His fingers trace equations on the tablecloth. "First, it was Dr. Chen from Berkeley. He just—vanished."

"Sir." The guard's warning carries deadly promise.

But Kai continues, his words rushing out between sips of coffee, disguising the conversation. "Three months ago, Rodriguez disappeared. They took his daughter. Then Williams and his wife …" He swallows hard. "I thought I could protect you by staying away. But I couldn't—couldn't leave without saying goodbye."

The pieces click, each one slotting into place with horrifying clarity. My breath catches in my throat as I stare at Kai, the weight of what he's not saying pressing down on me like a physical force.

My mind races, connecting dots I wish I could unsee. When humanity harnessed nuclear power, it lit up cities and fueled entire countries, but it also birthed destruction—the atomic bomb, a force capable of wiping out everything in its path.

And now fusion. Fusion energy that harnesses the power of the sun itself.

Clean, limitless energy—or a weapon of unimaginable scale.

My chest tightens as the implications hit me like a freight train. Whatever breakthrough Kai has been working on, whatever he's caught himself in, it's bigger than I could have imagined.

The guard shifts, his warning gaze drilling into me, but I barely notice. My eyes lock on Kai, his exhaustion etched into every line of his face. The slight dip of his head confirms it—he knows exactly what's at stake.

This isn't just about his research or them using me to control him.

It's about power—power to change the world or obliterate it.

The guard's hand twitches toward his weapon again, his jaw tightening. I sit back slowly, struggling to pull air into my lungs.

My brilliant, gentle brother—who taught me electron configurations using coffee beans, who still calls me 'Sissy' even though we're both adults—is caught in something bigger and darker than his quantum calculations could have predicted.

I reach across the table, not quite touching his hand. The first gesture of connection since takeoff. His fingers still, and for a moment I see the boy who used to chase away schoolyard bullies, who explained particle physics using Halloween candy.

"I understand," I whisper. And I do. Not the quantum mechanics or the fusion breakthrough, but the need to say goodbye. To have one last moment before everything changed.

I just wish Walt hadn't paid the price for that goodbye.

Exhaustion hits suddenly, the adrenaline of the past hours

crashing through me. My eyes feel gritty, my limbs feel heavy with fatigue. Even keeping my head up becomes a monumental task.

"Sleep." Kai's voice carries that familiar big-brother concern. "I'll watch over you."

"Like you watched over Walt?"

Pain flashes across his features. "I'll do better this time. I promise."

I want to argue, to stay angry, but my body betrays me. My eyes drift closed despite my best efforts. The last thing I see is Kai's face—torn between guilt and fierce protectiveness.

As for my dreams? They come in fragments: Walt's blood spreading across the pavement. His arms reaching as they dragged me away. His voice calling my name, growing fainter as he slips away.

I jerk awake with a gasp, momentarily disoriented. The cabin lights have dimmed to a soft glow. Most of the guards seem to doze.

Kai still watches me, his glasses reflecting the faint light. He hasn't slept. Probably won't until we land. The sight stirs something in my chest—anger and love tangled so tight I can't separate them.

He's still my brother. Still the boy who explained the universe to me, but he's also the man who got Walt shot. Who knew danger was coming but took me to dinner anyway.

How do you reconcile those truths?

His fingers tap out another equation—this one I recognize from childhood. The quantum formula for uncertainty. For all his brilliant calculations, he couldn't predict this outcome. Couldn't protect me from the consequences of his genius.

But he tried to say goodbye. Tried to give us one last moment before everything changed.

I close my eyes again, letting the engine's drone lull me back toward sleep. The last thought before unconsciousness claims me is a prayer:

Please be alive.

Please find me.

Because I'm not sure I can save us on my own.

When we land in Honolulu, they don't let us off the plane. I watch through the window as they refuel, the tropical paradise beyond the tarmac feeling like a cruel joke. So close to civilization, to phones and police and help—but might as well be a million miles away with armed men watching our every move.

"Almost halfway there," one suit comments as we take off again, heading west into an endless night. Somewhere ahead lies another country, another life I never asked for. Somewhere behind, Walt might be dead or dying, with no way to know where they've taken me.

Please be alive.

But even if he is—even if he survives ... How will he find me on the other side of the world?

SIXTEEN

Malia

___

THE JET TOUCHES DOWN HARD, rattling my teeth as Soviet-era concrete stretches endlessly before us. Dawn bleeds across the horizon in shades of rust and steel, casting long shadows across a place time forgot. The guards usher us down metal stairs onto the cracked tarmac, the brittle wind bitter enough to steal my breath.

Malikai stumbles beside me, his glasses fogging in the pre-dawn chill. A facility looms ahead—a sprawling complex of concrete and steel that looks like something from a Cold War nightmare. Thick pipes snake between buildings, steam hissing from joints like dying breaths. The main structure stretches at least ten stories high, its windows dark and vacant except for occasional flickers of movement.

"Move." The guard's accent is thick as he prods us forward. His expensive suit looks out of place against the industrial decay. Armed men patrol the perimeter fence, their weapons modern despite the dated surroundings.

"Kai, why are they doing this?"

My legs shake as we approach the main entrance. Whether from exhaustion or fear, I'm not sure anymore. The dress I wore to dinner offers no protection against the Kazakhstan winter. Walt's dried blood stains the silk, and I press my hand against it like a talisman.

"The quantum fusion, the containment fields are all a part of something bigger. These people aren't just building weapons; they're building chaos."

"Who? Who would do that?"

"Someone called the Third Sentinel, but he's just a pawn." Malikai's voice drops to a desperate whisper.

"A pawn? Whose pawn?" I keep my voice low, knowing this is something the guards can't overhear.

"I don't know, but the Sentinels are just pawns. They might run this facility, but they all answer to someone else."

"What do they want?" I try to pull closer, but the guards are already dragging us apart.

"Global destabilization," he manages to get out. "That's what they want, and we're the tools to make it happen."

The guards escort us through layers upon layers of security. The place feels like a maximum security prison. Security towers punctuate the fence line every hundred yards, their spotlights cutting through the lingering darkness.

The perimeter is a study in paranoia: three layers of fencing topped with razor wire, cameras covering every angle, and what look like motion sensors scattered throughout the dead zone between barriers.

The entrance itself feels like passing through the gates of hell. Thick steel doors groan open, revealing a stark corridor lit by harsh fluorescent tubes. The air carries a metallic tang that coats my tongue, mixed with the sharp bite of industrial cleaners. Everything feels aggressively sterile, as if they're trying to sanitize away any trace of humanity.

Other captive families huddle in the intake area—I recognize them from Kai's whispered descriptions on the plane. Dr. Chen's wife clutches their teenage son's hand, both pale and drawn. Rodriguez's daughter can't be more than twelve, her dark eyes huge in her thin face. Dr. Williams and his wife stand close together, shoulders touching as if afraid to lose contact.

A young woman about my age catches my eye—she must be Ally, Whittman's doctoral student. Her long blonde hair is tied back severely, but strands escape to frame a face that looks as shell-shocked as I feel. She offers a tiny nod of acknowledgment before a guard steps between us.

Power thrums through the building's bones, a low-frequency vibration that sets my teeth on edge. Whatever they're building, it's hungry for energy. The lights flicker occasionally, making the shadows dance along institutional green walls. Each time they dim, the guards' hands drift to their weapons.

I clutch my arms around myself, trying to hold what little warmth remains. The magnitude of our isolation hits me like a physical blow—we're in the middle of nowhere, surrounded by nothing but steppe and sky.

No one knows where we are.

No one is coming to save us.

The guards prod us forward through stark corridors, their boots echoing against concrete. Malikai's hand finds mine, squeezing with desperate strength. We haven't held hands since I was small enough to need help crossing streets, but now his fingers grip mine like an anchor.

I squeeze right back.

"Processing," one guard announces, gesturing to a steel door marked with Cyrillic letters. "Males left. Females right."

"No." Malikai's voice cracks as guards move to separate us. "Please, I need to stay with her. She's my responsibility, I have to—"

A guard cuts him off with a sharp jab to the ribs.

"Kai—" I reach for him, but hands grab my arms, yanking me toward the right-hand door.

"Malia!" He fights against the guards holding him, his glasses askew, his academic composure shattering. "Don't hurt her! I'll do whatever you want, just don't—"

The butt of a rifle silences him. As they drag him through the left door, our fingers stretch toward each other like children reaching for lifelines. His last look carries years of guilt and fear before steel doors slam between us.

I'm met inside by a woman in a pristine white lab coat that contrasts sharply with the appalling and depressive gray room.

"Strip." The woman's command carries no emotion. When I hesitate, she sighs. "Either you remove the dress, or we remove it for you."

My fingers tremble on the zipper. The silk whispers to the floor, leaving me exposed under harsh lights. The woman doesn't even blink when she sees I'm completely naked beneath the dress.

Images of Walt grabbing my panties, sniffing them, and stuffing them in his pocket flood my mind. His tempestuous eyes, dark and aroused, the low gravelly sound of his voice, and the delicious things he promised feel lost to me.

They photograph every angle, documenting existing bruises and marks with clinical precision. The woman notes Walt's blood on the dress before sealing it in a plastic bag—evidence of a life I'm no longer allowed to claim.

"Arms up. Turn slowly." Her latex gloves are cold against my skin as she searches for hidden weapons or communication devices. The medical exam that follows is thorough and humiliating. Blood draws, dental records, fingerprints—cavity searches. They document everything like I'm a specimen rather than a person.

They issue standard clothing—scratchy gray cotton pants, white T-shirts, and sturdy boots. Everything's identical and stripped of individuality. Even the underwear comes in uniform packets, sized and labeled like we're inventory rather than humans.

"Medical history?" The woman doesn't look up from her tablet as she rapid-fires questions. Allergies, surgeries, medications—building a file that makes me feel like property rather than a person. Each answer is meticulously logged.

My hair falls around my shoulders as they confiscate my hair tie—apparently, even elastics can be weapons. They take my watch, earrings, and even the small silver bracelet my mother gave me before she died. Each item disappears into labeled bags, becoming part of some vast cataloging system.

"Open your mouth." The dental exam feels invasive, with latex-covered fingers probing for hidden compartments or tools. They scan for implants or devices, treating my body like a potential security breach rather than flesh and blood.

Fingerprints come next. Then, retinal scans, DNA swabs, and voice prints. Every unique identifier is cataloged and filed away. They even measure and photograph my feet—apparently, shoe size can be used for identification if we try to run.

The final indignity is the tracking bracelet they lock around my wrist. The metal is warm from the soldering iron, a permanent reminder of my new status. The bracelet beeps softly, synchronizing with their security system. Now, they can track my every movement within the facility's confines.

"Medical ID number 2847-B," the woman announces, attaching a file to my new identity. "Familial leverage for Asset Singh. Security clearance level zero." She finally meets my eyes. "Welcome to the program."

SEVENTEEN

Walt

THE BEEP of the heart monitor is incessant, a constant reminder that I'm still here, tethered to this damn bed. The soft glow of the overhead lights feels harsher by the second, and I shift against the pillows, trying to find a position that doesn't make me feel like a caged animal.

My teammates take turns visiting me. Today, Ethan and Blake stand watch over me. Standing watch means making sure I don't try and get out of bed. Doc Summers was very insistent about that.

"I'm fine," I growl, my patience running thin. "It's not like I'm going to keel over the second I stand up."

"You're not going anywhere." Ethan leans against the wall with his arms crossed and raises a skeptical brow. "At least, not until Doc Summers says so."

"I'm healing. She said as much." I scowl, glaring at him from the bed. "I've been stuck here for days. I need to move."

"You need to heal," Blake retorts, his voice even though there's a warning edge. "Sitting still is part of healing."

"I'm not a damn invalid." I shove at the blanket draped over me, irritation bubbling under my skin. "I can walk to the door without dropping dead."

"You couldn't even sit up yesterday without passing out," Ethan reminds me, his tone dripping with calm condescension.

"That was yesterday," I snap. "Today's a new day. I'm stronger."

"Stronger, huh?" Blake steps closer, peering at me as if daring me to prove it. "You sure about that?"

I clench my jaw, my fists tightening against the bed. "Damn right, I'm sure."

Before I can launch into another tirade, the door creaks open. Doc Summers steps in, a tablet in one hand and a stethoscope draped around her neck. Her sharp gaze sweeps over the room before landing squarely on me.

"Those monitors," she begins, her voice steady but laced with authority, "say otherwise." She gestures toward the machines, blinking and beeping at my side, one brow arched as she approaches.

"The monitors are exaggerating. I feel fine." I huff, sinking back into the pillows.

"Yeah? And I'm sure the monitors just decided to lie about your heart rate when you threw that tantrum just minutes ago." She smirks faintly, setting the tablet down on a nearby counter.

"That wasn't a tantrum," I mutter, heat rising to my face. "That was frustration. There's a difference."

"Frustration or not, let's see how 'fine' you really are." Doc Summers ignores the comment, pulling the stethoscope from around her neck and slipping it into her ears. "Sit up."

I do as I'm told, though not without a grunt of pain. My muscles protest, a dull ache spreading through my torso as I shift upward. Doc places the cold metal of the stethoscope against my chest, her expression unreadable as she listens.

"You're improving," she finally says, pulling back and jotting something onto her tablet. "But not enough to go running laps around the building."

"I'm not asking for laps," I counter. "I'm asking for a little freedom. Let me get out of this bed, at least for a few minutes."

"Freedom?" Ethan snorts from the corner. "You'll probably fall flat on your face two steps in."

"I won't." I glare at him, then look back at Doc Summers. "I just need to move. Something. Anything."

Doc Summers sighs, crossing her arms as she studies me. "How about this? You stay put for another day. If your vitals look stable tomorrow, I'll let you sit in a chair instead of the bed. Deal?"

"A chair?" I grimace. "I was thinking more along the lines of a walk."

"You're thinking like an idiot," Blake mutters under his breath.

"Small steps, Walt. You don't go from near-death to marathons overnight. Push too hard, and you'll end up back at square one—or worse."

I chew on the inside of my cheek, torn between the need to get out of this bed and the sense in her words. Finally, I let out a resigned breath. "Fine. Tomorrow. But if I can stand, I'm walking."

Doc Summers smirks, a glint of amusement in her eyes. "We'll see." She pats my arm lightly before turning to Ethan. "Keep him in line, will you? No theatrics."

Ethan chuckles, his arms still crossed. "Oh, don't worry, Doc. I'm not letting him out of my sight."

"Babysitters. The whole damn lot of you." As the door closes behind her, I flop back against the pillows, muttering. "I'm fine."

The lie comes automatically as I struggle to sit straighter. Fire rips through my chest, but I keep my face neutral. I won't give them another excuse to keep me here one second longer than necessary.

"I know you want to find her. We all do." Ethan's expression softens slightly. "But you can't help Malia if you collapse from pushing too hard, too fast."

"Has Mitzy made any progress with the drive?"

His hesitation tells me everything. "The casing was too damaged. Whatever Malikai tried to give you ... The data's corrupted beyond recovery."

The words hit hard. Three days wasted, and our only lead is worthless. My hands clench in the sheets as monitors register my spike in heart rate.

"Dammit." The curse slips out as I slam my fist against the bed rail. Sharp pain lances through my chest, but I barely notice. "That drive was our only lead."

"Not necessarily." Blake kicks off from the wall and sits at the foot of my bed. "Mitzy's team is analyzing Malikai's research history. Three other quantum physicists have disappeared in the past month. All working on similar projects."

"Similar, how?" I force myself to focus past the fog of pain and medication.

"Quantum tunneling effects in fusion containment." Blake glances at the monitor above my head. It's alarming with the spike in my heart rate. "Malikai made some kind of break-through three months ago. Something that interested the wrong people."

"Has anyone claimed responsibility?" The question comes out rougher than intended. "Made demands?"

"Not yet." Ethan doesn't mince words. "But the pattern matches other disappearances. The targeting, the professional extraction teams—"

"The use of family as leverage." The words taste bitter in my mouth.

"Exactly," Blake adds. "Working theory is it might be connected to the Third Sentinel."

That catches my attention. "That's what the doc and Forest thought. The nuclear materials dealer?"

"He's evolved his game. Instead of stealing deuterium from research facilities, he's collecting the minds that can weaponize it." Ethan shoves his hands into his pockets. "I know it's not what you want to hear, but it is what it is."

"If Mitzy's right about Malikai's breakthrough …" The thought sends fresh fire through my veins. "How long before they decide she's outlived her usefulness?"

"Walt." Ethan's voice carries warning as the monitors register another spike. "Your body can't handle this level of stress right now. You need to—"

"What I need is to get out of this damn bed." I start pulling at the IV in my arm, but Ethan's hand clamps down on my wrist.

"Touch that IV again, and I'll have Forest sit on you." The threat carries weight—we both know the massive man would do it. "The team's working 'round the clock. You're not in this alone. We're all looking for her."

But they don't love her.

They don't wake up reaching for her.

They don't see her face every time they close their eyes.

They don't remember how she felt pressed against that wall, trembling with need as she confessed she was saving herself for me.

EIGHTEEN

Walt

———

A FEW DAYS LATER, the door to my hospital room opens, and in strides CJ carrying a tablet under his arm. Ethan and Blake follow on his heels. CJ yanks the bedside table close and sets the tablet down.

From his posture, something's changed.

"Got something interesting." He powers up the tablet, fiddles with a connection, and suddenly, we're in a briefing with Sam, Forest, Mitzy, and another face I recognize.

Robert Collins, tech billionaire and previous Guardian HRS client.

"We're on," CJ says.

"Walt." Sam's voice carries barely contained energy. "Sorry to disturb you, but Mr. Collins has information you need to hear."

I push myself straight in the bed, ignoring how the movement pulls at my stitches. "Mr. Collins. Last time we met, we rescued your daughter from a human trafficking ring."

"Please, call me Robert." He looks older than I remember,

new lines etched around his eyes. "And I'm here about Ally. She's missing—again."

I don't see how this can be related to Malia's kidnapping, but I play along. I don't have the energy for much beyond that. "Missing? Since when?"

"She was working on her doctoral thesis at CERN under her advisor, Dr. Wally Whittman." His hands clench at his sides. "Top quantum physicist, pioneer in fusion containment theory. Ally missed the defense of her doctoral thesis. Whittman also missed it. Neither of them showed up for work the next day. Her apartment is empty. There's no sign of a struggle."

"Wittman co-authored several papers with Malia's brother on quantum tunneling effects in plasma containment," Mitzy chimes in. The tablet suddenly flashes with several journal articles on cold fusion.

"Or weaponize them." Forest's gravelly voice carries grim understanding.

"Malikai?" My head snaps up. "You're sure?"

Forest turns to Collins. "When exactly did your daughter disappear?"

The conversation continues. I lean back because the act of sitting is too exhausting. It's a lot to process, but maybe we can find something in Ally's disappearance that will lead us to Malia.

"Found something." Mitzy's back in charge. I know this because the screen suddenly flickers and flashes with journal article after journal article. "Mr. Collins, we're following the abduction of Malikai Singh. He was taken three days ago by a professional extraction team. They took his sister as leverage. I cross-referenced papers published by Whittman and Singh and found something disturbing.

"What's that?"

"There's a Dr. Chen from Berkeley—a theoretical physicist and cold fusion specialist. He specializes in plasma containment. Dr. Rodriguez disappeared, as did his daughter. He's a theoretical physicist in quantum tunneling effect and applications to cold fusion. There's a Dr. Williams, same field of study—fusion dynamics—who also went missing with his wife. Now, we have Malia and her brother —the latest scientist taken, and your daughter and her mentor, Dr. Whittman. They're all connected through collaborations in publications in theoretical physics and/or cold fusion. It's the same pattern. The same people. Someone is collecting quantum physicists and using their families to ensure cooperation."

"Which means ..." Collins swallows hard. "Ally wasn't taken because she's my daughter this time. I feel as though I should be relieved that her life isn't in danger because of me, but she's still missing. She was taken because she's Whittman's doctoral candidate. Because she knows enough about their research to be valuable."

"That seems to be the case." Forest steps in with his rumbly voice. "We're going to do everything we can to get her back."

"We need everything you have on Whittman's research." Ethan's already reaching for his phone. "We also need to know what Ally was working on—anything you can give us. Mitzy, if you haven't already, find out what you can about the other scientists. There must be a thread we can pull that will show us where they might have been taken."

"I'll have Ally's lab notes sent over." Collins runs a hand through his hair. "But most of it's beyond me. Quantum mechanics, fusion dynamics ... And, of course, her phone. My people have already tried tracking it, but maybe you can find something we missed. Do whatever it takes to bring my girl home. Bring them all home."

Damn straight.

The video call ends with a sharp click, Collins' face disappears from the screen. The weight of his final words lingers in the room like a storm cloud.

Bring my girl home. Bring them all home.

I stare at the blank screen for a beat, the steady hum of the hospital room monitors filling the silence. My fingers twitch against the blanket, the restlessness clawing at me like a caged animal. They're out there—Malia and the others—somewhere.

And I'm stuck here, tied down by beeping machines and white sheets.

Helpless.

Useless.

I shove the blanket aside, the cool air biting my legs as I swing them over the edge of the bed. Pain ripples through my side, sharp but bearable.

"Walt." Ethan's warning comes too late. "What are you doing?"

"Getting dressed." Fire rips through my chest, but I force myself upright. "I'm not spending another minute in this bed while Malia's out there."

"You're supposed to be recovering." Ethan steps closer, but I hold up a hand to stop him.

"I've rested enough. There's no recovery while they're still out there." My feet touch the cold tile, and I exhale sharply, straightening despite the pull of stitches and the protests of my battered body. "Every second I spend here is another second wasted."

"And what exactly are you planning to do? Fall flat on your face before you make it out the door?" Blake crosses his arms, his expression dark.

"Whatever it takes." My jaw tightens as I take a step, the pain slicing through me like a hot blade. I don't let it stop me. "We don't have time, and I'm not sitting on the sidelines while the rest of you figure it out without me."

Ethan watches me for a long moment, the tension thick

between us. Finally, he lets out a low growl, shaking his head. "You're a stubborn bastard, you know that?"

"Yeah," I grunt, gripping the back of the chair for balance. "That's why you made me a Guardian."

"Fine." Ethan exhales through his nose, muttering something under his breath as he moves to the door. "But don't come crying to me when Doc Summers rips you a new one."

"She'll have to catch me first," I shoot back.

"Doc Summers will sedate you if you try to leave." Blake rolls his eyes and shakes his head.

"Let her try." I yank the IV from my arm, ignoring the trickle of blood. I manage two stumbling steps before my legs betray me. The room tilts sideways as darkness creeps in at the edges of my vision. Strong hands catch me before I hit the floor—Blake and Ethan, moving with tactical precision to keep me from face-planting.

"And this is why we can't have nice things." Doc Summers' voice cuts through the fog as they half-carry, half-drag me back to bed. "Do you have any idea how much damage you could have done?"

"Had to try," I mutter as they resettle me against the pillows. The world's still spinning, but I refuse to close my eyes. Won't give them the satisfaction.

"No, you didn't." She snaps on fresh gloves, already examining where I yanked out the IV. "You had to be stubborn and reckless because that's your default setting. Stuck on stupid. Hold still."

The sharp stick of a new IV makes me wince. "We're wasting time—"

"You know what wastes time?" She tapes down the line with more force than necessary. "Having to restitch wounds that won't heal because someone won't stay in bed. Having to monitor a patient who keeps spiking fevers because he won't rest."

"Doc—"

"No." She cuts me off, her dark eyes fierce. "You want to help Malia? Then, be a good patient. Rest. Recover. Heal. Because right now, you're barely able to stand, let alone fight. And when we find them—because we will find them—we're going to need you at full strength."

"Fine." I sink back against the pillows, hating how the simple act of trying to stand leaves me drained and feeling like I just finished a marathon. "Then, at least let me be useful from here."

"We'll have Mitzy set you up a virtual office," Doc Summers says, her sharp eyes narrowing as they rake over me. She doesn't miss a thing—the tension in my jaw, the way my hand grips the edge of the mattress like it's the only thing keeping me upright.

Her gaze flicks to CJ. "But if his vitals spike again—"

"They won't," I interrupt, my voice a growl.

Doc Summers doesn't dignify me with a response. Instead, she reaches for a syringe and attaches it to the IV port. "This isn't a negotiation, Walt. You need to rest, and I need you stable. You'll thank me later."

"Like hell, I will," I mutter, but it's already too late.

The sedative courses through my veins, a heavy, unwelcome warmth that drags me under. My protests fade, slurring into incoherence as the world blurs around the edges. The last thing I see is Doc Summers' silhouette and Ethan's disapproving scowl.

NINETEEN

Malia

AFTER *PROCESSING,* I'm escorted to a dormitory and shoved into a tiny apartment that is a study in Soviet minimalism—two bedrooms, one bath, and a combined living area. No kitchenette. I suppose kitchen utensils could become weapons; they don't want that.

The walls are bare concrete, painted institutional beige decades ago. A single window offers a view of an inner courtyard, its thick glass reinforced with wire mesh. Even if we could break it, the forty-foot drop would be fatal.

The door buzzes, then opens with a metallic groan. Guards shove Malikai inside, his lean frame stumbling from the force. He's dressed in the same gray uniform they gave me, his glasses slightly crooked from rough handling. His face is already bruising where the rifle struck him.

"Kai!" I rush forward, needing to verify he's real.

He catches me in a fierce hug, his body trembling. They've already erased the professor, the brilliant physicist. My big brother feels smaller somehow, diminished.

"I'm sorry," he whispers into my hair, the words carrying

years of guilt. "I'm so sorry, Sissy." His arms tighten as guards move to separate us. "Please," he begs them. "Ju-just give us a minute."

Surprisingly, they step back, though weapons remain ready. Perhaps even here, some small mercies survive. Or maybe they want to document our weakness and measure our bond to better use it against us.

"Home sweet home," Malikai mutters; his attempt at humor falls flat. The furniture is purely functional—metal-frame beds with thin mattresses, basic chairs, and a small table. No electronics, no decorations, nothing that could be used to communicate or cause harm. Even the mirror in the bathroom is polished metal rather than glass.

I explore my bedroom slowly, cataloging its limitations. The bed is bolted to the floor, and the mattress is sealed in a waterproof material that crinkles when I sit. A small dresser contains our issued clothing—everything identical and labeled with our ID numbers. A single shelf holds approved reading material—technical manuals and classic literature, nothing published in the last decade.

The bathroom door doesn't lock—privacy is a privilege we haven't earned. Even the toilet paper is counted and rationed, and our usage is monitored like everything else.

Air circulates through vents too small to crawl through, carrying the perpetual scent of industrial cleaner. The temperature remains constant, controlled by systems we can't access. Cameras in the corners track every movement—their red lights blinking steadily like malevolent eyes.

The window draws me like a moth to the flame. The courtyard below is barren concrete, divided into exercise yards by high fences. Other apartments face ours across the void, their windows identical to ours. I count six levels of housing units—enough for all the captured families plus additional space for the guards and whoever else inhabits this dreary space.

Are they expecting more prisoners? Or maybe it's left over from the Soviet era?

A panel by the door displays our schedules—mealtimes, permitted recreation periods, and designated shower slots. Everything is regulated and monitored. A speaker above it occasionally crackles with announcements in multiple languages.

Big Brother is always watching, always listening.

The worst part is how permanent it feels. This isn't a temporary holding cell—it's designed for long-term containment. They've thought of everything and eliminated every possible means of escape or communication. We're rats in a maze, our movements controlled, our lives reduced to schedules and rations.

I press my forehead against the cool glass, watching my breath fog the surface. Somewhere out there, beyond the fences, guards, and endless steppe, Walt is either dead or looking for me.

I don't know which possibility hurts more.

Malikai paces our small living space, his fingers tapping out quantum equations on his thigh—the familiar gesture feels like a betrayal. Those equations led us here, trapped in this concrete cage.

"I never thought …" He stops, staring at his hands like they belong to someone else. "The breakthrough was theoretical. Just numbers on a page." His voice cracks. "I should have destroyed everything when we achieved quantum tunneling in the palladium matrix. Should have known they'd come for it."

I sit on the metal chair, letting silence fill the space between us. The distance feels greater than the few feet separating us—it's measured in lies and omissions, in choices that can't be undone.

"They approached me six months ago." He removes his glasses and rubs his eyes. "Offered funding, resources, anything I needed. When I refused …" His hands shake as he cleans the lenses with his shirt. "They showed me photos. You at the coffee shop. They've been watching for months."

The revelation hits like a punch to the gut. While crafting lattes and falling in love, shadowy figures documented my every move.

In Guardian HQ?

How?

"That's why you came to dinner? To say goodbye?"

"I thought—public place, witnesses …" He laughs bitterly. "Stupid. So stupid. I underestimated them."

Grief etches new lines around his eyes, aging him years in days. My brilliant brother, who once explained quantum entanglement using coffee beans and sugar packets, looks lost in his own equations.

"Did you know they'd shoot him?" The question comes out sharp enough to draw blood.

"No!" His denial is instant, vehement. "God, Malia, no. I thought … I don't know what I thought. That I could slip you the drive, that someone would find it, that …" He presses his palms against his eyes. "I never meant for anyone to get hurt."

"But he did." I stand, needing distance. "Walt bled out on that pavement because of your choices."

"I know." His voice breaks. "I know, and I'll never …" He reaches for me, but I step back. "I'm so sorry, Sissy. I'd give anything to go back, to warn you, to—"

"To what?" The old nickname feels wrong now, tainted by betrayal. "To let me choose? To tell me the truth? When exactly in the past six months did you plan to mention that your research could get us killed?"

He flinches like I've struck him. "They'll kill millions if they weaponize this. Billions! You have to understand. In the wrong hands, the containment fields, the quantum tunneling effect—it's not just a power source. It's …"

"A doomsday device." The words taste like ashes. "And now they have exactly what they need. The research, the researchers, and the leverage to make you build it."

His shoulders slump in defeat. *I'm sorry* feels inadequate now, lost in the space between the brother I knew and the man whose choices landed us here.

"Well," I glance around the tiny, suffocating apartment, "I guess we should explore while we still can." The guards left after depositing Malikai, and they left the door open. I'm not letting that opportunity go to waste.

Beyond rows of other apartments, we come upon what looks to be a common area. It's bare except for bolted-down tables and chairs, all arranged to maximize surveillance camera coverage. That's where I meet Ally. She sits alone by the window, her fingers tracing equations in the condensation like ghostwriting.

"Quantum tunneling effect in crystalline matrices?" I recognize the formula from Kai's work. Her startled look shifts to curiosity as I sit across from her.

"You understand this stuff?" She gestures to the fading numbers.

"No. Pattern recognition. My brother tried teaching me. Mostly, I just memorized enough to follow his excited rambling." The almost-smile we share feels like the first real thing since arriving. "I'm Malia."

"Ally. Doctor Whittman's eternal doctoral student." Her attempt at humor carries an edge of bitterness. "Though I guess finishing my doctorate isn't a priority anymore."

She's closer to my age than any other captive—maybe twenty-five, with the intense focus I recognize in Kai. Her blonde hair is pulled back severely, but strands escape like acts of rebellion.

"How long?" I don't need to specify.

"A few days." She wipes away the equations. "They took us

from CERN—grabbed Whittman right after a lecture. I was—I was just in the wrong place. Wrong time. Wrong thesis topic."

The guards watch us from their posts, but she's learned their patterns. When the nearest one turns his patrol, she speaks faster and lower. "Chen was first. Then Rodriguez and his daughter. Williams and his wife a day before your arrival."

"My brother mentioned containment fields, fusion reactions …"

"More than that." Her voice drops further. "The power draws are massive." She glances at the guards. "Let's just say our chances of survival depend entirely on our success."

Understanding clicks. We're not just hostages for cooperation —we're insurance against sabotage. If the scientists try to stop the project, their families pay the price.

"Do you work in the labs?" I ask when the guard passes again.

"I do." She shakes her head. "Families aren't allowed below ground, but my thesis is based on sustainable nuclear fusion. Sometimes, at night, you can feel the whole building shake. And the power surges …" Her fingers tap restlessly on the table. "They're pushing the containment fields past safety limits. One failure, one miscalculation … I dream about CERN sometimes," she admits softly. "About equations and coffee runs and stupid department politics. When physics was beautiful instead of terrifying."

Her words echo something in my soul—memories of The Guardian Grind, of Walt's smile, of a life where coffee was just coffee and love was just beginning.

TWENTY

Walt

______

DAYS PASS and the sharp scent of disinfectant mingles with the faint aroma of coffee. Despite Doc Summers wanting me to take things easy, my hospital room is anything but peaceful.

Ethan leans against the wall, arms crossed, while Blake fiddles with a monitor. Rigel untangles cords with a look of pure concentration. Then there is Hank and Gabe arguing over where to position a chair. The room is crowded and chaotic.

My teammates are setting up my mobile office.

My chest tightens, but not from the lingering pain. It's the kind of tightness that comes from knowing you've got the best damn team in the world. They get it—they get me. They know I can't lie here, not when there's work to be done. Not when lives are on the line. Even when I can't be out there physically, they find a way to ensure I'm involved.

"Drink up." Ethan tosses me a bottle of water. "You've got five minutes to look human before we go live."

I don't bother to hide the faint grin tugging at my lips as I crack the seal. "You're all a bunch of overachievers, you know that?"

"Yeah," Rigel says, dragging a chair into place with a grunt. "And you're welcome."

Minutes later, Hank arranges the tablet at the perfect angle, and within moments, familiar faces fill the screen. Sam, Forest, and Mitzy take up their usual spots on the screen, the lines of tension evident even through the poor lighting, but it's the face at the bottom right corner that catches me off guard.

"Mia?" Her name comes out rough, almost a whisper. She looks good, but her eyes hold a weariness that wasn't there before. "They pulled you into this?"

Her lips curve into a faint smile, but it doesn't reach her eyes. "Like I had a choice."

I exhale slowly, the weight of the situation settling back over me. This is what we do—what we're built for. And if my team's here, working to keep me in the loop even when I'm stuck in a damn bed, then I sure as hell owe them my entire focus.

Time to get to work.

"Considering my history with Sentinel Three and the deuterium thefts ..." She gives a grim smile. "I might have insights about where large quantities of nuclear material disappeared to."

"It's official? We're thinking this is Sentinel?"

"The Third Sentinel's pattern changed after we stopped his deuterium operation," Mitzy adds, her fingers flying across her keyboard. "Instead of stealing materials, he started collecting the people who could weaponize them."

"But the deuterium shipments were for making nuclear weapons. These are cold fusion experts. Totally different."

"Maybe not as different as we'd like." Mia shrugs. "Whether to create a new super weapon or corner the market on sustainable fusion energy, they can disrupt global commerce."

"And that's exactly Malfor's game," CJ says. "Disruption followed by conquest, but on a global scale."

"Tell them what you found," Forest rumbles.

Mia leans closer to her camera. "Before we shut down the deuterium thefts, large shipments were going to supposedly decommissioned research facilities in Kazakhstan and North Korea. Places with existing infrastructure for nuclear research …"

"And the power grid to support it," Sam finishes. "Mitzy, overlay those locations with the scientists' last known movements."

The screen splits, showing a map dotted with red markers. "Chen's last cell phone ping was here." Mitzy highlights a point. "Rodriguez's credit card activity stopped here. Williams' final email came from this location."

"What about their research?" I ask. "There has to be a connection between what they were working on."

"We mentioned this yesterday," Mitzy says.

"Sorry, but the narcotics make my memory fuzzy. Can we go over it again?"

Mitzy splits the screen again, showing academic papers and grant proposals. "Chen specialized in plasma containment. Rodriguez focused on quantum tunneling effects. Williams worked on fusion dynamics. Whittman combined quantum tunneling effect and plasma containment. Malikai combined all three … They've all collaborated on various scientific papers in the field of cold fusion."

"Creating a breakthrough that could revolutionize how we control fusion reactions," Sam adds.

"Or weaponize them," Forest growls.

"Wait, can we break this down so that us ordinary folk can understand?" I lean forward, ignoring the pull of stitches. "Mia, you worked with deuterium. I thought that was for making nuclear bombs and your research in biochemistry. That's not what we're talking about, right?"

"The atomic bomb uses fission, breaking apart heavy isotopes, like plutonium and uranium, to release energy. We're talking fusion, smashing together light isotopes of hydrogen to create sustainable energy. It's what happens in the sun."

"So, deuterium is used for cold fusion research?" I lean forward despite Doc Summers' warning glare.

"That's what's been bothering me." Mia tilts her head, her brow furrowed in concentration as if she's turning the idea over. "They wouldn't steal just deuterium—they need palladium."

"Palladium?" Ethan frowns. "What's the connection?"

"It's crucial for cold fusion," Mitzy jumps in, splitting her screen to show chemical diagrams. "Palladium has a unique property—it can absorb massive amounts of deuterium into its crystalline structure. The Pons-Fleischmann experiment used palladium electrodes in heavy water—"

"Which failed spectacularly," Mia adds. "But here's what's interesting—looking at the power consumption data from Kazakhstan, they're pulling enough energy to run something exponentially larger than any previous cold fusion attempt."

Forest leans into frame, his ice-blue eyes intent. "Show them the thermal imaging."

Mitzy's fingers fly across her keyboard. A satellite image appears, showing heat signatures in deep reds and purples. "This is the facility two months ago." She pulls up another image. "And this is now. The energy output is off the charts."

"But cold fusion is supposed to produce energy, not consume it," Blake points out. "Why do they need that much power?"

"Because they're not trying to replicate the Pons-Fleischmann experiment. Pons and Fleischmann were specifically looking at cold fusion—fusion at room temperature," Mia's voice turns grim.

"Isn't that what we're talking about?" I cock my head to the side. I'm no rocket scientist, but I'm not dumb. Most of this is going over my head.

"Fusion reactions can occur in one of two ways," Mia explains, shifting into what I recognize as her teaching mode. "Cold fusion—like Pons-Fleischmann attempted—tries to achieve fusion at room temperature using chemical processes. Traditional fusion uses massive amounts of energy to heat plasma to over one hundred million degrees. What these power readings suggest ..." She pauses, her expression darkening. "They're trying to brute force fusion by combining both approaches. Using quantum tunneling effects in palladium to replicate high-energy conditions."

"And that's bad because ...?" Ethan prompts.

"Because they're essentially trying to create a miniature sun," Mitzy cuts in. "Without proper safeguards or proven containment methods. The energy readings from Kazakhstan show they're pumping more and more power into the system. If those containment fields fail—"

"We're looking at an explosion on the scale of a miniature sun," Forest rumbles.

"That's where Chen's expertise comes in," Mitzy continues. "He pioneered new plasma containment techniques. Combined with Rodriguez's quantum tunneling breakthroughs—"

"They're trying to force fusion at a molecular level," I realize. "Using the palladium matrix as a catalyst."

"Exactly." Mia nods. "If you could use quantum tunneling effects to bring deuterium atoms close enough together within the palladium structure—"

"While using plasma containment to compress everything," Forest adds. "They're trying to create a shortcut to fusion."

"That sounds incredibly dangerous," Ethan observes from beside my bed.

"It is." Mitzy pulls up more diagrams. "The pressure required would be astronomical. One containment field failure, one miscalculation in the quantum equations …"

"A runaway fusion reaction could vaporize everything within kilometers," Mitzy adds. "The devastation would be absolute and incredible."

The implications hit me hard. "That's why they need multiple experts. Chen for containment, Rodriguez for quantum mechanics, Williams for fusion dynamics—"

"And Malikai," Sam adds, "who found a way to make all three work together."

"With their families as insurance against failure," Forest's voice carries dangerous understanding.

My heart monitor betrays my spike in concern. Doc Summers steps closer, checking my IV with a warning look.

"So, the Kazakhstan facility …" I force my voice steady.

"Is showing all the signs," Mitzy confirms. "Massive power consumption, regular palladium shipments, specialized cooling systems being installed. They're building something big."

"And we're racing not only against them succeeding," Mia adds quietly. "But against a catastrophic failure. The energy readings from those containment fields are growing increasingly unstable."

"How long?" I ask, dreading the answer.

Mitzy and Mia exchange looks. "Impossible to say, but based on the power fluctuations?" Mitzy says. "Two months. Maybe less."

The room falls silent except for the steady beep of my monitors. Two months until they achieve cold fusion—or catastrophically fail and something much worse happens.

And Malia's caught in the middle of it all.

Our investigation continues over the next few weeks, the pieces slowly coming together. But all I can think about is Malia, on the other side of the world, being used as leverage.

TWENTY-ONE

Malia

ONE OF THE guards knocks on our door, gesturing for us to follow. "Facility orientation begins now. Deviation from approved areas will result in immediate consequences."

The tour starts with boundaries—massive steel doors mark where we can and cannot go. Red lines painted on the floors designate the limits of movement. Cross them without authorization, and the consequences are demonstrated. A guard steps over one line, and alarms shriek instantly. The response team arrives within thirty seconds, weapons ready.

"Living quarters are monitored continuously," our guide explains in accented English. "Common areas here, here, and here." He indicates sparse rooms designed for approved recreation. "Exercise yard access during designated hours only. All movements are tracked and logged."

The medical bay gleams with stainless steel. "Weekly health checks are mandatory. Any illness or injury must be reported immediately." The unspoken message is clear: Our well-being matters because without us, they lose their leverage.

Underground levels are strictly forbidden. Heavy blast doors and armed checkpoints guard access to the labs where our loved ones work. Sometimes, we hear machinery humming beneath our feet and feel vibrations through the concrete like distant earthquakes.

"Dining hall." The room is large but divided by barriers, keeping families separate. "Three meals daily, scheduled by section. Food hoarding is prohibited." Cameras watch even here, monitoring every bite and conversation.

The laundry facility operates on strict rotation. "Issued clothing only. Items are counted entering and exiting." Even clean socks are treated as potential security risks.

We pass other families being escorted through their permitted routines. Their eyes hold warnings they can't speak aloud. Every privilege is conditional, and every freedom can be revoked. Step out of line, and it's not you who suffers—it's someone you love.

"Communication between families is monitored." The guard indicates the common areas again. "Non-approved interactions will be terminated." Armed men stand ready to enforce these invisible boundaries between captives.

The tour ends where it began, at the line between permitted and forbidden spaces. We've learned our cage's dimensions and mapped the boundaries of our new existence. Everything is designed to remind us of our powerlessness, our complete dependence on our captors' whims.

But beneath the surface, I'm mapping too—counting steps between checkpoints, noting guard rotations, studying the facility's rhythms. They can cage my body, but my mind stays free, and I'm focused on only one thing.

Somewhere out there, Walt is alive. I refuse to believe he's dead. I need to stay alive long enough for him to find me.

Over the next few days, I meet the other scientists' families.

The Rodriguez girl—Maria—draws galaxies in her notebook while her father works in the labs below. She's twelve, with dark curls and eyes too old for her face. Her sketches are beautiful, swirling patterns of stars and planets far beyond our concrete walls.

"Papa used to take me to the observatory," she tells me, adding detail to a spiral arm. "He said quantum mechanics is like dancing with stardust." Her pencil moves in precise patterns— she has his gift for precision even if she doesn't understand the physics.

Mrs. Chen hovers near her teenage son, Kevin, as if afraid he'll disappear if she looks away. When guards aren't listening, they speak in rapid Mandarin. She teaches him traditional calligraphy using precious bits of paper and borrowed pencils, preserving their culture in this sterile place.

"My husband," she whispers during a rare private moment, "he warned them the containment fields were unstable. They ..." She touches her son's arm, where bruises fade to yellow. "They made their point about cooperation."

The Williamses are different—older, quieter, with the worn look of people who've survived worse. Dr. Williams' wife Helen knits with plastic needles they allow her for "therapy." Her fingers move constantly, creating and unraveling the same pattern.

Dr. Whittman's absence weighs on Ally like a physical thing. He's not just her advisor—he's her academic father, who believed in her theories when others dismissed them. Now, those same theories are being twisted into something monstrous.

Each family develops its own survival rhythms. The Chens practice tai chi in the exercise yard, moving through forms that look like meditation but keep their bodies ready. The Williamses share a private language of touches and glances, coordinated as dancers.

Maria Rodriguez collects scraps of paper, hoarding them like treasure. Her drawings grow more complex, revealing astronomical charts hidden in fantasy landscapes. She documents star positions and tracks time through celestial mechanics.

We're a forced community bound by shared fear and desperate hope. During mandatory recreation, we orbit each other carefully, aware that too much interaction draws guard attention. But messages pass in subtle ways—a borrowed pencil, a shared smile, a warning cough when surveillance approaches.

Dr. Chen's wife teaches me to fold paper cranes, her fingers moving deliberately as she demonstrates. "For luck," she says, but her eyes say something else. Even here, humans find ways to communicate.

We're beginning to recognize individual guards, learning their patterns and preferences. The night shift is stricter and more prone to violence. Morning guards are sluggish until their coffee kicks in. This knowledge becomes its own kind of currency among us.

Some nights, I hear crying through the thin walls. Other nights, the silence is worse. We're all haunted by the same question: what happens when the project is complete? When they no longer need hostages? Because there's no way they're going to let us go.

I hate this place, and my revulsion intensifies with each passing day. First thing in the morning, Malikai is prodded out of our tiny quarters, leaving me to spin my wheels until he returns late that night for dinner.

The dining hall operates with military precision. Each family unit is called forward in strict rotation, portions are measured precisely, and conversations are monitored by cameras and armed guards. The food is institutional but adequate: protein, starch, and vegetables. It is all carefully calculated to keep us healthy enough to serve our purpose as leverage.

The trays are molded plastic, sectioned like TV dinners.

The utensils are flimsy and designed to snap rather than sharpen. We eat at assigned tables facing inward, where cameras can track every movement. The room's acoustics are engineered to carry sound, so private conversations are impossible.

"You have twenty minutes," a guard announces as we're seated. The countdown begins, another reminder that even this basic human function is controlled. Some families pray before eating, while others stare at their food like it might be poisoned.

Hope dies slowly, but it fades with each day we're trapped in this prison.

Ally sits nearby, pushing reconstituted potatoes into geometric patterns. "Hospital food is better," she mutters, but she cleans her plate anyway.

We all do. No one knows when the rules might change or when food might become another form of control.

The Williamses share their bread with Maria Rodriguez, a small kindness that guards pretend not to see. These tiny rebellions keep us human—sharing food, trading small comforts, and watching out for each other's children.

I notice how families have developed silent routines. The Chens eat in synchronized bites, unconsciously mirroring each other. The Williamses alternate watching the room while the other eats. Maria draws star charts disguised as doodles in the condensation on her water glass.

Malikai sits beside me but might as well be miles away, lost in whatever equations consume him below ground. His fingers tap complex rhythms on the table—quantum calculations or desperate planning.

I can't tell anymore.

The food on his tray grows cold while his mind works in patterns I stopped trying to follow years ago.

Kitchen staff wear different uniforms—white instead of gray

—marking them as trusted personnel from elsewhere in the facility. They move, keeping their eyes down and avoiding contact. Sometimes, they slip extra portions to the children, another small defiance of our captors' rigid control.

Conversations stay carefully neutral—weather, bland memories, nothing that could be considered suspicious. But meaning hides in casual words. "The soup's too hot" means guard rotation soon. "Better yesterday" signals increased security. We're developing our own language beneath the approved one.

Guards patrol the perimeter, watching us watch them. Their hands rest on weapons even here, ready for any disruption of their ordered routine. They rotate positions every seven minutes exactly—we time it by the serving line's conveyor belt.

When the buzzer sounds, we rise in unison, conditioned already to respond. Trays go on a conveyor belt, and every scrap of food is documented. Wasting food means losing privileges.

Everything is measured

Everything has consequences.

And this is how my days pass—with agonizing slowness.

It's been weeks. How many? I'm not sure, but I'm slowly giving up hope for rescue. I know how the Guardians work. They're lightning-fast when it comes to their rescues. Which means, they don't know where in the world we are. I try. I do my best not to give up hope, but that gets harder every day.

"The power grid is their weakness," Ally whispers during evening recreation. We sit at a corner table, pretending to play approved board games while she draws circuit diagrams disguised as tic-tac-toe. "They're pulling massive amounts of electricity for the containment fields."

She's learned to talk without moving her lips much, a skill we're all developing. Her fingers trace patterns that look random but map the facility's infrastructure. "Three backup generators, but they can't support both security and the experimental equipment. That's why we get brownouts."

The information comes in fragments, pieced together from overheard conversations and careful observation. "Whittman says they're pushing the fields past safety tolerances. The quantum tunneling effect requires precise conditions—too much power, and the containment fails. Too little …"

She stops as a guard passes, pretending to concentrate on our game. When he's gone, her voice drops lower. "They're using palladium matrices to focus the reaction. The quantum mechanics are revolutionary—in a proper lab, with proper safety protocols, we could change the world. But they're rushing, pushing too hard."

Through the walls, we feel the facility's pulse—machinery humming, power surging through conduits. Ally has learned to read these rhythms, and she shares that with me. "That vibration? Cooling systems are struggling to keep up. The whine that comes after? Emergency vents are engaging."

She explains how she and the others work in shifts, pushing themselves to exhaustion. "They don't care about safety protocols or proper testing. They want results, no matter the cost." Her hands shake slightly. "Do you know what happens if those containment fields fail? If the quantum tunneling effect destabilizes?"

I shake my head, though I've seen the fear in Malikai's eyes when he returns from the labs. She draws another game board, but the intersecting lines form something else—blast radius calculations.

"Best case? Total system failure and explosion contained to the facility. Worst case …" Her pencil circles outward, marking distances. "Uncontrolled fusion reaction. Everything within fifty kilometers—gone. Maybe more. They're playing with forces they barely understand, and they won't listen to the safety warnings. They won't listen to us."

Guards approach, and we shift to actual gameplay. But her words sink in—we're sitting on a potential catastrophe. Our loved ones work under threat of violence to build something that could vaporize us all.

"Whittman's trying to build in fail-safes," she whispers as we pretend to pack up the game. "Ways to shut it down if …" She doesn't finish. We both know the stakes. Both know why they keep us here, where any accident or sabotage would take their hostages with it.

Time passes with agonizing slowness.

Days drag by.

Weeks pass.

Hope fades.

The shower's steady hiss should mask any sounds, but I still test each tile carefully, searching for loose grout or hollow spaces. The metal mirror comes off its mount with careful manipulation —nothing behind it but solid concrete. Even the ceiling panels are sealed, denying any hidden spaces.

Water runs into the drain in a perfect spiral. I've tried sending messages down it—tiny notes on dissolving paper—but camera coverage is too thorough. They watch even here, counting the minutes we spend washing and monitoring water usage for any anomalies.

Mrs. Chen taught me to fold paper into tiny boats before "accidentally" dropping them in puddles during yard time. The rain would carry them toward drainage ditches and maybe, impossibly, to the outside world. When guards caught on, they removed her paper privileges for a week.

I press my ear against the ventilation grate, trying to map air currents. The system is a maze of sealed ducts, carefully designed to prevent communication between sectors. Sometimes, I hear voices carried on the artificial breeze—fragments of conversations in Russian and Mandarin, languages I recognize but don't understand.

The window glass is too thick for signals, and exterior cameras catch any movement near them. I tried using reflected light from my plastic spoon until the guards confiscated it. Now, our utensils are counted after every meal.

Maria Rodriguez showed me how she marks time by scratching tiny dots into her soap bar. The marks wash away in the shower, leaving no evidence. But even if we track the days, we have no way to share them beyond our walls.

My latest attempt involves patterns walked in the exercise yard—precise steps that could be coordinates or messages. But the guards watch too carefully, redirecting us if we repeat any sequence too often.

I've memorized guard rotations, camera angles, every possible blind spot. But they've had years to perfect this system, to eliminate every conceivable method of communication with the outside world. Each failed attempt costs privileges—yard time, recreation access, and sometimes meals.

The truly cruel part is how they let us keep trying. They watch us test boundaries, attempt ingenious solutions, and exhaust ourselves against impossible odds. Our failures remind us of our powerlessness more effectively than any punishment.

Even the building itself fights against us. Concrete and steel are designed to contain, isolate, and break spirits through sheer architectural indifference. Every surface is sealed, every corner monitored, and every potential weakness eliminated through decades of trial and error.

The only messages that get through are internal—carefully coded gestures, innocuous words loaded with meaning, and warnings passed through subtle shifts in routine. We're building our own language of captivity, but it can't reach beyond these walls.

I'll try something new tonight: marking patterns in spilled salt at dinner, hoping they look random enough to escape notice. It won't work—nothing works—but I have to keep trying because the alternative is accepting this cage as permanent.

Hope is dangerous here, but it's all I have left.

TWENTY-TWO

Walt

—————

TEN DAYS AFTER THE SHOOTING, I sit on the edge of the hospital bed, struggling to button my shirt without wincing. Each movement sends fire through my chest, a constant reminder of the bullets that nearly ended me.

Doc Summers stands in the doorway, her small frame radiating authority as she watches my struggle. Her inquisitive eyes miss nothing—like how my hands shake, and I pause between each button to catch my breath.

"Two months," she announces, her tone brooking no argument. "Minimum. And that's only if you follow the recovery plan exactly."

"Two months?" The words come out sharper than intended. "Doc, I can't—"

"You can and you will." She steps forward, helping me with the last button when my fingers refuse to cooperate. "Unless you want permanent damage. You're lucky to be alive, let alone able to move."

I protest, but she cuts me off with a look that could freeze hell.

"Two paths, Walt." She begins checking my vitals one final time. "Follow the plan—intensive physical therapy, gradually increasing activity—and you'll return to full strength in two months. Maybe sooner if you don't push too hard." Her hands are gentle but clinical as she examines my healing wounds. "Or be a blockhead about it, try to rush things, and risk never regaining full function. Your choice."

The threat of permanent disability hits harder than the bullets did. I force myself to take a careful breath, ignoring how it pulls at my stitches.

"Walk me through it."

"Piper will give you the specifics of her physical therapy rehabilitation plan." Doc Summers' approval shows in the slight softening of her expression. "Week one is basic mobility—getting your range of motion back without tearing anything. In week two, you start gentle strength training. We'll look at modified combat drills if you haven't done anything stupid by week four."

"And if I follow all your rules?"

"Then, by eight weeks, you should be cleared for full duty." She steps back, crossing her arms. "But only if you listen to Piper. Push too hard too fast, and you'll set yourself back months. Maybe permanently."

The words settle like lead in my stomach. Two months of recovery while Malia is in enemy hands. Two months of healing while God knows what happens to her.

But Doc's right. I'm no good to anyone if I cripple myself trying to rush back into action.

"Fine." I carefully stand, testing my balance. "Two months."

"Deal." She hands me my discharge papers. "And Walt?" Her voice softens slightly. "We'll find Malia, and when we do, she needs you at full strength. Not half-healed and a liability in the field."

I nod, unable to trust my voice. Two months. I can do this. Have to do this.

The alternative—never being strong enough to save Malia—is unthinkable.

It feels like winning a battle when Doc Summers finally hands me my release papers. Until I try standing on my own for more than five minutes, and the room tilts like I've been on a week-long bender. It's humbling, infuriating, and exactly the fuel I need to push harder.

The next few weeks are a grind. Physical therapy has become my new mission; every session a war between my body and my will. Piper, the persistently perky therapist, is practically legendary among the Guardians.

She once dragged Bent, Angel Fire's brooding bassist, back from the edge after a debilitating accident, helping him regain full use of his arm. And when Bravo team's leader, Brady, faced a devastating recovery from horrific burns, she got him back to full operational status. If she could break through their stubborn walls … I'm doomed—or maybe saved. Depends on the day—and how much I'm cursing her by the end of each session.

The team converts my apartment's living room into a Command Center. While I do PT exercises, Mitzy's intel streams across multiple screens. Shipping manifests, power grid data, satellite imagery—a digital trail leading east. But we still have no confirmation on a location.

By the end of the first week, I'm walking laps around the gym, sweat dripping down my back as the ache in my chest dulls to something manageable. By the second week, I'm hitting the weights, testing my endurance with light sparring against Rigel. Every punch and every kick is a step forward and brings me closer to being ready.

The briefings continue, but we're stalled.

"You need to see this," Mitzy taps her tablet. She pulls up

satellite imagery showing convoy movements across Eastern Europe. "Sentinel Three's deuterium stockpiles are being relocated. All of them."

"Where?" I ask.

"That's just it," she swipes through more images. "They're moving everything east. Toward Kazakhstan. The timing can't be a coincidence."

"It's not." Forest enters, his massive frame filling the doorway. "Mia's sources confirm it. The deuterium and the quantum research are all connected. Malfor's been planning this for years."

"Planning, what?" The frustration in my voice mirrors what we're all feeling. Always one step behind, always reacting instead of acting.

"That's the million-dollar question," Forest says grimly. "But I bet Malia's brother is being forced to build the answer."

"Here. Three more deuterium shipments traced to Kazakhstan," Mitzy reports.

"Is that where we think they were taken? To Kazakhstan?" I ask.

"We're hamstrung looking into North Korea, but I'm not ready to rule it out just yet."

By week three, I can manage the climbing wall—barely five feet up before my shoulder screams in protest. Slowly, my body grows stronger, and my movements feel fluid again. The scar on my chest pulls slightly when I stretch; it's a faint tug, a reminder of what I survived. My reflection in the mirror isn't the same man from the hospital bed.

He's gone, and I'm back.

I step through the doors of HQ, the fluorescent lights harsh compared to the hospital's muted tones. My steps are slower than I'd like, and my chest is tight when I push too hard. Today's briefing is to go over surveillance of the facility in Kazakhstan."

"There are three main entry points," Sam briefs us, his image clear on the tablet propped by my exercise mat. There are underground access tunnels from the Soviet era, a loading dock for supplies, and the main entrance. All are heavily guarded."

"Have we given up on the North Korean facility?" I massage my chest, trying to loosen up the scar tissue.

"Not entirely," Mitzy says. "*Smaug* continues to perform flyovers. We're not seeing the same level of activity there. Our best bet is Kazakhstan, but I'd like to be certain before putting together a mission packet."

Week four marks my return to modified training. I stand in front of a punching bag, sweat dripping down my face. My fists slam into the bag with an almost mechanical rhythm—jab, cross, hook, repeat. The dull ache in my chest reminds me to hold back, but I push through the pain. Between treadmill sessions, I join the others for tactical updates as we piece together the facility's layout.

By week six, I'm cleared for light sparring. It's not full contact, but it's enough to keep me from climbing the walls. The mats feel familiar under my bare feet. I roll my shoulders, the scar on my chest pulling faintly, a reminder of how far I've come —and how much further I still need to go.

"Two on one," Hank announces with a wicked grin, tossing his towel onto a bench. "We'll take it easy on you."

Gabe snorts, adjusting his wraps. "Sure we will."

I narrow my eyes, squaring up. "You both against me? Real fair."

"Life's not fair," Hank shoots back, circling me. "Thought you'd know that by now."

Hank lunges, drawing my attention, and before I can counter, Gabe sweeps in from the side, his movements fluid and precise. I block one strike, but the other lands square on my shoulder, forcing me back. Hank seizes the opportunity as I stumble, closing in with a powerful grip on my arm. Gabe mirrors the move, grabbing my other arm, their hands intertwining as they pin me between them.

Their synchronized movements are impressive and intimidating. It's like they can read each other's minds, anticipating every step and every punch. I struggle to keep up.

My muscles scream in protest as I sidestep, deflecting Gabe's jab with my forearm. The impact stings, but it's nothing I can't handle. Before I can reset, Hank charges from the opposite side, a freight train of muscle and speed.

His powerful blows land with precision, each strike carefully timed to complement Gabe's quick, darting movements. They're a well-oiled machine, working together with a seamless rhythm that's both beautiful and terrifying to behold.

I pivot, my breath catching as I twist to block his strike. My chest protests, a sharp reminder of my limitations, but I grit my teeth and push through. Hank's forearm collides with mine, the force jolting through me, but I hold my ground.

"Still standing," I grunt, shoving him back a step.

"Not for long," Gabe quips, slipping behind me. His foot sweeps low, aiming for my legs, but I sidestep at the last moment. Sweat drips down my temple as I twist to face him, keeping both of them in my line of sight.

They're relentless, coming at me from every angle. Hank's brute strength pairs seamlessly with Gabe's quick, calculated strikes, like two parts of the same machine. It's unnerving how well they move together—Hank charging like a battering ram while Gabe darts in to exploit the openings Hank creates. It's not just coordination; it's instinctual like they know what the other thinks before a move is made.

Hank lunges, drawing my attention, and before I can counter, Gabe sweeps in from the side, his movements fluid and precise. I block one strike, but the other lands square on my shoulder, forcing me back.

"You two always fight like this?" I growl, sidestepping a brutal hook from Hank.

"Like, what?" Hank smirks, ducking low as Gabe moves in above him.

"Like you're one damn person," I snap, managing to deflect Gabe's jab.

Hank's fist barrels toward me again, forcing me to shift focus. I catch Gabe's wrist mid-strike, twisting just enough to send him off balance, but Hank's already there, a heavy hand shoving me backward. My feet slide on the mat, but I plant myself, bracing for the next hit.

"You're slowing down, old man," Hank taunts, his grin wide and infuriating.

"You talk too much," I growl, lunging forward. My fist connects with his shoulder, the satisfying thud cutting his laughter short.

"Good," he grunts, shaking it off. "Better."

Gabe sweeps in again, and I sidestep, turning his momentum against him. He stumbles but recovers fast, his grin sharp. "Still got it, huh?"

"More than you," I snap, a small smirk tugging at my lips despite the ache in my chest.

They come at me again, and I know they're holding back just enough to keep me from breaking—but not enough to make it easy. Each hit, each dodge, and each stumble builds my strength. They push me to my limits, testing me, forcing me to adapt, and I can feel it—day by day, fight by fight—I'm getting stronger.

Hank calls a halt with a sharp whistle, signaling the end of the session. My muscles scream in protest, every breath burning like fire in my lungs. Gabe claps me on the back, nearly sending me forward, his grin wide and unapologetic.

"Not bad," he says, clearly enjoying my exhaustion a little too much.

I straighten, rolling out my shoulders despite the ache settling deep into my bones. My chest heaves, my hands rest on my knees, and sweat pours down my back, but I'm standing. Barely, but standing. Hank and Gabe exchange a look, their grins approving.

"You'll be ready," Gabe says, tossing me a water bottle.

I chug the water, the ache settling deep into my bones.

Gabe's phone buzzes from where he left it near the edge of the mats. He wipes his face with a towel before checking the screen. His easy grin slips into something sharper, more focused.

"We've got a briefing. An update just came through."

Hank tosses me a clean towel. "Let's hit the showers first."

The exhaustion dragging at my limbs suddenly feels distant, replaced by a familiar edge of anticipation. It's been too long without a solid lead—weeks of chasing shadows, debating whether the hostages are being held in Kazakhstan or North Korea. Every dead end frustrates me.

But maybe something's shifted. Whatever update came through … It could be the break we've been waiting for.

TWENTY-THREE

Walt

BY THE TIME we enter the briefing room, Ethan's already there, stone-faced and ready for business. Rigel and Blake are seated, their attention locked on the monitors as they flicker to life.

Sam stands at the front of the room, arms crossed, brows drawn tight in focused thought. Near the head of the long table but slightly off to the side, CJ leans back in his chair, a pen moving absently over a sheet of paper in front of him. Across from him, Mitzy types steadily on her laptop, her expression sharp and unreadable.

As I drop into a chair, my gaze snags on CJ's paper. He isn't doodling random shapes like I first thought—he's sketching out the Kazakhstan facility's layout with precise, calculated lines. His pen pauses, taps twice against the table, then resumes its steady glide, tracing the edges of a building that's haunted every strategy session we've had.

Before I can process what he might be thinking, Mitzy's voice cuts through the low hum of the monitors. "I've got updates."

Tension coils tight in the room. Whatever she's found … It's time.

"Main lab complex is here; there are many levels below ground." Mitzy overlays blueprints with heat signature data. "I'm almost positive we're on the right track." She turns to me. "The North Korean facility shows no signs of activity."

"Power consumption is climbing," Sam notes.

"The facility's power grid is their weakness," Mitzy explains.

"Can we kill the main power?" CJ rumbles.

"Not that simple." Sam zooms in on the facility layout. "Lose containment at the wrong moment …"

"And we risk triggering an uncontrolled fusion reaction," Mitzy finishes. "We need a precision strike. Take out security without compromising the containment systems."

"What about the patrol patterns?" I ask.

"Iron tight," Blake says, pulling up surveillance footage. "Their patrols have so many overlapping redundancies there's nowhere the facility isn't covered. No blind spots. No gaps. Every entrance, every corridor—they've sealed it tighter than a vault."

"Getting into that place is going to be difficult," Ethan says.

"An assault is a no-go." CJ pulls at his chin. "We've looked at this a hundred ways, and there's no way to infiltrate the facility without setting off alarms. I hate to say it, but we're stuck."

"There has to be a way in." The thought of Malia in their hands sends fresh fire through my veins. I lean forward, studying the holographic display hovering above the briefing room table. The Kazakhstan facility rotates slowly in a blue wireframe schematic, each defensive position highlighted in angry red.

"*Smaug's* latest pass confirms it." Mitzy's fingers dance across her tablet, zooming in on the compound's perimeter. "Three-layer security fence, motion sensors every ten meters, thermal cameras covering every approach vector. No blind spots."

"What about tunnels?" Ethan asks from his position at the head of the table. "Soviet-era facilities usually had escape routes."

"All sealed." Sam's rumbling voice carries barely contained frustration. "Concrete plugs every fifty meters. They aren't taking chances."

I study the hologram, looking for any weaknesses we might have missed. The last ten weeks of recovery have given me plenty of time to memorize every detail of this place, but understanding it hasn't made breaching it any easier.

"Air insertion?" Blake suggests.

Sam shakes his head. "Anti-aircraft battery here and here." Red markers flare on the display. "Plus high-altitude radar coverage. We couldn't get a chopper within five kilometers without being detected."

"What about going in as a supply convoy?" Rigel leans forward, his usual swagger replaced by tactical focus. "They must need regular deliveries for that many people."

"All supplies are transferred at a forward checkpoint ten kilometers from the main facility," Mitzy explains, her tone clipped. "Everything's thoroughly searched and repacked into their own trucks. No outside transport gets past the perimeter."

Blake pulls up a satellite image, highlighting the barren stretch of land surrounding the facility. "The place is smack in the middle of the steppes. Miles of open terrain with only one main access road cutting through."

Mitzy nods, overlaying the supply route on the map. "The closest natural cover is a mountain range about ten kilometers out. But from that distance, the facility's sensors would pick up any approach long before we got close."

"They'd see us coming from miles away," Ethan says grimly. "Plenty of time to neutralize us."

The room falls into tense silence, the stark reality sinking in. Every possible route is a death trap—or worse, a failed mission before it even starts. There are five scientists, with their families, trapped inside, and we have no way to get to them, let alone get them out.

"I need to know what's on the inside before we even think about an assault. The only way I can do that is with the bumblebees." Mitzy breaks the tension. She pulls up specs for Guardian's micro-surveillance drones. "They're small enough to slip through ventilation shafts, map the interior layout …"

"And confirm where they're holding the hostages," Sam finishes, nodding slowly. "Good. Do it."

"But then what? What good does it do us to know where the hostages are being held if the place is impenetrable?" Every day feels like a failure.

"Let's focus on what we can do. We need to establish a forward staging area in-country." CJ pulls up a topographical map of the region. "The bumblebees have a limited range—we need to get within five kilometers of the facility without detection to release them. I'm open to suggestions."

"These mountains here." I point to a ridge line. "Natural cover, high enough for clear transmission signals."

"Still too far to launch the drones." Mitzy shakes her head. "I need a way to get close enough to launch them."

"But there's no way." Rigel pushes back from the table. "With one road in and one road out, how can we get within those five klicks?"

"Can we depend on any local assets?" Ethan asks.

Sam shakes his head. "Too risky. We go in completely self-contained. No contact, no paper trail."

"That complicates things. We need our own power supply, communications relay, the works," CJ notes. "Plus enough supplies to maintain a surveillance post for at least a week, maybe a month."

"I can have my equipment ready in thirty-six hours," Mitzy

says. "But getting it in the country without raising flags ..." She glances at Sam.

"I've been working that angle with my CIA contacts." Sam pulls up flight manifests. "There's a mining company already in place, controlled by U.S. interests. They're the perfect cover for bringing in heavy equipment. It's twenty klicks out, though. Not ideal, but better than where we sit now." He turns to Mitzy, his concern about the bumblebee deployment limitations clear.

"Once we're set up, how long will it take us to have usable intel?" I force myself to focus on logistics rather than my growing impatience.

"Forty-eight hours to get the bumblebees deployed and complete their initial sweeps," Mitzy calculates. "Another twenty-four to process the data and build accurate interior schematics."

"That's three days minimum before we even know what we're dealing with inside," Hank observes.

"Three days they're still in there," I growl, but we don't have a choice. Going in blind would be suicide.

"Sounds like we have a plan," Sam rumbles. "Hopefully, things will look different once we've got boots on the ground. Let's get the teams prepped and ready our equipment. I want us wheels up within forty-eight hours."

"What does a forward staging area matter if there's no way in?" Rigel blows out a breath. We're all feeling the same frustration.

"When we find a way in, we'll be twenty klicks away, rather than two days' worth of travel moving in our assets." CJ leans back and pulls at his chin. "We'll find a way to rescue the hostages."

"Local weather might be a problem." I study weather projections and stare at the terrain map. "At that altitude, conditions can change fast."

"Already modeling it," Mitzy confirms. "We'll need at least

three days of clear weather for reliable drone operation. The long-range forecast looks good starting next week."

"Then that's our window," Sam decides. "Five days to get the staging area set up and operational. Three days for surveillance. By next week, we'll know exactly what we're up against, and we'll be positioned to act."

I force myself to accept the timeline even as my instincts scream to move faster. But Sam is right—*we do this smart, or we don't do it at all.*

"I wanted to talk about something else." Mitzy's voice cuts through the chatter as we stand to leave.

"What's that?" Sam asks.

"I've been monitoring all known Sentinel intelligence channels. There's no chatter. No movement from other Sentinel operations. It's like they've been ordered to stand down."

"You think Malfor's keeping them away deliberately?" Ethan asks.

"Has to be. The Third Sentinel's quantum facility is a prime target, but there is no response from the Eighth Sentinel's intelligence networks. That feels wrong."

"He's letting us come." I realize, the thought settling cold in my gut. "Why? What does he gain by losing the scientists?"

"Maybe he already has what he wants," Forest rumbles. "The research, the breakthroughs … Maybe we're just cleaning up loose ends for him."

The team disperses, but I linger, staring at the facility's imposing outline on the display. Eight days. Eight more days of waiting, wondering, and hoping we're not too late.

I force myself to accept this is the smart play, but my hands clench under the table as I stare at the facility's defenses. Somewhere in there, Malia's waiting. Probably wondering if I survived. Definitely wondering if help is coming.

The first forty-eight hours drag like centuries. I haunt the equipment bay as Blake and Rigel check every piece of gear, triple-check the weapons, and verify each comm unit. My recently healed wounds ache from the constant motion, but sitting still feels impossible.

"If you're going to hover," Blake finally says, tossing me a crate of backup batteries, "at least make yourself useful."

The work helps but doesn't quiet the voice in my head counting every minute that passes.

The journey takes another full day—a carefully choreographed dance of multiple vehicles and routes to avoid detection. The mining operation provides perfect cover, but every checkpoint and delay sets my teeth on edge. Hank and Gabe try to lighten the mood with their usual banter, but even they grow quiet as we near our destination.

Setting up the mining operation takes two more days. Sam oversees the installation of our comms array, disguised as geological survey equipment scouting the mountain range. The satellite dishes blend seamlessly among legitimate mining gear, while every piece of tactical equipment is stashed in carefully marked crates.

On day six, the Rufi units deploy with their precious cargo. I watch through binoculars as the robotic canines navigate the rugged terrain, their movements eerily fluid and precise. Their radar-shielded exteriors keep them invisible to the facility's surveillance grid—a crucial advantage given the vast, exposed steppes.

Each Rufi carries a compartment housing the bumblebee hive—a swarm of micro-drones engineered for stealth reconnaissance. They're nearly undetectable to humans—just another cluster of harmless insects—but their one flaw is limited range. With a maximum flight distance of five kilometers, the Rufis have to get them close enough to deploy.

If the drones can breach the facility undetected, they'll map the interior, locate critical systems, and, most importantly, confirm whether the hostages are inside—or if we've been chasing ghosts all along.

"Five klicks to target," Mitzy updates through comms. *"Rufi units maintaining stealth protocols. No indication of detection."*

The waiting becomes almost physical—a weight pressing against my chest that has nothing to do with healing wounds. I find myself touching the scar where the bullet nearly took me out of the game permanently—nearly kept me from being here for this mission.

Nearly kept me from finding her.

Finally, in the pre-dawn hours of day eight, we gather in the Command tent. The first wave of bumblebee drones prepares for deployment. These micro-drones represent over a week of preparation, careful planning, and agonizing patience.

"Drones launching now," Mitzy's voice carries clearly through our comms.

"How long before the bumblebees can give us internal layouts?" I ask.

"We'll need at least 36 hours to map the critical areas. More to process the data, but we should know soon." Mitzy places a hand on my shoulder, doing her best to provide comfort.

"When those drones give us the interior layout," Sam says, his voice sharp with conviction, "I want multiple plans ready to go."

We grind through scenarios until the maps are burned into my mind—every corridor, every access point, every weakness we can exploit. But each idea crumbles under the brutal reality of the facility's defenses.

"We've already ruled out ground insertion," Ethan growls, pacing the room. "There's only the one road in with checkpoints along the way."

"Air's out too," Blake adds, tapping the map's perimeter.

"SAM sites blanket the area. They'd see us coming and shoot us out of the sky before we hit the ground."

"What about the supply convoys?" Rigel suggests, but even he sounds doubtful. "We could intercept one—"

"Supplies transfer ten kilometers out," Mitzy cuts in, arms crossed, frustration etched into her face. "Everything gets searched, repacked, and driven in by their transport under their guards. I don't know how we'd smuggle in an entire Guardian team."

Silence stretches, heavy and suffocating. Every route, every angle, everything—blocked.

Sam rubs a hand over his face. "We need a miracle."

No one speaks. No one moves. The room feels like it's closing in, the oppressive weight of failure pressing against my chest. Outside, the wind howls across the desolate steppes, relentless and unforgiving—just like the facility we're trying to breach.

I catch what sleep I can between planning sessions, but my dreams are filled with images of Malia. Sometimes she's scared, sometimes she's calling for me, but I always wake up reaching for her. The wound in my chest aches with phantom pain, a constant reminder of how I failed to protect her that night.

Finally, Mitzy's voice crackles through our comms with the update we've been waiting for. *First wave entering the ventilation system. Tracking signals strong.*

I watch the drone feeds with Ethan while Blake and Rigel maintain our perimeter security. The rest of the teams wait at the mountain staging area, ready to move the moment we have actionable intelligence.

Mitzy's fingers do their magic. The hologram shifts, overlaying heat signatures in ghostly orange. "They're keeping everyone here." She highlights a section three levels below ground.

"What kind of security is inside?" Ethan asks.

"Card readers, biometric scanners, armed guards at every checkpoint. The whole level's designed as a containment zone—probably repurposed from the facility's Cold War days."

"Show me the ventilation system again." I lean forward, ignoring the twinge in my chest.

"Here." Blue lines thread through the hologram-like veins. "But they're not stupid—everything larger than six inches is reinforced with steel mesh. That's why we're using the bumblebees. Anything bigger won't fit."

"What about the power infrastructure?" Blake asks.

"Multiple substations feeding into the main reactor core," Sam says, "but like CJ said—we can't risk cutting power without potentially triggering a catastrophic reaction."

I study the rotating hologram, frustration building in my chest. Every potential approach hits another wall.

They've thought of everything.

"Get creative. Run scenarios," Ethan orders, his voice tight with the same frustration we're all feeling. "Every possible insertion point, every method of approach. There has to be a way in."

"And we need to find it fast." Mitzy pulls up another display showing power consumption graphs. "These readings are getting more unstable. Whatever they're building in there, it's either close to working—"

"Or close to failure," Forest rumbles.

Ice slithers through my veins. Malia's not just trapped in there—she's caught in the middle of an experiment that could vaporize everything within kilometers if things go wrong.

We're nowhere near an actionable mission plan, but we know the most important thing.

This is the right place.

TWENTY-FOUR

Malia

STRANGE NOISES ECHO through the facility's bones as darkness falls. The building creaks and groans, settling into its nighttime rhythm. Machinery pulses beneath us—a constant mechanical heartbeat reverberating through the concrete.

From somewhere deep below comes a high-pitched whine—cooling systems struggling against the heat of whatever experiments consume the night shift. The sound rises and falls in patterns I'm learning to read. Higher pitch means increased power draw, and sudden silence means emergency protocols are engaging.

The elevator doors open with a pneumatic hiss that echo through the dining hall's evening quiet. Harsh fluorescent light spills from inside, casting long shadows as the night shift scientists emerge. The acrid scent of ozone clings to their lab coats, mixing with the institutional smell of instant coffee and bleach-cleaned tables.

Dr. Chen stumbles out first, catching himself against the doorframe. His lab coat bears dark sweat patches, and his security badge dangles forgotten from one pocket. The usual precise movements of his hands have deteriorated into tremors as he fumbles with his access card. The scanner beeps three times before accepting it.

"Another breach?" Mrs. Chen's whisper carries in the unnatural quiet. She reaches for his hand but hesitates as if afraid he might shatter at her touch.

He shakes his head, but the tremor in his hands betrays him. "Almost. The containment fields are getting harder to maintain. The quantum effect ..." His voice trails off as a guard shifts closer, his radio crackling with static. A muscle twitches in Chen's jaw as he swallows whatever he meant to say.

Dr. Williams follows, his shoes scuffing against polished concrete. The usual immaculate knot of his tie has come undone, and he tugs at his collar like it's strangling him. Dark sweat stains map exhaustion across his shirt. His wife hurries forward, pressing a plastic cup of water into hands that shake so badly he nearly drops it.

Rodriguez stumbles next, listing to one side until he catches himself on a chair back. His daughter Maria is already moving to support him, her small fingers wrapping around his arm. The fluorescent lights cast harsh shadows under his eyes, aging him a decade in a day.

"Papa?" Maria's voice breaks on the word.

"I'm fine, mija." His attempt at a smile cracks at the edges. "Just tired." The lie bitter in the air between them.

Whittman practically carries Ally through the doors, both of their faces gray beneath the institutional lighting. Her usual enthusiastic chatter about quantum theory has given way to hollow-eyed silence. She moves like a puppet with cut strings as Whittman guides her to a chair. Even the guards exchange glances, their practiced indifference cracking at the sight of the scientists' state.

The ventilation system cycles with a mechanical groan, stirring papers on empty tables. The sound seems to echo forever in the strange quiet that has fallen over the dining hall. Something about their collective exhaustion feels wrong—deeper than physical fatigue.

Malikai is the last to exit, his glasses smeared and askew. His fingers tap equations against his thigh in an endless loop. When he sees me, he tries to smile, but it looks more like a grimace. Purple shadows beneath his eyes make him look haunted.

"That bad?" I slide a cup of facility-issued coffee toward him, the bitter scent rising between us like a question.

"Worse." His voice comes out raw, as if he's been shouting. He takes a shaking breath that rattles in his chest. "The containment fields—"

The first tremor cuts him off, a violent shudder that runs through the facility's bones. Coffee sloshes over cup rims, leaving brown rings on metal tables. A high-pitched whine pierces the air as cooling systems scream in protest, the sound drilling into our skulls.

Dr. Chen lurches to his feet, knocking his chair backward with a metallic clang that echoes like a gunshot. "No. Not now. We just stabilized—"

Red emergency lights flash to life, painting everything in shades of blood. Through the windows, strange aurora-like ribbons of light rise from the lab sector—colors that have no names in any human language, moving in ways that hurt the eyes to watch.

"The fields are collapsing." Whittman's voice cracks as he stares at his tablet's readings. His hands shake so badly that he nearly drops it. "Everything we did … It's not holding."

The air thickens with static electricity, making hair rise and skin prickle. Papers lift from tables, defying gravity for heartbeats before settling again. The facility's foundations seem to shudder as if reality is being twisted out of shape in the labs below.

Malikai's face drains of what little color remains. The look he exchanges with Chen sends ice through my veins. Before I can process what's happening, he's moving toward the elevator with desperate purpose, each step carrying him closer to whatever waits below.

Malikai grabs Chen's arm, their white-knuckled grips betraying the terror neither man will voice. "The quantum cascade ..." His voice catches. "If it reaches critical threshold—"

"Everyone dies." Chen's face hardens with resolve, years of academic theory crystallizing into deadly reality. "Not just in the facility. Not just us."

The lights flicker, casting strange shadows as backup generators strain against growing power demands. That high-pitched whine from the cooling systems rises another octave, becoming almost unbearable. The air feels wrong, charged with energy that shouldn't exist outside theoretical papers.

"We have to go back down." Malikai turns to me, and I see something terrible in his eyes—the weight of a decision already made. "Sissy—"

"No!" I lunge forward, fingers twisting in the stiff fabric of his lab coat. The material is still warm from the labs below, carrying that strange ozone scent that clings to everything down there. "You're exhausted. You can barely stand. Let someone else—"

"There is no one else." His hands cup my face—a gesture straight from childhood, from skinned knees and nightmare comfort. But his fingers tremble against my skin. "No one else understands the quantum tunneling effect like Chen and I do. We're the only ones who might be able to stop this."

"Then I'm going too." Dr. Williams struggles to rise, but his legs buckle. The metal chair scrapes against the concrete as he catches himself. "I can help—"

"You can barely walk," Chen cuts him off, voice gentle but

brooking no argument. "Stay with Helen. Keep the others safe." His eyes find Mrs. Chen's face across the room. Two decades of marriage pass between them in that look. *Someone has to survive to tell the world what happened here.*

Mrs. Chen's spine straightens like steel, but tears track silently down her face. She doesn't try to stop him. She understands— her husband's mind might be the only thing standing between us and the apocalypse.

"Kai, please …" Tears blur my vision as Malikai pulls away from me. The taste of copper fills my mouth—I've bitten my lip without realizing it. "I can't lose you too."

The facility shudders again. Through the windows, those impossible lights paint the night in colors that human eyes were never meant to process. The laws of physics themselves seem to be unraveling in the lab below.

Malikai's palms are cold with fear, but his voice stays steady. "I have to fix this, Sissy. We created this monster. We have to try to stop it."

His forehead presses against mine—our childhood gesture of absolute promise. His fingers tap our secret code against my cheek, a rhythm that means more than words ever could: *Stay safe. Love you. Always.*

Another tremor rocks the facility, stronger than before. Lights strobe in panic patterns as circuit breakers pop like gunshots. The elevator doors slide open with a sound like a mechanical gasp.

Chen and Malikai sprint for the opening, lab coats billowing behind them like pale wings. Guards move to stop them, but Petrov barks something in Russian that makes them step back. Even they understand—we're all dead if someone doesn't contain this.

"Get them out!" Malikai shouts as the elevator doors begin to close. His voice carries pure desperation. "Promise me you'll get them all out!"

The other scientists try to follow, but Whittman holds them back. Years of quantum theory have taught them the brutal math—too many minds in that lab could be as dangerous as too few. When Ally tries to push past, Whittman physically turns her away.

"You don't need to die for this," he says. "Go with the others."

"But—"

"Don't argue." He spins her toward us with surprising strength. The look in his eyes brooks no argument.

The men's badges flash urgent blue as emergency protocols engage. Warning klaxons shred the air with mechanical shrieks. The elevator doors slide closed with terrible finality.

"Kai!" I lunge for the elevator, but strong hands lock around my arms. The metallic doors seal with a sound like a tomb closing.

"Your brother gave orders." Petrov's breath is hot against my ear, his fingers digging into my biceps hard enough to bruise. "You're leaving. Now."

The facility shakes harder, deep groans echoing through steel and concrete. Light fixtures swing wildly, casting frenzied shadows. That high-pitched whine from the cooling systems suddenly cuts out—a silence more terrifying than any noise.

"Move!" Petrov's voice cracks like a whip. "Everyone topside! Now!"

I grab Ally's hand, her fingers ice-cold against mine. Her quantum physics training makes her the only one who truly understands what's happening below. The raw terror in her eyes tells me everything I don't want to know.

Guards herd us toward emergency exits, their practiced control fracturing around the edges. Even they can feel it—the air growing thick and strange. Static electricity makes every touch spark painfully.

"They're going to die down there." Maria's sob cuts through the chaos as we run. Her father's absence beside her feels like an open wound.

"They know what they're doing." Mrs. Chen's voice carries the strength of mountains, but her fingers curl into white-knuckled fists. "They're the best minds in quantum physics. They're trying to save us all."

We sprint through corridors I've walked a hundred times, but everything looks alien under the strobing emergency lights. Left at the security station, through the decontamination chamber, and past the guard post where Ivan always snuck us extra coffee. My mind catalogs each turn, each doorway, mapping an escape route we might never need.

The heavy blast doors leading outside require two guards' key cards. Their hands shake so badly that they have to swipe three times. Warning klaxons continue to shriek, the sound bouncing off concrete walls until it feels like it's coming from inside my skull.

"Faster!" Petrov shoves us through the opening. "Move!"

Night air hits like a physical blow after months of filtered ventilation. Stars wheel overhead, impossibly bright and strange. The facility squats behind us like a crouching beast, those uncanny lights still dancing through its windows. Even the darkness feels wrong, as if the quantum uncertainty below has begun infecting the world above.

Through the haze of steam and warning lights, I catch fragments of conversation between two guards, their voices tight with tension.

"The Third wants another progress report," one mutters in heavily accented English. "Third time today."

"Let him wait," his companion responds. "We answer to someone higher now. Malfor is monitoring the containment field data."

"You think it's true? About what they're building?"

"I think if those fields fail, we won't live long enough to find out."

The exchange sends chills down my spine. Even here, at the heart of the Third Sentinel's operation, Malfor's invisible hand pulls the strings. Whatever they're forcing Malikai to build, it's important enough to draw the attention of the shadow behind all the Sentinels.

Guards establish a perimeter, their rifles pointed outward, though there's nothing to shoot. Beyond the fence, Kazakhstan's endless steppes stretch toward darkness. But distance won't save us if those containment fields fail.

"How long?" My voice sounds foreign in my ears as I grip Ally's hand. "How long before we know if they …"

"The containment fields are already critical." Her fingers are still ice-cold, trembling against mine. "If they can't stabilize the reaction in the next few minutes …" She swallows hard. "The quantum cascade effect could—"

A new sound cuts through the night—a deep thrumming vibrates in our bones. The ground shudders beneath our feet. Machines scream through the facility as physics strains against human control.

Mrs. Chen murmurs prayers in Mandarin, the soft words carrying on the night wind. Mrs. Williams clutches her hand, though they've barely spoken through months of captivity. Strange how fear strips away all our carefully maintained distances. Maria presses against her father's side, face buried in his shoulder.

The facility's exterior lights flicker and die, plunging us into starlit darkness. The air feels charged, making every breath taste like lightning.

"The backup generators shouldn't have failed." Ally's voice

shakes as she stares at the building. "They're routing all power to the containment fields."

"What happens if the fields collapse completely?" I force the words out past the knot in my throat.

"Don't." She shakes her head sharply. "Don't ask me that. Please."

But her silence tells me everything. The quantum cascade effect—Malikai tried to explain it once. How quantum tunneling could theoretically create a chain reaction, in reality unraveling from the inside out. The math is beyond me, but the fear in his eyes wasn't.

Another tremor rocks the ground. The guards shift uneasily, some crossing themselves. Even Petrov's iron control shows cracks as he snaps orders into his radio, demanding updates that never come.

Strange harmonics rise and fall through the facility walls— machinery fighting forces it was never meant to contain. I imagine I can hear voices beneath the mechanical screaming. Malikai's equations. Chen's calculations. The desperate race to stop what they created.

"Please," I whisper to the uncaring stars. "Please let him survive this."

"Do you feel that?" Ally's fingers dig into my arm. "The vibrations—they're changing."

"Is that good or bad?"

The deep thrumming cuts out suddenly, leaving a silence that rings in our ears. For one endless moment, even the facility holds its breath.

Then everything goes wrong at once.

And through it all, one thought burns like fire in my mind: Kai is down there.

My brilliant, gentle brother who taught me physics with

coffee beans. Who protected me from playground bullies and quantum mechanics with equal dedication. Who went back into hell because his mind might be the only thing standing between us and the apocalypse. He's down there.

The ground shudders again, gentler this time. Like aftershocks from an earthquake that happened in another dimension.

The tremors gradually subside, each one weaker than the last. The air feels different—lighter somehow, the strange static charge dissipates.

A crackle of static breaks the silence. Petrov's radio comes to life, voices speaking rapid Russian. His shoulders relax fractionally as he listens.

"All clear," he announces, his usual iron control sliding back into place. "Containment has been restored."

Relief ripples through the group, though no one dares celebrate. We've learned that hope is a dangerous thing in this place.

"Inside." Petrov gestures toward the entrance. "Orderly lines. Now."

The return journey feels surreal after what we witnessed. Guards scan badges and check credentials with mechanical precision as if the laws of physics hadn't just bent to breaking.

The metallic clang of the facility's reinforced doors slams shut behind us, locking us back inside. The facility's corridors smell different—sharp ozone mixed with burned metal. Emergency lighting casts everything in shades of amber rather than blood red. Our footsteps echo against concrete, marking time like a metronome returning to normal rhythm.

Where is he?

My gaze darts toward the elevator where he vanished, swallowed by flashing hazard lights and shouted commands. He should be back by now.

A faceless guard barks orders, forcing us to move, but I can't shake the memory of his face—the fierce determination in his eyes as he stayed behind, shielding me with everything he had left.

My brother. My only family.

Fear gnaws at my chest, cold and relentless. What if this time —he doesn't come back?

TWENTY-FIVE

Walt

"SIGNAL SPIKE!" Mitzy's sharp voice slices through the pre-dawn stillness of the Command tent. Her fingers move with practiced urgency over multiple keyboards, summoning a cascade of data streams onto the holographic display. On the central screen, jagged power curves climb sharply, overlaying muted thermal imaging of the reactor sublevels. "Something's happening inside the facility."

I push away from the tactical table, the sudden shift from quiet planning to crisis tightening my gut. "What kind of spike?"

Mitzy doesn't look up. "Major power fluctuations. The bumblebees are detecting facility-wide alarms. Emergency protocols are firing across every sector."

Forest steps in from the shadows, his broad frame casting long, sharp lines against the dim tent lights. His voice is low, deliberate. "Show me."

The schematic updates in real time, lighting up with warning signals: power surges in multiple sectors, emergency overrides activating at every critical checkpoint. Mitzy splits the screen to show energy diagnostics alongside live feeds from the drones.

"They're dumping power into the containment fields," she says. "Massive loads. Way beyond capacity. They're trying to stabilize the reaction, but the system isn't designed for this."

Ethan abandons his half-finished coffee to study the screens over her shoulder. "This doesn't look like a drill."

Mitzy shakes her head, flipping to another set of feeds. "It's not. These readings are …" She trails off, the unease in her voice thick.

"Unprecedented," I finish for her, stepping closer. The heat maps from the reactor level glow like a furnace while red warning indicators flash across every subsystem.

"Their backups just kicked in," Mitzy says, highlighting a fresh surge in power output. "They're rerouting everything into the containment fields. This is an all-out fight to keep that reactor stable."

"Can the fields hold?" Forest asks.

"For now," Mitzy replies, her tone clipped. "But look at this." She pulls up a new graph, the jagged lines spiking and falling erratically. "The system's oscillating. If they lose control, the energy discharge will—"

"Blow everything," Sam's voice crackles through comms. He's stationed in the mountains, watching from the theoretical blast zone. *"Thermal imaging confirms a massive heat bloom at the reactor level. Looks like they're on borrowed time."*

"Rufi units are reporting heightened guard activity," Blake adds. "They're locking down entry points and doubling up patrols. This isn't containment—they're preparing for a worst-case scenario."

I run a finger over the scar on my chest. The memory sharpens my focus. "Where are the hostages?"

Mitzy redirects the bumblebee feeds to the residential wing. The footage is grainy but clear enough to show armed guards moving civilians through narrow halls. Families huddle together, as they're herded toward a central corridor.

"They're evacuating," Mitzy confirms, toggling through more feeds. "Multiple groups converging on the exits. Security teams are maintaining tight formations."

Ethan leans in beside me, his tone sharp. "Track their evacuation routes. Entry points, exit routes, guard patterns—I want a full accounting of their movements."

The display splits, focusing on a group moving out of the residential wing. Mrs. Chen clutches her teenage son's hand like a lifeline while armed men guide them forward. The Williams family moves in unison, their steps perfectly synchronized, as if they've been through worse together.

"There's Ally." Forest gestures toward a different feed. A blonde figure—Whittman's doctoral student—crosses through a checkpoint, standing out starkly against the sterile gray walls. "And there's Malia." Mitzy flips through the feeds before I can ask, doing what she can to get a close-up.

I can't tear my eyes from the screen. My heart pounds as the bumblebees zero in on a figure among the evacuees.

Malia.

Even through the poor resolution, her posture is unmistakable—rigid, unyielding. Her head stays high, defiance etched into every line of her body. But there's something else—her gaze darts between the guards and the corridors, calculating.

"She's looking for an opening," I murmur, mostly to myself.

"Rufi units confirming movement at all exits." Blake's voice crackles over comms. *"External security establishing perimeter control points. Whatever shook them, they're not taking any risks."*

Mitzy's voice breaks through my focus. "Power levels are still climbing. They're redirecting everything to buy more time, but it's not enough. They're relocating to hardened shelters outside the main facility," Mitzy says, overlaying schematics onto the footage. "We missed those on our initial survey." She shakes her head, but Forest places a hand on her shoulder.

Her voice is clipped and monotone as she reports out details. "Cold War-era bunkers. Reinforced to withstand pretty much anything short of a direct nuclear strike."

"Smart," Forest mutters. "If the containment fields fail, those might be the only survivable places in the blast radius."

"How long do they have?" I ask, already dreading the answer.

She hesitates. "Minutes. Maybe an hour if they're lucky." Mitzy stiffens, her hands flying over the keyboard. "We're missing two hostages." Her words hit like a punch. "Malikai and Dr. Chen aren't with the evacuees."

My grip tightens on the table as I force my mind to keep working. "Where are Malikai and Chen?"

Mitzy's face falls. She pulls up thermal imaging, overlaying it onto the schematic. Two faint heat signatures are moving deeper into the facility.

"They're heading toward the reactor level," she confirms.

The tent goes quiet as the weight of it sinks in. Whatever's down there—it's bad enough to evacuate the facility and dangerous enough, or worse, for two men to risk their lives trying to stop a catastrophe.

Forest's jaw tightens. "They're walking straight into the fire."

Hank lets out a low whistle, his usual humor gone. "They must think they're the only ones who can stop this."

"Or they're buying time for the others," Gabe mutters grimly.

"Show me the containment field data again," I order.

Mitzy brings up another graph. The lines are steadier now, but the strain is evident. "The fields are stabilizing—for now. But the power draw is …" She trails off, shaking her head.

I study the schematic, my mind racing. "This evacuation—it's too smooth. Too organized."

Ethan narrows his eyes. "What are you thinking?"

"They've drilled for this." I tap the schematic, highlighting the routes. "These movements, the guard rotations—they've practiced this. If we can replicate these conditions ..."

"We can force another evacuation," Ethan finishes, his tone sharp with understanding. "No need to breach an impenetrable facility if we can get the guards to bring the hostages to us."

"Exactly, but we need to get to them before they can funnel them into those bunkers."

The tension in the room shifts, the weight of realization settling over the team.

"Let's assume it blows. How bad?" My voice cuts through the heavy silence, sharp and focused. "Chernobyl bad? Worse?"

Mitzy doesn't look up from her screen, her fingers flying over the keys. "Fusion and fission are two completely different animals. Fission—what you're thinking of—is what's used in nuclear power plants and atomic bombs. It splits heavy atoms, like uranium or plutonium, into smaller ones, releasing energy. But it also leaves behind radioactive waste that stays deadly for thousands of years."

"Like Chernobyl and Fukushima," Forest adds.

"Exactly." She gestures at her screens, frustration sharpening her tone. "Fusion is the opposite. It fuses light atoms—hydrogen isotopes like deuterium—into helium, releasing energy. It's cleaner, way more efficient, and doesn't create the same kind of long-lasting waste. But it's dangerous as hell if something goes wrong."

Blake frowns. "Cleaner? Then why the hell are we worried about a five-kilometer blast radius?"

"Because it's still a nuclear reaction," Mitzy snaps. "And this isn't about radioactive fallout. If those containment fields fail, all that energy—the power of a star—gets released at once. No waste, no lingering radiation. Just heat and force. Twenty-seven million degrees of heat. Everything nearby gets vaporized into plasma."

Gabe crosses his arms, brows furrowing. "So, no wasteland? Just instant destruction?"

Mitzy nods. "Right. Fusion doesn't poison the land for centuries. But if this reactor goes critical? It'll vaporize everything within the blast radius. The damage is in the heat and the pressure wave."

"Don't forget about the neutrons. There's still radiation," Forest presses, his tone grim.

Mitzy exhales sharply. "If they're using tritium, the neutrons can irradiate nearby materials—short-term radioactivity, not thousands of years. Days or weeks, tops. But the immediate problem is the energy release."

Walt shakes his head, his mind racing. "I thought this was cold fusion?"

Mitzy snorts, shaking her head as she pulls up another diagnostic. "Room-temperature fusion is a pipe dream. Even if it worked, it'd still need containment fields to hold the reaction."

I lock eyes with her. "So, worst-case scenario?"

Mitzy exhales, her fingers hovering over the keyboard. "If it blows? I'm beginning to think five klicks is a vast underestimation of the blast radius. Those bunkers? It's hard to say how protective they might be. Twenty-seven million degrees is a lot of heat. We've never seen anything like that outside the sun and some very controlled reactions here on Earth. Outside that blast range, there's no fallout, no long-term radiation."

I force myself to turn away. "We can't move until we're certain the reactor is stable. If those fields fail, nothing else will matter. But if they fix it—we have to be ready. Who knows when this will happen again." My voice is steady, but the weight of it presses heavily on my chest. "Mitzy, can you replicate the conditions for an evacuation?"

"Maybe. Why?" Her fingers fly across the keyboard. "The bumblebees mapped their entire emergency protocol system. I can simulate a fire in a non-critical sector. Big enough to force an evac, but far enough from the reactor to avoid a real catastrophe."

"They expected something like this could happen. They built these protocols for a reason, and they drilled them repeatedly." I trace the paths on the holographic display. "We've been thinking like intruders, trying to breach a fortress. But this evacuation— this is our way in."

"Walt has it right." Ethan narrows his eyes, following my line of thought. "We have to trigger another evacuation and make them move the hostages outside."

I nod, the plan solidifying in my mind. "Exactly. They're conditioned to respond to these alarms. We replicate the conditions for an evacuation and use their protocols against them."

Forest crosses his arms, his expression skeptical. "And what if triggering another evacuation destabilizes the reactor further? Or worse, tips them off to our presence?"

"We avoid touching anything connected to the reactor," Mitzy answers firmly. "The bumblebees are mapping their system. I assume their fire suppression systems and environmental controls are separate from containment operations, but I need more time to confirm."

"Do it," CJ says.

"That's risky," Blake points out. "What if the guards figure out it's fake before we can reach the hostages?"

"Timing," I say, stepping forward. "This has to be perfect. We hit them as soon as the alarms go off before they realize it's a false alarm. Multiple teams, coordinated strikes. We intercept the hostages en route to the bunkers and extract them before the guards can regroup."

"We need to bring in more teams. Alpha and Charlie can't handle something like that alone." Ethan taps the display, highlighting the evacuation paths.

"You work on that," Mitzy says, her fingers flying over the keyboard. "I'll work on the bumblebees. I should have something in a few hours, but I need to see what's happening down in that lab first."

I turn back to the holographic display, a plan solidifying in my mind.

TWENTY-SIX

Walt

———

DAWN BREAKS harsh and cold over the Kazakhstan steppes. Inside the converted Quonset hut serving as our Command Center, banks of servers and monitoring equipment push the temperature well above the freezing point outside. The scent of burnt coffee mingles with electronics.

I pace the length of the Command Center, my boots echoing against the metal floor as I work off my frustration.

"I've got an update." Mitzy's announcement cuts through our tense silence. "Power levels dropping. Look at these numbers."

The facility's power grid tells the story of dropping energy curves. Emergency systems powering down. Cooling units cycling back to normal operation.

"Containment fields holding at eighty percent capacity," Mitzy confirms. "It's stable—for now. But all that energy? It's waiting for an excuse to explode."

The tactical display shows thermal images of two figures stumbling away from the reactor controls—spent but successful. They've prevented catastrophe, for now, but their exhaustion is evident even through the grainy feed.

"If the fields destabilize again," she says, "they might not be able to fix it a second time. The good news is that I can access their fire suppression systems and environmental controls. I'm confident I can trigger another evacuation without touching the reactor control systems or power backups."

"We need options for getting in there," CJ says, studying the facility's defensive layout. "Ground approach is suicide—they'll see vehicles coming from twenty klicks out."

"Air infiltration is out," Blake adds. "Their anti-aircraft coverage is too tight for choppers."

"What about HALO?" I trace a finger along the tactical display. "Mitzy, show me their radar coverage again."

She pulls up the sensor grid overlay. "They've got overlapping sweeps, but there's a gap. Their radar coverage syncs up every three minutes, creating a blind spot." Her fingers move efficiently across the keyboard. "Thread the needle during that window; theoretically, you could drop in undetected."

"How big's the window?" Ethan asks.

"Ninety seconds, max. You'll need perfect timing on the jump."

"No pressure," Gabe mutters.

"Distance to target from drop point?" CJ asks.

"Two klicks to the facility perimeter. There's enough shielding in your tactical gear that you should be able to evade their ground radar once you're down. I'll do my best with the bumble-bees to create interference with their ground radar."

"Two klicks ... Let's say five minutes from the drop zone to the facility." CJ studies the approach vectors.

"That's a rough pace in full tactical gear." Ethan shakes his head. "I say we call it six, maybe seven minutes. That leaves less than three minutes to secure the hostages."

"It's doable," Forest says, his tone matter-of-fact. "We've executed tighter insertions before."

Mitzy continues, "Once you're on the ground, the Rufi will assist. They'll secure corridors for exfil and monitor guard movements in real time. Or, you can use them to create havoc."

"How?" I ask.

"Scare the shit out of the guards. Herd them away from the hostages." There's a wicked gleam in her eyes as if she's been waiting to put the Rufi to use like this. "I'll feed everything directly to your HUDs."

I step back from the table, letting the details sink in. Every step of the plan is razor-thin, dependent on perfect timing and flawless execution. One misstep, one delayed alarm, and the whole operation falls apart.

"We're betting everything on this evacuation protocol," I say, my voice steady despite the weight of the words. "If Mitzy's fire alarm doesn't trigger the response we need …"

"It will," she interrupts, her voice firm. "The bumblebees have mapped every circuit, every sensor. When those alarms hit, they have no choice but to evacuate."

"That gets us in. But extraction's another matter," CJ says. "We can't exactly HALO out with civilians."

"No, but we can use vehicles for exfil," I say. "Stage them here, in the mountain pass."

I trace an overland route across the steppe, skirting the rugged mountain range on the map. The peaks are jagged and imposing, cutting like teeth against the desolate expanse of the steppe.

"It's the last place they'll expect. Keeps the vehicles out of sight and off the main road. The mountains provide natural cover."

"I agree," Gabe says. "Bring the vehicles in the moment we hit the ground. How long will it take them?"

"It's ten kilometers from the mountains to the facility. Say, ten minutes?" Mitzy glances at her screen, no doubt doing the calculations.

"Rough terrain," Blake observes. "High risk of mechanical failure."

"We'll stage redundant vehicles," Mitzy cuts in, her tone cool and precise. "My team can handle transport. You don't have enough operators to cover everything."

CJ's jaw tightens. "We've never put tech teams in combat situations."

"With respect …" Mitzy arches a brow, deadpan. "Unless you're planning to clone yourself in the next six hours—you don't have a choice."

"Fine. The techies drive." CJ's tone is curt, irritation barely leashed. "How long can you keep their systems confused once we initiate?"

Mitzy turns, leveling him with a pointed look. "The same ten minutes." Her voice is cool, precise, and edged with snark. "That's how long you have from when the fire alarm goes off until they figure out it's fake. Same clock. Same countdown. Ten minutes." She arches a brow, daring him to push further.

Ethan shakes his head. "That's not much time."

"It's all we've got." I watch the feed from the residential wing, where Malia and the other hostages are being escorted back to their quarters. "We need to warn them somehow. Get them ready to move."

"Too risky." CJ shakes his head.

"I have an option." Mitzy reaches for one of the microdrones. "Remember the Holbrook extraction?" Mitzy reaches into a case beside her station, pulling out one of our microdrones. "Remember how we used one of the drones with Blaze? I can send a drone to Malia. We can get a message to her."

"Lock it down," CJ finally orders. "I want every team

prepped and ready. The moment those containment fields stabilize, we move."

The Command Center erupts into focused activity. Through it all, I keep watching that grainy feed of the residential wing, where Malia waits with no idea that rescue is coming.

TWENTY-SEVEN

Malia

MY SHOES SCUFF against polished concrete as I pace the hallway outside the elevator. Back and forth. Six steps one way, spin, six steps back. Crimson emergency lights bleed across institutional walls, transforming the sterile gray surfaces into a landscape of raw, bleeding tension.

"They've been down there too long." Ally's whisper barely carries over the hum of fluorescent lights. She stands rigid beside me, her fingers twisting the hem of her institutional gray shirt.

"Please," I say softly. "Not now." I'm unable to bear hearing the statistics she's about to quote. My brilliant brother, descending into that hell of quantum physics gone wrong. "Just—don't."

Another circuit. Six steps. Turn. Six steps back. The elevator display remains stubbornly dark, offering no hints about what's happening in the levels below. Somewhere down there, Malikai and Dr. Chen are fighting forces that could tear reality apart at the nuclear level.

My throat burns with unspoken prayers as I make another

turn. The guards watch us with predatory attention, their hands hovering near holstered weapons.

Mrs. Chen appears at the end of the corridor, her usual composure cracking around the edges. Her son, Kevin, hovers close beside her, trying to appear strong despite the fear evident in his young face. None of us say what we're all thinking—that our loved ones might not return.

Other faces peek around corners—the Williamses watching from their doorway with collective dread. We're all united by a singular, terrifying uncertainty: will our loved ones return? The Rodriguez girl's eyes are red from crying, though she tries to hide it.

"Containment fields are holding," Ally mutters technical reassurances. "The quantum tunneling effect must be stabilizing, or we'd be …" She trails off, but we all know how that sentence ends.

The guards shift restlessly, their boots squeaking against freshly waxed floors. One speaks rapid Russian into an encrypted radio, his glances growing more frequent—suggesting our fate hangs by a thread far more complicated than mere scientific experiment.

The elevator suddenly flickers to life, casting an eerie blue glow across my trembling skin. My heart leaps into my throat as I watch the numbers slowly climb, one basement level at a time, each illuminated digit bringing them closer—or bringing news I can't bear to hear.

B7 ... B6 ... B5 ...

Ally leans closer, her voice a desperate whisper. "They're alive," she says, scientific certainty replaced by a fragile hope. "They have to be, or the guards would be moving us already."

B4 ... B3 ... B2 ...

I press my sweating palms against my thighs, feeling the coarse institutional fabric dig into my skin.

B1 ... G ...

The elevator machinery whines—a mechanical dirge that will haunt my nightmares. Around us, breaths are suspended in a collective, razor-sharp silence. Even the guards have gone motionless, their eyes locked on those illuminated numbers. Whatever happened down there affects them, too—we're all within the theoretical blast radius.

A soft, almost apologetic ding punctures the silence, somehow more terrifying than the endless waiting.

"Please," I whisper, the word a fragile prayer carrying the weight of every hope, every desperate plea I've ever known. "Please ..."

The elevator doors part with a mechanical groan, and my heart stops. Malikai and Dr. Chen lean heavily against the far wall, their lab coats stained with sweat and something darker that might be blood. The harsh fluorescent lights make them look like ghosts—pale, drawn, barely standing.

"Kai!" I lunge forward, but a guard's iron grip restrains me. Malikai stares through me, his eyes glazed, like he doesn't recognize me.

The acrid smell of ozone and burned metal rolls out of the elevator. Dr. Chen's glasses hang crookedly from one ear, and angry red marks circle his eyes where radiation gear must have pressed too tight. Both men's hands shake with fine tremors—the kind Ally warned me about after too much exposure.

"Clear the elevator." The guard's command spurs me into action.

I rush forward, shrugging off the guard's grip as Malikai staggers from the elevator. His knees buckle, shoulders slumping like gravity doubled its hold on him.

His breath comes in ragged gasps, each one a battle he's barely winning. Fine tremors ripple through his hands, still curled into tense claws, as if he's holding onto something he can't let go of. His face is ashen, sweat slicking his skin in uneven patches.

"Malikai …" I grip his arms, feeling the unsteady twitch of strained muscles beneath my fingers. He sways dangerously, and I brace to keep him upright.

His eyes flutter, unfocused and glassy, searching for something—someone.

I tighten my hold, voice trembling. "You did it."

He sags against me, a shuddering breath escaping his lips—relief, fragile and fleeting.

"Whatever you did down there …" My voice breaks as I press my forehead to his. "It worked. We're still here."

The guard ushers us toward medical. Each step becomes a Herculean effort, Malikai's feet leaving ghostly scuff marks on the sterile concrete, his breath a ragged symphony of exhaustion. His breath comes in short gasps, and heat radiates from his body like he's running a fever.

"Almost there," I murmur as he stumbles again. The institutional lights cast harsh shadows under his eyes, aging him decades in hours. His fingers clutch my shirt with desperate strength as if I'm the only thing anchoring him to reality.

Ally appears on his other side, taking some of his weight. Her fingers brush his wrist, checking his pulse with scientific precision. The look she gives me carries volumes—too fast, too thready, but steady enough to mean survival.

"The quantum cascade," he mutters, his words slurring slightly. "Had to realign manually … Chen found the resonance pattern … Beautiful mathematics …" His voice drifts into equations I can't follow, numbers tumbling out in an exhausted stream.

Medical looms ahead—massive steel barriers, cold and unyielding, that usually mean invasive exams but now promise rest.

Behind us, soft, shuffling steps scrape against the concrete, slow and uneven. Dr. Chen, leaning heavily on his wife, moves with weary determination. She murmurs gently, her words low and soothing.

A hush settles, stretching thin and expectant, the air charged with unspoken relief and lingering dread.

Then—

A single clap breaks the strained silence—sharp but steady, like a stone skipping across still water. Dr. Wittman's weathered hands come together again—slow, deliberate, not to demand attention, but in simple acknowledgment—and gratitude.

Another clap joins his, higher-pitched, crisp—Maria Rodriguez, followed by her father's deeper, more measured rhythm. Then another. The Chen's teenage son adds his voice with sharp, decisive strikes.

Applause builds, spreading like a rising tide, filling the cavernous space with life and relief. Even some of the guards, usually cold and unreadable, soften, their stoic masks cracking under the weight of what they've survived.

Malikai's head lifts slowly, his eyes searching. When he sees the source of the sound, a weak but genuine smile tugs at his lips —the first real expression I've seen since the elevator doors opened. His fingers tighten around mine, faint but unmistakable —the silent code from our childhood. *"It's okay."*

Dr. Chen raises a trembling hand in acknowledgment, his wife pressing her lips to his temple, tears tracking silently down her cheeks.

Malikai's smile falters, shadowed by something deeper— resentment, exhaustion, rage kept in check.

"None of this should've happened. They are pushing us too hard, and we're making mistakes." His voice is rough, raw with lingering defiance.

My throat tightens. He's right. They were forced into this ... Used.

"You still saved everyone." My voice trembles despite my best effort. "You and Chen walked into hell—and came back."

His weight shifts as he tries to straighten, shoulders squaring despite his exhaustion—as if he can still carry the burden of what they made him do.

The applause fades naturally, replaced by the soft murmur of relieved voices. For now, we're not hostages, guards, scientists, or security. We're simply people who stared into the atomic abyss and lived to tell about it.

"That's enough." Petrov's voice cuts through the momentary warmth like a blade. "Everyone back to quarters. Now."

The guards herd us toward our assigned rooms. Their boots echo against concrete, a rhythm I've learned to hate. Malikai stumbles between two of them, his exhaustion making him clumsy. I try to stay close, but a guard's arm blocks my path.

"Keep moving." The order comes with a nudge from his rifle barrel.

The sense of unity shatters as we're separated into family units. The Williamses disappear first, then the Chens, their teenage son glancing back with worried eyes. Next the Rodriguez's. Little Maria clinging to her father's hand.

"Doctor will check him in the morning." Petrov's tone brooks no argument. "For now, everyone stays in their quarters."

The corridors feel longer tonight, each step carrying us further from that brief moment of shared humanity in the dining hall. Overhead lights flicker—aftereffect of the power surges from below.

Or warnings of what's still to come.

TWENTY-EIGHT

Malia

———————

DARKNESS PRESSES AGAINST MY EYES, but sleep refuses to come. The institutional mattress crinkles with every restless movement. In the next room, Malikai's breathing is labored, with each inhale carrying a slight wheeze that terrifies me.

My mind races through the day's events like a broken film reel: the alarms, the evacuation, the terrible waiting while my brother descended into atomic hell. Every time I close my eyes, his exhausted face is all I can see, and I can't forget the way his hands shook.

The facility creaks around us, settling into its nighttime rhythm. Or maybe those creaks are warnings—containment fields straining against forces they were never meant to hold.

How long until the next breach?

How many times can Malikai and Chen pull off a miracle?

Every distant mechanical sound could be the beginning of another emergency.

I can't help but feel like we're all just waiting to die.

The thought hits with crushing certainty. Even if Malikai and Chen keep the reactor stable, we know too much—we've seen too much. We become disposable liabilities when our captors get their quantum fusion weapon.

A soft buzz cuts through my dark thoughts. At first, I think it's just another facility sound—ventilation, power conduits, or failing containment fields.

But this is different. Organic somehow. Almost like …

I sit up slowly, my ears straining. The sound fades and returns, weaving through the artificial hum of the building's systems. It's impossible. We haven't seen a single insect since arriving. The facility's environmental controls are too strict, and the decontamination protocols are too thorough.

As the buzz draws closer, it carries harmonics that don't quite match natural wing patterns. Something about the pitch feels manufactured, precise in a way that nature never is.

My heart rate picks up as I track the sound's movement. Years of watching Malikai work with precision instruments have taught me to recognize artificial patterns. This isn't random insect flight.

This is—purposeful.

Guards pass outside, their boot steps regular and heavy. I force my breathing to stay steady, fighting the urge to search openly for the source.

Moonlight filtering through the mesh-reinforced window catches something in the corner. It is small, dark, and hovering with impossible precision. My breath catches as I study its silhouette against the pale concrete.

It's not an insect—not quite. The wing movements are too regular and controlled, and the body proportions are slightly wrong for any species I know. As I watch, it adjusts its position with microscopic precision, maintaining a perfect distance from the surveillance cameras' sweep.

The drone moves again, drifting closer with deliberate care. Its flight path traces a perfect arc between camera blind spots.

Only one organization I know of has this level of technology. Only one team would attempt something this insane.

Hope blooms dangerously in my chest as I track the drone's approach. Somehow, against all odds, he found me.

Under the moonlight, I catch glimpses of metal where chitin should be—microscopic joints and servos disguised as insect anatomy. My fingers twitch with the instinct to reach for it, to verify it's real and not just another hallucination born from months of captivity.

But even that small movement could give everything away.

The drone drifts closer, defying every natural law of insect behavior. Real bees don't hover with military precision. Don't navigate between camera sweeps with calculated grace. Don't maintain perfect distance while scanning with nearly invisible sensors.

My muscles coil tight with the effort of remaining motionless as it enters my personal space, close enough that its wingbeats stir my hair.

Fighting these defensive instincts feels like drowning—every nerve ending firing with the need to move, react, and protect myself. But I think of Walt teaching me about maintaining cover, about the importance of stillness under surveillance. His voice echoes in my memory: *"Sometimes survival means letting the enemy get close."*

But this isn't an enemy. It's salvation.

I remain frozen, hardly daring to breathe, as this mechanical miracle carries hope close enough to touch.

The bumblebee drone lands in my hair, its tiny feet catching and pulling individual strands. Every point of contact sends shivers down my spine as it moves deliberately through my tangled curls.

Oh God, this is so wrong.

The sensation is nothing like a real insect—too heavy, too

precise, each step calculated rather than organic. My scalp crawls as it navigates closer to my ear, and I bite my lip to keep from whimpering.

The urge to shake my head, to dislodge this artificial thing crawling through my hair, is almost overwhelming. Bile rises in my throat as I imagine its metal legs tangling in my curls, getting stuck, and having to explain to guards why there's a mechanical bug in my hair.

It reaches my ear canal, and I nearly lose it completely. The mechanical legs scrape against my skin as it positions itself, sending violent shivers through my body that I desperately try to suppress.

Oh God, oh God, oh God, this is so gross.

It's like having a spider crawl directly into your ear, except this spider is made of metal and circuits. My fingernails dig into my palms, and the pain gives me something to focus on besides the horrifying sensation of the drone finding its final position.

A soft click echoes through my skull as the device engages. The sound seems to vibrate through my bones, and for one terrifying moment, I'm certain the guards must hear it too. But their boots continue their regular patrol outside my door—*click, click* against concrete. Still, I hold my breath, waiting for alarms to blare, doors to burst open, and everything to fall apart.

Instead, Mitzy's voice crystallizes in my head, so clear and precise it's like she's standing beside me. Her words bypass my actual ears, sending her message directly to my brain through bone conduction. The technology is incredible, but I can only focus on fighting my gag reflex as the drone shifts slightly, adjusting its position.

"Don't respond," her voice whispers through my skull.

Sweat trickles down my temple. The urge to cough, shake my head, and do anything to dislodge this invasion of my personal space is unbearable.

Mitzy's voice hums through my skull, each word vibrating directly into my bones. *"Listen carefully. We're coming. I can't tell you when or how—but you'll know what to do when you see it."*

Really? That's it?

After all this technological wizardry, after sending a mechanical bee through supposedly secure ventilation systems and making it crawl through my hair—which, by the way, still makes my skin crawl just thinking about it—that's all she can tell me?

"The most important thing …" Mitzy continues, oblivious to my internal frustration. *"When you get outside, you need to be ready to run. Don't stop, don't look back, just run."*

When? How? What kind of signal? I wish I could ask questions.

"One last thing …" There's a pause, a softening in her tone that makes my heart skip. *"He's been obsessed with finding you. Hasn't slept, barely eaten. Nothing else matters."*

Walt's alive!

The words hit me like a thunderclap, stealing the breath from my lungs. He's alive. A sob catches in my throat, half-formed and disbelieving. I press my hand against my mouth as if that will contain the rush of emotion surging inside me—relief so sharp it aches.

He didn't die in that parking lot. He's been searching, fighting, surviving—just like I have.

I squeeze my eyes shut, feeling the sting of tears I can't stop, a ragged laugh breaking free despite myself. He's out there. He's been out there this whole time.

Walt's alive—and he's coming for me.

The mechanical bee disengages before I can process that last bit, its legs untangling from my hair. I watch it disappear into a ventilation grate as if it was never here at all.

I arrange myself in what I hope passes for natural sleep positioning, but my heart hammers against my ribs so hard I'm amazed the biometric sensors don't sound alarms. My mind races with hope so fierce it burns.

He's alive.

Of course, he survived those bullets.

Of course, he came looking for me.

And when I see him again …

I press my face into the thin institutional pillow to hide my smile, but my imagination runs wild. I'll kiss him. I'll grab his stupidly handsome face and kiss him like our lives depend on it. Then I'll run wherever he tells me to run, but that kiss comes first.

TWENTY-NINE

Walt

PLANNING CONTINUES AT A FEVERED PACE, making sure we account for as many variables as possible. No plan is perfect, but we try.

"HALO insertion here." Sam indicates, marking our drop zones. "Teams exit at 30,000 feet, free fall to 2,500 before chute deployment. Weather window gives us perfect conditions—high cloud cover for concealment, minimal wind interference."

Ethan takes over, highlighting approach vectors. "Two klicks from the Rufi perimeter to the facility. We hit the ground running. Once on the ground, Mitzy initiates the alarm. That gives five?—six minutes max to reach the target. Alpha team sets up here and provides overwatch while Bravo and Charlie breach the perimeter. Delta maintains our exit corridor."

The tactical display shifts to show our staged vehicles—a mix of local vehicles that won't draw attention. SUVs, cargo vans, and even a tourist bus. Everything is carefully chosen to blend in. With the teams engaged at the facility, it's up to Mitzy and her techs to man the vehicles.

"Guardian transport teams are staged here and here." CJ

marks rally points in glowing blue. "Multiple extraction routes mapped. Once we secure the hostages, we move them to these positions. Mitzy, your team needs to be ready."

"They will be. My guys are pumped." Mitzy brings up feeds from the Rufi in position. "The Rufi units will be on chaos patrol, providing support and separating the guards from the hostages." Their thermal signatures dot the landscape in precise patterns.

"Then we're ready." CJ glances around the room, looking for confirmation from those of us gathered. "Bravo and Delta just landed. We'll meet up with them at the airstrip. Ethan and Max, get your teams on the bus. Mitzy, your team knows what to do."

"We're on it." She gives him two thumbs up.

Two hours later, we're gearing up for the HALO insertion. The cargo bay of our high-altitude transport thrums around us as teams perform final equipment checks. Through small windows, stars wheel past—bright points in the darkness that will guide us down.

I verify my oxygen system one final time, muscle memory taking over. The familiar weight of tactical gear settles me—plate carrier, comms, weapons all exactly where they should be. Around me, my teammates check seals, verify frequencies, and run systems diagnostics.

"HALO insertion points are locked." Sam's voice carries through our comms. "Weather window is perfect—high clouds, wind at 3 knots."

"The Rufi units have our landing zones mapped," Mitzy confirms. "Eight units maintaining surveillance from two clicks out. They'll guide each team to designated rally points."

I make final adjustments to my jump gear, checking straps and connections I could verify in my sleep. Through the window, Kazakhstan's steppes stretch endless and dark below us.

"Two minutes to drop." The pilot's voice comes crisp through our comms.

"You good?" Forest asks, somehow graceful despite his massive frame in full tactical gear. For some reason, he's decided to join the teams on the ground, letting Sam and CJ execute this mission from Command.

"Better than good." I verify my oxygen one last time. "Ready to end this."

"Ninety seconds."

The cargo bay door opens with a hydraulic whine, letting in the thin, cold air of aerial heights.

"Thirty seconds."

"Hold on, Malia," I whisper into the rushing wind. "I'm coming."

The jump light turns green.

Wind howls through the open bay door, carrying the bitter ozone scent of high-altitude air. My hands tighten on the frame as I count. One … Two …

I push off into nothingness.

Ice crystals sting my face in the microsecond before my goggles seal. The wind transforms from a howl to a roar, pressing against my body with physical force as I arch into the free fall position. My lungs burn with each filtered breath through the oxygen mask, the thin air barely satisfying despite the pure O2 mix.

Stars blaze overhead, so bright they cast shadows at this altitude. The curved horizon glows faintly—the first hint of dawn is still hours away.

Far below, Kazakhstan's steppes stretch into endless blackness, a vast, empty void swallowing the horizon. No roads. No towns. No signs of life. Just darkness, broken only by a single, solitary pinprick of light—a cold, sterile glow etched into the emptiness, like a fallen star clinging stubbornly against the void.

Our target.

Dark silhouettes plummet through my peripheral vision—my

Guardian brothers maintaining perfect spacing as we slice through the night sky. A flash of hand signals catches starlight: position check, course correction, altitude confirmation. The altimeter on my wrist glows faintly—28,000 feet and dropping.

Moisture crystallizes on my goggles as we punch through a thin cloud layer, the anti-icing system humming as it clears my vision. My body remembers this dance—the subtle adjustments of arms and legs to maintain position, the way my breath syncs with the fall. The ground below sharpens into recognizable features with each passing second.

The altimeter blinks: 3,000 feet. My fingers curl around the ripcord. The team spreads out in a perfect pattern, visible as darker shapes against the stars. At 2,500 feet, I pull.

The chute snaps open with bone-crushing force. My harness digs into my shoulders as free fall transforms into a controlled descent. The wind's roar cuts off so abruptly that my ears ring in the sudden silence. Only the whisper of air through shroud lines remains as my canopy joins others blooming against the starlit sky.

The last thousand feet pass in near silence. The ground resolves into patches of scrub and rock, terrain features I've memorized from countless briefings.

My boots crunch into frozen soil. Knees flex, distributing impact through my legs as the chute collapses behind me. Around me, dark shapes touch down in perfect sequence—the soft impacts and rustling fabric barely audible above the wind sighing across the steppes.

"Clear," Hank whispers through comms, already stripping his jump gear.

"Clear," Gabe confirms from somewhere to my left.

Everyone checks in. Acknowledgments come in quick succession as we secure equipment. The material whispers against itself as we collapse chutes into shallow depressions already scoured by the wind.

"Contact," Forest's voice carries through comms. *"Local patrol, two klicks north."*

"Hold positions," Ethan responds. *"Let them pass."*

The Rufi units materialize from the darkness, their mechanical forms barely visible as they join us. They move with uncanny grace across the broken ground, their advanced sensors sweeping the area in complete silence.

"Rally point secure," Blake reports. *"Ready to move."*

"Check your counts," Ethan orders softly. *"Two klicks to target. Ten minutes to breach point."*

"Like a walk in the park," Hank murmurs, falling into formation.

"A very cold park," Gabe adds, his breath fogging in the bitter air.

"Cut the chatter," Forest rumbles. *"Movement west."*

Two kilometers of open steppe stretch between us and the facility. We move out, each team flowing along pre-assigned formations.

"Teams set," Ethan's voice barely carries over the wind. *"Maintain intervals."*

The bitter wind knifes through layers of tactical gear, carrying the scent of snow yet to fall. Stars wheel overhead as we cross the empty ground, our shadows barely visible against the darkness. My boots find purchase on the uneven ground, each step measured and silent.

"Nine minutes," Blake reports.

The facility grows more distinct with each stride—hard-edged shadows against the star-filled sky. Floodlights cast pools of harsh illumination, creating a maze of light and shadow. We planned for six minutes, worst case seven, and make it in just over five minutes.

"Teams check in," CJ calls through the comms.

"Alpha in position," Max reports in.

"Bravo ready," Brady follows.

"Charlie on mark," Ethan calls in our status.

"Delta holding perimeter," Jenny announces her team's position.

The scar tissue on my chest pulls tight in the cold. My fingers brush the spot where bullets tore through, the memory of copper-scented blood and Malia's scream driving my legs faster.

"Final approach," CJ says. *"Go."*

The only change we made to our initial plans was for Mitzy to wait until we are just outside the wire.

Our boots crush frost-brittle grass as we close the final distance. The concrete walls loom closer, exhaust vents breathing steam into the frozen air.

The Rufi units spread wider, their mechanical joints silent as they maintain our perimeter. Their sensors sweep the darkness, invisible to any watching eyes.

"Stand ready."

The facility looms ahead, its brutal, fortress-like architecture crouched defiantly against the desolate landscape. Steam billows from rooftop vents in a steady rhythm—slow, deliberate—like the measured breath of some slumbering beast poised to wake.

"Mitzy." Ethan's voice carries deadly focus. *"Light it up. Execute. Execute."*

Inside the facility, alarms wail.

THIRTY

Malia

THE NIGHT STRETCHES ENDLESSLY around me as I pretend to sleep, every distant sound making me wonder if this is it—if this is the signal. Beneath the anxiety and uncertainty, beneath the frustration at Mitzy's vague warnings, one thought burns bright enough to warm me despite the facility's perpetual chill: Walt is coming.

Every sound, shadow, and tiny deviation from routine sends my heart racing with false hope. But nothing changes. The facility drones on with mechanical precision—meals at exactly the same time, guard rotations like clockwork, scientists descending into the labs below to work on whatever horror they're building.

Malikai looks worse each time he returns from the underground labs. The radiation burns on his neck have barely healed. His hands shook so badly this morning that he could scarcely hold his spoon at breakfast. When I tried to help, he stared through me, lost in quantum equations I'll never understand.

"We can't keep going like this," Ally whispers during evening recreation. We sit at our usual corner table, pretending to play approved board games while guards patrol the perimeter. "The containment fields are becoming more unstable. Each breach takes more out of them."

I want to scream at her that help is coming. I felt metal legs in my hair and heard Mitzy's voice in my head. But I can't. I can't risk whatever plan is in motion. Can't endanger whatever signal I'm supposed to recognize.

Maybe I imagined the whole thing. Maybe isolation and fear finally cracked something in my mind, making me hallucinate a mechanical bumblebee and the promise of rescue.

The thought haunts me as I lie in bed that night, staring at the ventilation grate where the drone disappeared.

How many more times can Malikai descend into atomic hell before something breaks permanently?

The first hint that something's wrong comes just after midnight. A faint haze drifts from the air vents—too thick to be steam and too white to be smoke. The scent hits me before I fully process what I'm seeing: burning electronics with an undercurrent of something chemical.

Alarms shriek to life, their sudden wail making me jump despite weeks of drills. Red emergency lights strobe against institutional walls as smoke pours from every vent. The sprinkler system engages with a mechanical groan, releasing torrents of water that turn the smoke into a ghostly fog.

"Everyone out!" Guards burst through doors, their usual precision fracturing around the edges. "Move! Move! Move!"

I'm already grabbing my shoes when they reach our quarters. Malikai stumbles from his room, disoriented from whatever nightmares haunt his sleep. The guard's shove sends him reeling, but I catch his arm before he falls.

"Stay together!" The command carries over chaos as other families spill into the corridor. Water drums against concrete, smoke swirls in psychedelic patterns under emergency lights, and machinery screams in mechanical agony somewhere beneath it all.

My fingers find Ally's hand in the confusion, gripping tight enough to hurt. She squeezes back with equal desperation as guards herd us toward the emergency exits. The Williamses appear through the haze like ghosts, then the Chens, their teenage son pressing close to his mother's side.

"Keep moving!" The order is sharp and cold as we are directed through decontamination chambers that haven't been used since the Cold War. Ancient steel doors groan open, letting in the bitter night air that cuts through our soaked clothes.

The quarter moon offers barely enough light to navigate by, but the facility's external floodlights compensate for the lack of light. White beams sweep the perimeter, reflecting off water droplets to create halos in the smoke that still pours from every vent and window.

Is this it?

The signal Mitzy promised?

Every shadow could hide rescue; every strange sound could be the start of something. But all I see are more guards, more guns, and concrete walls closing in.

"Faster!" Petrov's voice carries over the chaos. "Everyone inside! Now!"

The bunker's entrance gapes like a mouth, ready to swallow us into underground darkness. My grip on Malikai and Ally tightens as we're shoved forward. The smoke is thinner out here, but the facility's floodlights paint everything in harsh contrast— too bright, too sharp, too exposed.

The quarter moon hangs like a broken fingernail above us, offering barely enough light to cast strange shadows across the compound. Every sweep of the perimeter lights makes me flinch, waiting for—something.

What was it Mitzy said? *When you get outside, be ready to run.*

Run where?

The steppes stretch endlessly into the darkness beyond the fences—cold, unyielding, and unforgiving. Guards pace with military precision, rifles ready, eyes sharp. Every breath feels like borrowed time. There's no way out—just isolation and the brutal certainty of another underground cage.

A sharp crack splits the air. The facility's lights shudder and die with a mechanical groan, plunging the world into absolute darkness. The hum of electrified fences falls silent, leaving only the ragged sound of my breathing.

A heartbeat of stillness.

Then everything ignites.

Blinding flashes tear through the night as explosions detonate in rapid succession, burning jagged afterimages across my vision. Guards shout in multiple languages, their commands tangled in panic.

Thump-thump-thump. Projectiles arc through the air—not bullets, too deliberate, too controlled. They burst overhead, raining down clouds that reek of scorched metal and sharp peppermint.

Gunfire cracks, muffled and strange, like someone's smothered the rifles with thick cloth. Shadows twist in the flashing light, soldiers scattering as precise strikes tear through their formations.

A metallic whir slices through the chaos, distinct and deliberate. My head jerks toward the sound just as the first RUFI unit bursts from the darkness—sleek, powerful, lethal. Its robotic frame gleams in the flickering light as it leaps, muscles of titanium and hydraulics propelling it forward like a predator unleashed.

Guards spin, weapons snapping up too late. The RUFI collides with the nearest one, sending him sprawling. Another unit surges from the opposite flank, driving two more guards back with a low, resonating hum that sounds almost alive.

More RUFI units follow, fanning out with terrifying precision. They strike like wolves, herding the guards away from us.

Every move is calculated, cold, and unstoppable.

I stand frozen amid the hostages, breath locked in my chest. The guards scatter, their tight formations dissolving into fractured clusters. One tries to regroup, barking desperate commands—but the machines are faster, merciless in their pursuit.

Around me, hostages tremble, pressed together in a terrified huddle. But the RUFI units never come for us. They carve a protective perimeter around us, driving the enemy away—forcing distance between us and the armed chaos erupting beyond.

And for the first time in what feels like forever, I think: We might survive this.

"Get down!" Malikai tries to pull me toward the bunker, but I plant my feet.

No. I'm not going back underground.

Never again.

I catch glimpses of shadows moving with deadly grace through the chaos and smoke. Dark figures flow between guard positions, precise as dancers, lethal as striking snakes. The sounds of combat are oddly muffled, like everything's happening underwater.

"NOW!" The command cuts through the noise—a voice I'd know anywhere. My body responds before my mind fully processes. I yank Malikai and Ally toward the source. Other figures emerge from the smoke—massive shapes that resolve into Ethan and Rigel, covering our retreat with strange weapons that fire clouds of that peppermint-scented gas.

"Run!" Ethan directs us toward a gap in the fence I swear wasn't there seconds ago. "Don't stop! Don't look back!"

I pull Malikai and Ally forward, forcing them to match my pace. I yell at the others to follow.

Behind us, more explosions rock the compound. The smell of gunpowder grows stronger, making my head swim.

"Keep moving!"

The command slices through the chaos, sharp and relentless. Shadows surge through the smoke—figures in tactical gear, helmets concealing their faces, head-up displays glowing faintly in the flickering light. But I know them—not by sight, but by the way they move.

One figure breaks left, fluid and precise, his motion a blend of strength and speed. Blake. No one else moves with such ruthless control, calculated yet explosive. Another charges forward like a battering ram—Rigel, unmistakable in his raw, unyielding power.

Ahead, two more figures flank the hostages with perfect synchronicity, clearing a path through the gunfire. The way they cover each other, an unspoken rhythm born from countless missions—that's Hank and Gabe.

Something kicks up dirt near my feet—real gunfire. My grip tightens around Malikai and Ally's hands as we sprint toward the distant break in the fence. Every step feels like pushing through thick, choking air.

Then, the RUFI units barrel past, relentless and unstoppable. They strike like living nightmares—lethal machines driving the guards away from us, cutting through the chaos with brutal precision.

And then he emerges.

Through the swirling smoke and flickering firelight, Walt materializes like a vengeful ghost—a force forged from war, fierce and unyielding. His every movement is lethal artistry, precise and fluid. He drops two guards, never faltering, never slowing.

My breath locks in my chest. Even masked, even in the madness, it's him. His presence hits like a physical force—unchanged, undeniable.

Through the smoke, through the inferno, through the hell separating us, he finds me.

It isn't his face—I can't see it beneath the matte-black helmet, the polarized visor concealing every feature. It's him. I feel it in the way he moves—unstoppable, lethal, and deliberate.

His head snaps in my direction, his body shifting with electric precision, locked onto me like I'm the only thing in the world that matters. Recognition blazes in the way he freezes for a fraction of a second—a heartbeat stretched thin—before surging toward me with fierce, singular intent.

My knees threaten to give out, my breath catching like I've forgotten how to breathe. Walt.

He moves like a weapon unleashed—swift and unrelenting. Two guards appear in his path, but they never have a chance to raise their weapons. He cuts them down, never breaking stride.

Every step, every breath screams him. No voice, no face, but I know. Deep in my bones. The universe narrows to this moment, suspended on the edge of something too vast to name.

Then his voice cracks through the chaos like a gunshot, sharp and commanding—unmistakable.

"RUN!"

And I run.

THIRTY-ONE

Malia

"THIS WAY!" I grab Malikai's arm, half-dragging him as I turn to the others huddled behind us. "Mrs. Chen! Dr. Williams! Everyone—follow me!" My voice carries over the chaos, stronger than I knew it could be. Months of captivity fall away as survival instinct takes over.

Gunfire erupts from above—sharp cracks of rifle fire cutting through the night. On the roof, dark figures move with military precision. Guardians lay down covering fire, buying us precious seconds to escape. The guards return fire, muzzle flashes painting strobe-light snapshots of the battle.

"Kevin, stay close to your mother!" I shout as Mrs. Chen and her teenage son sprint past, their gray uniforms ghostly in the darkness. The Williamses follow, Helen stumbling until her husband catches her arm. Dr. Rodriguez shepherds Maria ahead of him, while Dr. Whittman assists Dr. Chen, making sure no one falls behind.

Malikai stumbles beside me, his breath coming in ragged gasps. Ally appears on his other side, helping me support his weight as we run.

"Contact rear!" someone shouts behind us, their voice sharp and urgent. The sharp bark of automatic weapons cuts through the frigid night as Charlie team engages, holding back the pursuing guards.

The thin quarter moon casts a faint, silvery glow over the desolate Kazakh steppes, barely piercing the choking clouds of steam rising from the facility's vent shafts. The vapor rolls across the ground like something alive, twisting in the icy wind.

The bitter cold bites through our thin uniforms, searing exposed skin with each gust. Every breath sends clouds of white vapor spilling from our mouths as we run, desperate and breathless.

Then I feel it—a deep vibration thrumming beneath our feet, faint at first but growing stronger with every step. It's not just movement—it's alive, like some massive beast stirring underground, restless and waiting.

The earth beneath us seems to pulse, wrong and unnatural, as though the facility itself is awakening—and whatever's coming next is far worse than the guards at our backs.

"The quantum cascade," Malikai gasps between steps. "If the fields collapse—"

"Less physics, more running!" Ally cuts him off, adjusting her grip on his arm.

The RUFI appear from the darkness like mechanical ghosts, their articulated legs carrying them easily over the rough ground. The robotic dogs take up flanking positions, weapon mounts ready but invisible in the darkness. Their presence is both reassuring and unsettling—machines that move like living things.

The ground shudders again, a deep resonance that makes my teeth ache.

More guards pour through the steam and chaos, but Guardian operators are there to meet them. The sound of close-quarters combat echoes off concrete walls—the meaty thud of hand-to-hand fighting mixed with sporadic gunfire.

"Keep moving!" Walt's voice carries over the chaos. He appears beside us again, rifle firing in controlled bursts at pursuers I can't see. "The extraction point is two klicks east!"

Two kilometers across the open steppe?

With no cover, no concealment, nowhere to hide if they catch us?

Just darkness and the bitter wind whipping across the grasslands. The stars wheel overhead, shockingly bright after months of artificial light, their cold light offering little comfort.

"Maria!" I call out as the young girl stumbles. "Stay with the group!" She regains her feet, her father's hand tight on her arm as they run. The Williamses help her up, all of us moving together now. Months of shared captivity have made us family—no one gets left behind.

Malikai's legs give out completely. Ally and I struggle to keep him upright, but he's dead weight between us. My muscles scream in protest—months of limited exercise in captivity haven't prepared me for this. Then Walt is there, slinging his rifle and taking Malikai's weight from us.

"I've got him," he says, easily supporting my brother's larger frame. "Keep moving!"

I want to stop. I want to touch Walt. I want to verify he's real and not another dream. The last time I saw him, he was bleeding out on American concrete. Now he's here, solid and alive, helping my brother run to freedom.

But there's no time for a reunion. No time for anything but survival.

The RUFI units spread out behind us, forming a defensive line between us and our pursuers. Their mechanical forms blend into the darkness as they set up firing positions, buying time for the Guardian teams to extract.

The perimeter fence looms ahead—three layers of razor wire illuminated by failing security lights. But sections have been breached with surgical precision, creating corridors of escape. We push through the gaps, the cold metal snagging at our clothes.

The ground pulses again, stronger now. The air itself feels wrong, charged with impossible energies. Each breath tastes like metal and ozone.

"The quantum tunneling effect is cascading," Malikai gasps as Walt half-carries him through the fence. "The reaction—"

"Not our problem anymore," Walt cuts him off. "Everyone through the fence! Move!"

We emerge onto the open steppe. The wind cuts through our thin uniforms like knives, but the cold is almost welcome after the facility's sterile warmth. It tastes like freedom.

Charlie team provides covering fire as more Guardians emerge—Alpha, Bravo, and Delta teams leap-frogging back in practiced retreat—thirty-five people running for our lives across the frozen steppe.

Kevin Chen practically carries his mother now; the Williamses support each other, and Maria and her father run hand-in-hand. Dr. Whittman brings up the rear with Dr. Chen.

We're running on pure adrenaline.

"Wait!" Malikai tries to turn back, his face ghostly in the facility's pulsing light. "The containment fields—I can still stabilize them! If they collapse—"

"No time!" Walt's grip tightens on my brother's arm. "That cascade effect is exponential now. Nothing can stop it."

The truth hits like a physical blow—we can run until our lungs shred and our bodies collapse, but there's no outrunning this. If those containment fields fail … If quantum tunneling triggers an uncontrolled reaction …

The world itself will end here.

For one horrifying second, I see it—an unstoppable chain reaction ripping free, consuming everything. The frozen steppes igniting in a cataclysmic flash. Earth, air, us—all of it obliterated, burned away until nothing remains but searing light and endless fire.

No escape. No survival. Just obliteration

The ground thrums beneath our feet, the deep vibration rising, relentless and merciless—counting down to something far worse than death.

We can't stop it.

We can't survive it.

But still—we run.

"We need more distance!" Walt shouts over the growing mechanical howl from the facility. "Don't stop! Keep moving!"

Then I hear it—the growl of powerful engines approaching fast. Headlights cut through darkness as vehicles converge on our position. A massive deuce-and-a-half military truck leads the convoy, followed by Jeeps and armored SUVs bouncing over the frozen terrain.

"Load up!" To my surprise, Mitzy's at the wheel. Her voice cuts through the chaos—sharp and commanding, if a bit high-pitched.

The vehicles screech to a halt around us. Rear doors fly open, tailgates drop. No time for organized loading—we pile in wherever there's space. The Williamses practically throw Maria and her father into an SUV before climbing in after them. Mrs. Chen and Kevin squeeze in beside them, the vehicle's suspension groaning under the weight.

"Move, move!" Guardians help Dr. Chen and Dr. Whittman into another vehicle. More Guardian teams emerge from the darkness, some bleeding, all running full-tilt toward the convoy.

Walt half-carries Malikai toward the deuce-and-a-half. "In! Everyone in!"

We scramble into the truck's cargo bed, helping others after us. The metal deck vibrates beneath us as more people pile in.

No time for comfort or organization. Just survival.

The Rufi units maintain their defensive line, buying precious seconds for the evacuation. Then, as the last Guardians reach the vehicles, the robotic dogs move.

They leap through the air with impossible grace, mechanical legs propelling them in perfect arcs. One by one, they land in the deuce's cargo bed, metal paws finding purchase on the deck.

"That's everyone!" someone shouts. "Go, go, go!"

The convoy lurches into motion, engines roaring as drivers push their vehicles to maximum speed. The facility recedes behind us, but its otherworldly glow only intensifies.

"We'll never outrun it," Malikai's voice carries raw desperation. "The reaction radius—"

"How far?" Walt demands, his arm tight around me as another bump jolts us.

"Ten miles minimum. Maybe more. I don't know—we never tested—"

"Faster!" Mitzy's voice crackles through the radio. "That reaction's going critical!"

Ten minutes to cover ten miles. Ten minutes before whatever's happening in those labs consumes everything within range.

The trucks' engines scream as the drivers push their vehicles. Sixty, seventy miles per hour over terrain that threatens to shake us apart. The other vehicles keep pace, their headlights cutting through the darkness as we race against physics itself.

Behind us, the facility's glow paints the steppe in impossible colors. The quantum cascade builds like a wave about to break.

The convoy races across the steppe, each vehicle pushing its limits across the broken terrain. In the deuce's cargo bed, we cling to whatever we can grab—sides, benches, each other—as the truck bounces over frozen ground. My hands grip cold metal, knuckles white, while Walt's arm anchors me against his side.

Through the billowing dust of our passage, a deeper darkness rises against the stars—the mountains, our only hope of shelter from what's coming. The vehicles spread out, giving each other room to maneuver as we eat up the distance. Five miles. Six. Seven.

The ground trembles beneath our wheels, each vibration stronger than the last. The quantum cascade is building, reality itself beginning to unravel behind us. Malikai's face is ghost white in the strange light, his eyes fixed on the growing anomaly we're fleeing.

Eight miles. The mountain range looms closer, black against the star-filled sky. Our convoy hooks right, the drivers somehow keeping formation as we race around a massive outcropping. The trucks and SUVs bounce violently as we hit rougher ground, suspension systems screaming in protest.

Nine miles. We curve around the mountain's bulk, placing it between us and the facility. The facility disappears behind the ridge, and we continue to race over the rugged ground.

Ten miles becomes eleven. Eleven becomes twelve.

For one heartbeat, everything stops—sound, motion, even the air itself seems to freeze.

The night explodes.

A wall of pure energy erupts from where the facility stood, a tidal wave of raw power that paints the clouds in colors human eyes were never meant to process. Even behind the mountain's shelter, the light bleeds around the edges of our rocky shield— like staring into the heart of creation itself.

Seconds later, the shock wave slams into the mountain. The massive ridge absorbs the full force of the blast, its ancient bulk becoming our salvation. Quantum energy crashes against stone, the mountain's mass deflecting that impossible fury upward into the atmosphere. Our vehicles rock as the ground trembles, but the ridge splits the destructive force like a blade through water. The diverted energy shoots skyward, carrying energy high into the stratosphere.

For one blinding millisecond, day blooms in the Kazakhstan night—brighter than noon, brighter than the sun itself. Then darkness crashes back as the quantum cascade burns itself out, leaving only afterimages dancing across our vision and the mountain's steadfast bulk shielding us from where the facility used to be.

Before I can move, Walt reaches up, his gloved fingers finding the release latches beneath his helmet. A sharp twist, a hiss of decompressing seals, and he yanks the helmet off, letting it drop with a dull thud.

His face—rugged, fierce, alive—fills my world. His skin is warm beneath my trembling fingertips, not the cold, blood-stained memory that's haunted me for months. Harsh lines of exhaustion carve deep into his features, but his dark eyes blaze with fierce relief, burning through the lingering shadows of fear.

"I told you I'd find you," he rasps, voice raw, his hand lifting to cup my face—rough, familiar, real.

Something inside me shatters. I crash into him, my hands framing his face as I press my lips to his, desperate, wild, claiming him. Every ounce of longing, fear, and hope I've held back surges into that kiss, fierce and consuming.

His arms crush me against him as I crawl into his lap, fingers tangling in his tactical vest, holding on like he might disappear. His hands dive into my hair, anchoring me just as fiercely—as though he's the one afraid of losing me.

All I feel is Walt's heartbeat pounding beneath my palm.

All I taste is his kiss—warm, real, unmistakably his.

He came for me—rescued me—and nothing else matters.

The mountain trembles while Walt and I reconnect in the back of a military truck, surrounded by hostages, Guardians, robotic dogs, and my brother.

And I don't care.

THIRTY-TWO

Walt

IN THE BACK of the truck, Malia's lips find mine with desperate intensity. I pull her close, needing her pressed against me. Her tears dampen my cheeks as we kiss—relief, fear, and joy all mingling together. My hands tremble as I cup her face, still hardly believing she's here, she's safe, she's in my arms.

"I knew you'd come," she whispers against my mouth. "I never stopped believing."

The convoy rumbles around the mountain, returning to our mining camp staging area. Malia stays curled against my side, her fingers tangled in my tactical vest as if afraid I'll disappear. I keep one arm around her, my other hand resting on my weapon—old habits die hard.

Across from us, Hank and Gabe position themselves to either side of Ally. The blonde physicist seems shell-shocked, but something in her posture eases as they bracket her with their protective presence. Hank murmurs something that makes her lips twitch in an almost-smile while Gabe's hand rests casually on her shoulder, steadying her against the truck's motion.

The mining facility comes into view as our convoy crests the final ridge. Rufi units bound out to secure the perimeter, their robotic movements eerily graceful against the harsh landscape. I help Malia from the truck, my hands lingering on her waist. Around us, other Guardians assist the hostages, offering steady hands and quiet reassurance. Chen helps his wife while Rodriguez sweeps his daughter into a fierce hug.

The mining camp transforms into a processing center as we debrief the rescued hostages. Medical teams check everyone over while intelligence officers gather preliminary statements. Malia gets pulled away for her medical exam, but her eyes find mine across the Command tent. The moment she's cleared, she's back in my arms, her mouth seeking mine with renewed desperation.

She tugs me outside into the biting Kazakhstan wind. Her kisses turn hungry and demanding. When her hands slip beneath my shirt, I catch her wrists.

"Not here," I murmur against her lips. "Not like this. Your first time deserves better than a frozen mining camp in Kazakhstan."

"I don't care where," she breathes. "I just want you."

"Soon." I press my forehead to hers. "I promise. But I'm going to make it perfect."

Inside, the scientists gather for debriefing. Malikai's voice carries an edge of warning as he discusses the technology they were forced to develop.

"The power was too unstable, too dangerous," he explains. "If it had worked … If someone weaponized it—entire cities could have been erased from existence."

"The quantum cascade effect destroyed everything," Chen adds, relief evident in his tone. "All our research, all our break-throughs—gone. And thank God for that. The world isn't ready for that kind of power."

"Perhaps some discoveries aren't meant to be made yet." Dr.

Whittman pulls Ally to his side. He looks down on her with fatherly love. "The world isn't ready for that kind of power."

I keep catching glimpses of Gabe and Hank with Ally throughout the evacuation process. The way they move in sync to keep her sheltered from chaos, how naturally they include her in their usual banter. Something is building there—subtle but unmistakable. When she stumbles from exhaustion, they're both there instantly, supporting her between them.

The camp dismantles with military precision. Equipment disappears into unmarked trucks, evidence of our presence erased as thoroughly as the quantum research. Soon, nothing remains but tire tracks in the frozen ground as our convoy heads toward the airstrip where Guardian HRS's 747 awaits.

The loading process is efficient, and everyone is eager to leave this place behind. I help Malia up the stairs, unable to resist stealing another kiss once we reach the top.

"Get a room," Rigel calls out, but his grin is wide as he passes us.

The flight home feels surreal after so much tension and planning. The cabin is filled with quiet conversation and occasional laughter as the adrenaline crash hits.

Our medical team directs the rescued hostages to the onboard facilities—private bathrooms with showers and clean clothes waiting for them. Throughout the long flight home, they emerge transformed, prison grays replaced with civilian comfort.

I catch Ally disappearing into the showers, with Hank and Gabe following close behind.

Malia dozes against my shoulder, her hand resting over my heart as if reassuring herself it still beats. I kiss her hair occasionally, breathing in her scent, still amazed that she's here.

Malia showers last. She tugs at my hand, her smile soft but insistent, her fingers curling around mine as if she can pull me along by sheer will.

She tilts her head toward the narrow corridor leading to the showers, her cheeks flushed with exhaustion and something else —something raw, unspoken, that latches onto my chest and squeezes.

"Come on," she whispers, her voice husky and low, meant just for me. Her eyes meet mine, wide and trusting, and that's what does it—the trust.

"Malia," I say, my voice rougher than I would like. I lace my fingers with hers, squeezing just enough to keep her tethered to me but not enough to follow her. Her lips part, her brows knitting together in confusion. "You need to go …" I keep my voice steady even as the words catch in my throat. "Alone."

"Why?"

I exhale hard through my nose, running a hand over my jaw. "Because if I follow you in there …" My voice cuts off. I can't say it. Can't give her the weight of that truth, not here, not now.

Her head tilts, her lips pressing into a determined line as she waits, silent but expectant.

I close the space between us, my hands finding her face. Her skin is soft under my calloused palms, her pulse thrumming under my thumb. I press my forehead to hers, letting the steady rhythm of her breaths ground me.

"If I go in there," I murmur against her skin. "I won't be able to stop. You deserve more than this," I say, my voice rasping. "Not here. Not rushed. Not with your brother sitting ten feet away." I brush my thumb over her cheek, my heart thundering. "When it happens, it'll be right. Perfect."

"It'll be now, and it will still be perfect." Her lips tremble, her lashes lowering as her gaze falls. She leans into my touch for a brief second before stepping back. "Don't say no."

THIRTY-THREE

Walt

I TAKE A DEEP BREATH, unmoving, as a war rages inside me. Her trust is a precious gift, one I don't take lightly. I want this—God, I want this—but I need to be sure she's ready.

Slowly, I lift my gaze to meet Malia's. The trust in her eyes sends a shiver down my spine. "Malia," I start, my voice rough with emotion. "Are you sure about this?"

She steps closer, her body nearly pressing against mine. Her hand resting on my chest, her eyes never leaving mine. "I've never been more sure of anything. I want this. I want you." Her face lights up with a radiant smile. She tugs on my hand again, and this time, I follow her, my boots heavy on the floor.

Unable to resist, I cup her face, my thumbs stroking her cheeks. The gentle touch sends electricity zinging through me. Her sweet, inviting scent envelops me as I savor her closeness. Her eyes flutter shut as I caress her skin, a soft sigh escaping her lips.

"I want to memorize every inch of you," I murmur, my voice low and reverent. "I want to worship you like you deserve."

Malia's pupils dilate, blown wide with desire. She turns on the water, testing it until it's just right. It doesn't take long before steam fills the small space.

Malia's hand slides from mine, her eyes locked onto mine, a silent conversation passing between us. She steps out of her shoes, her feet bare on the cool tile floor. I mirror her actions, my socks whispering softly as they meet the floor.

I turn her toward me, my hands cradling her face as if it were the most delicate thing in the world. I can feel the heat of her skin under my palms, the slight tremble of anticipation. Her breath is soft and warm, feathering against my lips as I lean in. Our lips meet in a slow, tender kiss. It's a soft exploration, a whispered promise. Her arms wrap around my neck, her fingers toying with the hair at my nape, sending shivers down my spine.

The kiss deepens, our breaths mingling, our hearts synchronizing. My tongue explores her mouth languidly, savoring her taste. It's like honey and sunshine, warmth and sweetness. I trail kisses down her jaw, her skin soft against my lips.

As my lips brush against her neck, her pulse flutters beneath my touch. Her breath catches, and the soft gasp that escapes her lips is a melody that sends a shiver down my spine, my body responding to hers like a finely tuned instrument.

The warmth of her skin, the taste of her, the sound of her breath, every sensation envelops me, drawing me in, inviting me to explore further.

I pull back slightly, my hands finding the hem of her shirt. I raise it slowly, my fingers brushing against her soft skin, my eyes never leaving hers. I want her to feel cherished, respected, loved. She raises her arms, allowing me to slip the shirt off. It floats to the floor, forgotten. Her skin is bare before me, her cheeks painted with a soft blush, her breath coming in gentle waves.

"Is this what you want?" I whisper, my voice low and husky. I want to hear her say it, to know that she's sure.

Her eyes meet mine, no hesitation, no doubt. "Yes," she breathes, her lips parting slightly. "I'm ready."

I reach behind her, my fingers finding the clasp of her bra. I unhook it slowly, feeling her breath hitch again. The straps slide down her arms, the fabric falling to the floor. I take a moment to appreciate her, to admire the curve of her shoulders, the sweep of her collarbone, the rise and fall of her chest. She's not just beautiful, she's radiant, her skin glowing under the soft light, her eyes shining with trust and desire.

I trace a line from her shoulder to her elbow with the back of my fingers, enjoying the silky smoothness of her skin. Her breaths come in quick, shallow bursts, her chest rising and falling rapidly. Goosebumps bloom across her flesh, a delicate pattern emerging beneath my gaze, tracing the path my fingers had taken moments before.

The cool air meets the warmth of her skin, creating a dance of sensation that prickles and teases. The soft hiss of her breath, as it slips between her lips, stirs something primal within me, a longing to both protect and possess.

Her body's responses, so immediate and honest, fuel my desire to explore every inch of her, to learn the language of her body and speak it fluently. The flush of her skin, the hitch of her breath, the shiver that runs through her—each is a whisper of her need, a secret shared between the two of us in this intimate dance.

I lean in, my lips replacing my fingers, trailing soft kisses down her arm. I want to take my time, explore every inch of her, and make her feel as cherished as she makes me feel.

The steam from the shower envelops us, a warm, damp embrace that heightens every sensation. The world outside fades away, leaving just the two of us lost in a private dance of intimacy and tenderness.

I turn my attention to my shirt, grasping the hem and pulling it over my head in one fluid motion. My muscles stretch and flex, and I hear the soft hitch of her breath as she watches me. The shirt joins the growing pile of discarded clothing, fluttering to the floor beside her bra. Her eyes trace the lines of my chest, pausing on the ink that marks my skin. I stand still, allowing her gaze to roam, enjoying the heat that trails after it.

Tentatively, she reaches out, her fingertips featherlight as they brush against my skin. She traces the curves of my chest, pausing at the puckered skin of my healing scars. Her touch is gentle and reverent as if she's aware of the pain lingering beneath the surface. Each touch is a spark, igniting a slow burn beneath my skin, a mix of pleasure and emotion that catches in my throat.

Her fingers drift lower, mapping the dips and valleys of my abdomen. Each muscle twitches slightly under her touch, my body responding to her exploration. I watch her, entranced by the expressions flitting across her face.

There's curiosity in her eyes, wonder in the soft "O" of her lips, desire in the flush of her cheeks. Her brows furrow slightly as she concentrates as if she's trying to memorize every line and contour.

She looks up at me, her heavy gaze meeting mine. There's a question there, a silent ask for permission to touch, explore, and know my body intimately. I nod slightly, encouraging her, inviting her to learn my body as I intend to learn hers.

Her fingers continue their journey, tracing the line of hair that disappears beneath the waistband of my jeans, then retracing the path upward.

My breath deepens, my lungs filling with the steamy air, the scent of her, the scent of us. Her touch is more than a physical sensation, it's a conversation, a connection.

It speaks of trust and intimacy, of shared pain and expectant pleasure. I let her explore, learn me, and heal me with her touch.

And in her eyes, I see a reflection of my desire, my need, and my love.

Stepping closer, my hands find the waistband of her pants. I pause, looking into her eyes. There's a soft glow there, a mix of anticipation and trust. I want to drown in that look, to wrap it around me like a blanket. She nods, her lips parting slightly, a silent invitation.

I slowly slide her pants down, revealing more of her to me. Dropping to one knee, I hook my thumbs in the waistband, easing the fabric down her legs. She steps out of them, her hands resting lightly on my shoulders for support.

Kneeling before her, I look up. She stands before me, clad only in her underwear, her body a landscape of soft curves and smooth skin. A rosy flush spreads across her chest, creeping up her neck, a visible sign of her desire and nervousness.

I want to replace that nervousness with warmth, with pleasure, and with a love so profound it chases away every shadow.

I press a soft kiss to her hip, feeling her shiver beneath my lips. Her skin is warm and soft, inviting my touch. I trace a path with my fingertips, following the curve of her waist, the flare of her hip, and the length of her thigh. Each touch is a conversation, a give and take, a call and response. Her breathing steadies, her body leaning into my touch, her nerves slowly giving way to pleasure.

I take her hand, pressing a kiss to her palm. Her fingers curl around mine, holding on tightly.

My lips brush against her stomach, a gentle caress that makes her muscles quiver and dance beneath my touch. I hook my fingers in the waistband of her underwear, pausing to look up at her. Her eyes are twin pools of trust and desire, a silent granting of permission.

I slide the fabric down, her body revealing itself to me inch by inch. As I rise, I pause, inhaling deeply. Her scent, warm and intoxicating, fills my lungs, a heady aroma that makes my mouth water and my heart pound. It's a primal, intimate thing, her smell; I'm drawn to it and captivated by it.

My lips nearly brush against her thighs, the urge to taste her overwhelming. I want to bury my face between her legs, to lick and suck, to lose myself in her, but I hold back, my breath ragged with the effort of restraint.

I don't want to rush this, don't want to scare her or move too fast. I want to savor every moment, every sensation, every breath. I want to memorize her body, learn its language, and understand her needs.

Continuing my ascent, I press against her, my body aligning with hers. Her breath hitches as she feels my arousal, my body hard and ready, yearning for her. I want her to understand what she does to me, to feel the depth of my need.

Her scent still fills my senses, a constant reminder of the pleasure that awaits us, the intimacy we'll share, the love we'll make. For now, however, I'm content to explore her, learn her, and let our connection deepen and grow.

My lips find hers again, our kiss a slow, sensual exploration. My hands roam her body, learning her curves, her secrets, as if they're a language only my touch can decipher.

She presses against me, her hands dropping to my belt. She looks up, a silent question in her eyes. I nod, a soft smile playing on my lips, granting her the permission she seeks. Her hands tremble slightly as she unbuckles my belt, the metal clanking softly as it gives way. She unfastens my pants, the zipper hissing as she slides it down.

Kneeling, she pushes my pants down my legs, her hands trailing after, feeling the muscles of my thighs, the coarse hair of my legs. I step out of them, the fabric a puddle at my feet. My breath is ragged, my body aching with need and anticipation.

"This is your doing," I whisper, my voice rough with emotion. "This is what you awaken in me."

Her eyes widen, wonder and desire warring in their depths. She tugs at my briefs, pulling them down my legs, her knuckles brushing against my skin. I'm laid bare before her, vulnerable, exposed, every inch of me yearning for her touch.

Her breath is warm against my skin, her cheeks flushed, her lips parted. The steam from the shower envelops us, creating a world where only the two of us exist.

I reach down, pulling her to her feet. I kiss her deeply, my body pressed against hers, our skin touching from chest to toe.

I guide her under the spray of the shower, the warm water cascading over us like a tropical rain. Steam billows around us, creating a cocoon of heat and intimacy. I want to wash away her doubts, her fears, and her inhibitions, leaving only the two of us. I take a moment to appreciate the sight of her, the water flowing over her body, her breasts heaving with each breath.

She reaches out, her delicate fingers wrapping around my length with a featherlight touch, a tentative exploration that sends a jolt through my body. A shiver runs through me, and my breath hitches, a low rumble building in my chest, a primal response to her touch. My head falls back, a low groan rumbling from deep within my chest, unbidden and uncontrolled. It's the sound of a need so profound it steals my breath away.

It's a raw, intimate moment.

I rein in my passion. More than anything, I wish to turn her hands away, to kiss every inch of her instead, and show her delight slowly. To guide her through a journey of sensations without rushing, without surrendering to the fire that threatens to consume me.

Her touch is more than just a physical sensation. It's an emotional connection, a silent whisper of trust and intimacy. It fuels my desire to make this moment unforgettable for her, to take my time, to explore her, to pleasure her.

I gather her in my arms. Her body soft and yielding against mine. Her heart beats steady and strong, a rhythm that calls to me and grounds me. Our lips meet in a languid kiss, a tender melding of mouths that speaks volumes without a word. It's a kiss that starts slow, a gentle brush of lips that evolves into something deeper, more profound.

Her breath hitches as she kisses me back, her body melting into mine. Her heartbeat quickens, matching mine beat for beat. Our connection is palpable, a silent language that only the two of us understand, a dance of love and desire that's uniquely ours. We luxuriate in the intimacy of our kiss, the joy of our closeness, and the promise of more.

Malia's hands glide up my chest, her fingers curling around my shoulders as she draws me deeper into the kiss. Our tongues entwine in a languid dance, the water cascading around us like a sacred rite, cleansing and pure. Her trust in me is explicit, a silent offering that humbles me.

I turn her gently, my hands resting lightly on her shoulders. Water streams down her hair, darkening it, and I follow the path with my fingertips, massaging her scalp in slow, tender circles. She sighs, her body relaxing under my touch, her eyes fluttering closed.

Emboldened, I explore further, my fingers tracing the curves of her neck, the lines of her shoulders, the expanse of her back. I press kisses to her nape, my lips lingering on her soft skin, leaving gentle impressions of my devotion. She turns to face me, her eyes still closed, a soft smile playing on her lips. I capture her mouth in another kiss, this one more insistent, more fervent. Her body arches into mine, a low moan rumbling in her throat. My hand slides down her stomach, my fingers curling around her hip, anchoring her to me.

"Let me take care of you," I murmur, pulling back slightly, my gaze locked on hers. The words are a promise, a vow to cherish and honor her.

Taking the soap, I lather it in my hands, working up a rich foam. My touch is soft and reverent. I start at her shoulders, my hands sliding down her arms, her back, her stomach, washing away the day's worries, the past's hurts. Her eyes follow my movements, dark with desire and wonder.

Kneeling before her, I wash her legs, my hands running down her calves, her ankles, and her feet. She steadies herself on my shoulders as I lift each foot, my thumbs circling her insteps, my fingers cleaning between her toes. I look up at her, water flowing over her body, her eyes filled with such profound emotion it steals my breath away.

As I rise, she leans into my touch, a soft, languid sound unfurling from her lips, a melody of pleasure and anticipation. My hands, guided by instinct and adoration, cup her breasts, learning their weight, their shape, their sensitivity. Her breath quickens, and my touch becomes leisurely, my fingers stroking and tracing the ever-hardening peaks, feeling sensations ripple through her, which set my heart racing.

Her back arches, a silent invitation, a surrender to the dance of give and take. My lips drift from hers, tracing a path down her neck, her throat, her chest. I pause at her breast, taking her nipple into my mouth, the feel of it against my tongue a sensual jolt. She responds with a moan, her fingers digging into my shoulders, anchoring herself to me.

My hands roam her body, tracing each curve, each contour, a slow, sensual journey of discovery. Her skin is soft and smooth, her muscles quivering beneath my touch. Her breath catches, her body trembling, a symphony of pleasure building within her, rising toward a joyous crescendo. Time slows down, each moment stretching, expanding, filling with love and light. I savor each second, each sensation, each shared breath.

Reluctantly, I break the kiss, my eyes meeting hers. I slide my fingers lower, gently exploring her most intimate place. I part her folds, my fingers finding her center, circling it softly, tenderly. She moans, her body trembling.

I slide one finger into her, then another, my thumb continuing its gentle rhythm. Her eyes widen, her breath hitching, her body responding, hips moving in sync with my hand. It's a dance, a rhythm, a song that only the two of us can hear, can feel. Each movement is a testament to our connection; each gasp a whisper of love and desire.

"Walt …" Her eyes flutter open, her gaze finding mine as my fingers delve into her secrets. Her head falls back, eyes drifting closed, a surrender to the sensation building within her. I lean in, my lips pressing tender kisses to her neck, my fingers never ceasing their delicate dance.

Her body tenses, a bowstring drawn taut, her inner muscles fluttering around my fingers. She's on the precipice, a moment away from flight. I intensify my touch, my fingers moving with more urgency, my thumb circling her sensitive bud with increased fervor.

Driven by a need to bring her to the height of pleasure and guided by her soft whispers, I drop to my knees. I press kisses to her stomach, her hips, her thighs, each touch reverent, a silent worship of her body, her essence. I look up at her, our eyes meeting, a silent communication passing between us. Hers are filled with desire and trust, a mix that sends a wave of emotion crashing through me.

I lean in, my tongue finding her center, an intimate kiss that makes her grip my hair tightly. But it's my fingers that dance with her, that draw out her pleasure, that send her soaring. I take my time, learning, discovering what makes her gasp, what makes her moan, what makes her body tremble.

Her breath hitches, her body tensing, her muscles coiling in anticipation. I want to witness her face as she surrenders to her release. Her eyes meet mine, a profound connection that steals my breath away.

Then, she's soaring, her body convulsing around my fingers. Instead of the taste of her, I drink in the sight of her release, the cry of completion that rings in the small steamy cubicle, the beauty of her face as she falls apart and comes back together again. It's a melody that fills the small space, a sacred and intimate expression of surrender.

Her body trembles as she rides the waves of her climax. As the tension melts away she wilts into my arms, spent, her body leaning heavily against my steadying frame. I rise, wrapping my arms around her, a shield, a sanctuary, holding her until the last ripples of her orgasm subside.

I gently stroke her back and hips. Her breath slowly returns to normal, her body relaxing, going limp against mine.

"You okay?" I ask, my voice barely above a whisper.

Malia nods, her eyes still glazed with pleasure. "Yeah," she whispers. "I'm more than okay."

"I love you," I murmur, my voice husky with the weight of my emotions. Her eyes fill with soft tears. "I want to know every inch of you." I underscore every word I speak with my kiss.

THIRTY-FOUR

Walt

MALIA TILTS HER HEAD BACK, her gaze meeting mine, desire pooling in her eyes. She reaches between us, her fingers wrapping around my length, her touch both tentative and eager. A low groan resonates from deep within my chest, my head falling back, my body instinctively pressing into her hand. Her touch is a spark, a live wire, setting my body alight with need and longing.

She explores me, her strokes measured, her eyes locked on mine, gauging my reactions. My name is a whisper on her lips, a secret song.

"Malia," I breathe, my voice hoarse with desire. Her grip tightens, her rhythm steadying, a dance of give and take, a silent conversation between our bodies.

I guide her, my hand covering hers, showing her the rhythm and pressure that brings me the most pleasure. She's a quick study, her confidence growing with each stroke, her touch becoming more sure, more insistent.

She kisses my chest tenderly, her lips lingering before she sinks to her knees. Her eyes sparkle with mischief and desire, a combination that sends a wave of anticipation crashing through me.

Water cascades down her hair, her face, as she takes me into her mouth.

The warmth and wetness of her mouth envelop me, a sensation so intense it sends a jolt through my body. She starts tentatively, her tongue exploring, her lips wrapping around me. I sense her nervousness, eagerness, desire to please and learn.

I guide her gently, my hand in her hair, fingers gently tightening and releasing, a silent encouragement, a steady rhythm.

"That's it, love," I murmur, my voice husky with desire and emotion. "Nice and slow."

She looks up at me, her eyes wide and trusting, seeking approval, her mouth stretched around me. The sight of her on her knees, looking up at me with those big, beautiful eyes, is almost more than I can bear. But I hold back, reining in my desire, wanting to savor this moment, this connection.

She takes more of me into her mouth, her head bobbing up and down, her hand wrapping around the base of my shaft. She's learning quickly, her confidence growing with each stroke.

I let out a ragged sigh, "Ah, Malia. Just like that, love."

She senses my restraint and pulls back slightly, looking up at me with a question in her eyes. I smile down at her, brushing a wet strand of hair away from her face, my touch tender, my eyes filled with love and reassurance.

"You're doing amazing, love," I assure her, my voice soft. "But let's slow down. I want to enjoy this, enjoy you. I want to savor you."

She nods, her eyes filling with understanding and a newfound confidence. She slows her pace, her tongue swirling around my head, her lips sucking gently.

I groan, my body trembling with the effort of holding back, but I do it, for her. I want her to feel good about this, about us. I want her to know that she's in control.

I drink in her face, the truth of her feelings shining in her eyes, a beacon guiding me to let go. Tension grips my body as my fingers tangle in her hair. My breath hitches, muscles coiling tight as sensation builds, a gathering storm at the base of my spine.

"Malia," I groan, her name on my lips a symphony of surrender and adoration. She looks up at me, eyes wide and eager, her mouth a sanctuary of exquisite pleasure.

The sensation swells, threatening to overwhelm me. Every nerve is a live wire, every muscle taut, poised on the precipice. My grip on her hair tightens, my hips moving instinctively as I chart our course to the release we both crave.

"I'm close," I whisper, my voice hoarse with pent-up passion. She doesn't waver, her mouth and hand moving in perfect harmony, driving me closer to the edge.

And then, with a final, deep thrust, I shatter. A low, primal sound escapes my lips, a raw, unfiltered expression of my climax. Waves of pleasure crash over me, and she takes everything I give her, her hand gripping me tightly, guiding me through the storm.

My body convulses, hips jerking as I surrender to the intensity of my release. She meets my passion with her own, her throat working as she swallows, her mouth never ceasing its rhythmic embrace.

The pleasure is all-consuming, a blaze of sensation that leaves no part of me untouched. I groan, my body shuddering as the last waves of my orgasm ebb away.

As I drift back to reality, I gently draw her to her feet, wrapping my arms around her and holding her close. My body is still trembling slightly, my breath coming in quick gasps. I press a tender kiss to her forehead, my voice filled with gratitude and awe.

"That was—incredible," I murmur, my heart still pounding in my chest. I can feel her smile against my skin, her body soft and pliant in my arms.

In this moment, she is my world, my universe, and my everything.

And I'm utterly, completely hers.

She tilts her head back, her eyes dancing with curiosity and a hint of mischief. "Was that okay?" she asks, a playful smile gracing her lips.

A warm chuckle rumbles deep in my chest, my heart still pounding with residual pleasure. "Incredible," I murmur, pressing a soft kiss to her forehead, a surge of affection and amusement washing over me. "You are incredible."

Her grin widens, her eyes sparkling with pleasure and satisfaction. "I'm glad," she whispers, her voice laced with mischief and delight. "Because I plan on doing it again."

Laughter bubbles up from within me, a sound filled with happiness and contentment. In this moment, with Malia in my arms, I am exactly where I am meant to be. Our connection is a tangible force that wraps around us, binding us together.

Her expression turns thoughtful, her fingers tracing patterns on my chest. "You know," she says, her voice soft but steady, "technically, I'm still a virgin."

I smile, pressing a tender kiss to her lips, feeling her melt into me. "My love, we've shared so much already. When we come together fully, it will be special, unhurried. Not here, not like this." I gesture vaguely to the shower cubicle, my voice filled with promise. "It will be somewhere comfortable, somewhere meaningful."

She nods, her eyes filled with trust and understanding. "I like that plan," she whispers, her voice tinged with anticipation. A shy smile plays on her lips as she looks up at me. "Can I ask you something?"

I brush a wet strand of hair away from her face, tucking it behind her ear, my touch gentle, reverent. "Of course, anything."

She takes a deep breath, her cheeks flushing slightly. "When you … When we … Will you be all growly and bossy?" she asks, her eyes casting down shyly, her voice barely above a whisper.

I raise an eyebrow, a playful smile tugging at my lips. "Growly and bossy?" I ask, intrigued by her request.

She blushes even more, her eyes meeting mine before flitting away again. "You know, taking control. It's kind of—exciting, in a scary, fun kind of way," she admits, her voice softly vulnerable, a secret shared just between the two of us.

I smile, my heart swelling with love and tenderness. "If that's what you want, my love, then that's what you'll get," I promise, my voice a low rumble, a preview of the growly, bossy lover she desires.

At this moment, I would give her anything, be anything she needs. Her pleasure and her happiness are my only concerns, my only goals. I chuckle, my thumb tracing her cheek, a tender caress that makes her lean into my touch.

"You like it when I'm growly, huh?" I tease, my voice a low rumble as I lean in to press a soft kiss to her lips. "I'll keep that in mind." I pull back, my eyes meeting hers, a silent promise passing between us. "I'll be growly whenever you want. Just say the word."

Her grin is shy, her eyes sparkling with excitement and trust. "I want you to be growly all the time," she admits, her cheeks flushing a delicate pink. She peeks up at me, her eyes filled with a beautiful blend of embarrassment and desire.

A surge of heat rushes through me at her words, a primal response to her honesty, her trust. I cup her cheek, my thumb brushing her jawline, a reverent touch that makes her eyes flutter closed. I lean in, pressing a fierce kiss to her lips, feeling her melt into me, her body molding to mine.

"Are you sure about this? Because that hits my buttons. It might be too intense for you if I take charge like that. It might be better to walk before we run."

She looks up at me, her eyes filled with curiosity and a hint of confusion. "What does that mean?" she asks, her voice barely a whisper.

I brush a wet strand of hair away from her face, my touch gentle, my eyes never leaving hers. "It means, are you sure you don't want to take things slow at first? To explore each other gently, softly?"

"Honestly? No." Her voice is filled with conviction, her eyes reflecting memories of our past encounters. "I'd rather start intense," she admits, her cheeks flushing slightly. She pauses, her eyes reflecting memories from our past encounters.

"I liked it when you shoved me up against the wall at work," she admits, her voice soft but sure. "And I liked how you took control in the bathroom at the restaurant and what you did in the booth. Just because I'm a virgin doesn't mean I don't know about sex or that kind of stuff. I've read all the books and I know what interests me. That kind of thing hits my buttons as well. I don't want my first time with you to be soft and gentle."

She draws in a deep breath, her eyes shining with resolve. "Being taken hostage taught me one thing: seize life with both hands. I don't want to wait. I want to experience it all right from the start."

I drink in her face, the determination etched in every line, the resolve burning in her eyes. A surge of respect and desire courses through me.

"Alright, love." My voice is low and steady, a rumble of promise and passion. "You're in for a wild ride. But remember —" I pull back slightly, my eyes locking onto hers, "—you hold the reins. One word from you, and everything stops." I lean in, pressing a fierce, passionate kiss to her lips, sealing our agreement, our promise.

"I know." Her smile is radiant, her eyes filled with trust and anticipation. "And I will."

I press a soft kiss to her forehead, a surge of protectiveness and desire washing over me. I pull her into my arms, her body molding to mine, a perfect fit. We stand there for a moment, our hearts beating in sync, a shared rhythm, a silent song.

"I love you," I murmur, my voice hoarse with emotion.

"I love you more," she whispers, her arms wrapping around me, holding me tight. We remain like that, locked in our embrace, the world around us fading away.

Eventually, I reach out, turning off the water. I grab a towel, wrapping it around her carefully. I dry her off gently, reverently, before securing another towel around my waist. We dress in silence, her slipping into fresh clothes, me into—well, my options are more limited.

Taking her hand, I lead her back to our seats, our fingers entwined.

We curl up together, her body pressed against mine, our breaths slowly returning to normal. I kiss her forehead, a sense of contentment washing over me. This is where I'm meant to be. Right here, with her.

After so much tension, the flight home feels surreal. The cabin fills with quiet conversation and occasional laughter as the adrenaline crash hits.

Across the aisle, Ally sits between Hank and Gabe. Their usual larger-than-life personalities soften as they coax her to eat something. She picks at the meal until Hank starts dramatically taste-testing everything, making her laugh despite herself.

Gabe's hand rests casually on her knee, and she leans into the touch like a flower seeking sunlight. Hank drapes an arm over her shoulder, his fingertips drawing circles on her skin. The look they exchange over her head carries volumes—possession, protection, and something deeper. Something that suggests they might have finally found what they've been searching for.

The rest of the flight passes in a blur of tender kisses and quiet, intimate moments. Our bodies remain entwined, fingers interlaced, breaths synchronizing—a silent dance of reassurance and desire. Each touch, each kiss, a testament to the reality of us, a whispered promise of more to come.

Around us, the scientists huddle together, their voices a low hum of urgency and relief. The quantum cascade obliterated their research, and yet, they seem almost giddy; their words tumbling over each other as if giving voice to their experiences somehow validates them.

"I love you," I whisper against her lips during one such moment. "God, I love you so much."

Her smile could light up the sky. "I love you more," she breathes and kisses me back.

Many hours later, as we descend, I glance across the aisle one last time. Ally is finally asleep, her head resting on Hank's shoulder, Gabe's jacket draped over her like a protective blanket. They watch over her with matching expressions of tender protectiveness.

The cabin is filled with a sense of hope. It's there in Malia's smile, in Ally's peaceful slumber, in the tight embraces of families reunited. It's a tangible force, a silent promise that life, love, and light will always find a way to pierce through the darkness.

The wheels touch down, and a wave of relief washes over me.

We're home.

Malia is safe.

And we're together.

THIRTY-FIVE

Malia

AS I STEP off the plane, the warm California sun envelops me, a welcome respite from the weeks of darkness and despair. Walt's hand wraps around mine, a reassuring grip as we make our way through the small group of scientists, their families, and the Guardian teams: Alpha, Bravo, Charlie, and Delta. The sound of muted chatter and the occasional cry of relief fills the air.

Skye Summers greets us with a warm smile. "Welcome back. We need to get you and the others processed through medical. Just a precaution, but we want to ensure everyone is healthy and safe."

I nod, still trying to process the events of the past few weeks. Walt's hand tightens around mine, a gentle reminder that I'm not alone.

As we wait in line, I catch glimpses of the other hostages, haggard but relieved. My brother, Malikai, gives me a nod of acknowledgment before turning to the medical team. I watch as they examine him, my heart still racing with anxiety.

The medical examination is quick and efficient. I'm

pronounced healthy, if a bit exhausted. Walt stays by my side, his eyes never leaving mine as we wait.

Finally, we're cleared to leave. Walt leads me away from the plane toward a sleek, black SUV parked away from the chaos. His expression softens, and he turns to me, leaning down, his voice low and gentle.

"Do you want to stay with your brother?" he asks, his eyes searching mine. "I understand if you do, but …"

His words are laced with meaning, and I can't help but think about the lingering tension between us, the desire that's been building since we first met. I know what he's offering—and I know exactly what I want.

"I want to stay with you." My voice is steady and sure.

"My place it is then." A slow smile spreads across his face, and he nods, opening the door for me.

I slide into the SUV and can't help but feel a thrill of anticipation. Tonight is the night, and I can't wait.

As we drive away from Guardian HQ, the SUV winds up a narrow road, the sound of the waves growing louder. Finally, we arrive at a cozy cottage perched over the California cliffs, the rugged beach below a stunning backdrop.

Walt opens the door, gesturing for me to enter. The interior is warm and inviting, the scent of wood and sea salt filling my senses.

I wander through the living room, taking in the eclectic decor. Walt watches me, his eyes burning with intensity.

"Want a drink?" he asks, his voice low and husky, but he doesn't wait for a response.

I shake my head, my heart racing with anticipation. We both know why we're here, and it's not for small talk or drinks.

Walt's eyes narrow, his jaw flexing as he steps closer. Tension vibrates through his body, the coiled power waiting to be unleashed. His gaze is intense and hungry, and there's no mistaking his intent. He reaches out, his fingers closing around my wrist, pulling me firmly against his chest.

His eyes narrow, his jaw flexing. "You sure about what you said on the plane? No taking things slow?"

I nod, my heart racing with anticipation. "I'm sure."

His mouth claims mine in a fierce, dominant kiss, his tongue delving deep, taking what he wants, what he's been craving. His hands grip my hips, holding me tightly against him, his body hard and insistent against mine.

He breaks the kiss, his breath coming in ragged pants, his eyes flashing with desire.

"Tonight, I make you mine," he says, his voice a low, primal growl.

I melt into him, my body responding to the growl in his voice, the power in his touch. This is what I've been craving, what I need. My legs weaken, and in an instant, I'm swept off my feet.

Walt lifts me, his strong arms cradling me securely as he strides toward the bedroom. His grip is firm, his intention clear.

I gasp softly, my arms instinctively wrapping around his neck, my body pressing against his. My heart races with anticipation, and my breath comes in quick, shallow breaths. Walt's stride is determined. His eyes never leave mine, and his gaze is filled with primal, possessive hunger.

He carries me through the doorway, his body hard against mine, sending shivers down my spine. His strength is palpable, his dominance undeniable. And I am more than ready to be claimed, to be taken, to be made his completely.

As we pass the threshold, Walt's dominance unfurls like a dark, velvet cloak. He sets me down, his hands still grasping my arms, holding me in place. His eyes burn into mine, his voice low and commanding.

"Undress for me," he orders, his words sending shivers down my spine.

I hesitate for a moment, my heart pounding in my chest.

"Now, Malia." His grip on my arms tightens, his fingers digging into my skin. I swallow hard, my hands rising to the buttons of my shirt. I undo them, one by one, my fingers trembling slightly.

Walt's gaze is intense as I reveal my skin inch by inch. His power and control envelop me like a vise. My breath hitches, and my body responds to his dominance and sheer presence. Yet, I feel safe and protected with Walt.

When I reach the last button, Walt's hands close around my wrists, pulling my arms down.

"Stop," he says, his voice rough. "I want to admire you for a moment."

I stand before him, my heart racing, as Walt's eyes roam over my body. His gaze is like a physical touch, making my skin prickle with goosebumps.

Then, without warning, Walt's mouth crashes down on mine, his kiss brutal and possessive. His hands grasp my face, holding me in place as he devours me. It's not a kiss; it's a claiming.

As we kiss, his hands roam, pulling me close, holding me tight. His fingers dig into my hips and my waist as if he can't get enough of me.

Suddenly, Walt breaks away, his chest heaving with exertion. He tears at his clothes, ripping his shirt off and revealing his chiseled chest. His hands are rough and urgent as he undoes his belt and steps out of his pants.

I watch, mesmerized, as Walt reveals himself to me. His eyes are wild, feral, as he stands before me, naked and unashamed.

For a moment, we stand there, our chests heaving, our eyes locked in a fierce, primal stare. Then, Walt's hands close around my waist, pulling me into his chest, and I know I'm in for the ride of my life.

THIRTY-SIX

Malia

WALT'S GAZE DROPS, his eyes tracing a path down my body, leaving a trail of heat in its wake. He reaches down, wrapping his large hand around his engorged length, stroking himself with a firm grip. My breath hitches, my eyes widening as I watch him pleasure himself.

"This," he growls, his voice rough and low, "is what you do to me. This is how you make me feel."

I swallow hard, my mouth going dry as I watch his hand move, his hips thrusting slightly with each stroke. He's hard and ready, his body taut with desire.

He continues to stroke himself, his breath coming in ragged gasps. Then, suddenly, he reaches out, grabbing my hand. He wraps my fingers around his shaft, his hand covering mine, guiding me.

"Like this," he rasps, his voice hoarse with need. "I want you to feel what you do to me. I want you to know how much I want you."

His hand moves mine up and down, his hips thrusting in time

with our combined grip. He's hot and hard in my hand, his skin like velvet over steel. His pulse, his desire, throbs in my palm.

Walt's breathing grows more ragged, his eyes wild with need. Suddenly, he pulls my hand away, his fingers digging into my wrist.

"Enough," he growls, his voice low and dangerous. "I want to go slow," he says, his voice softening slightly. "I want to savor every moment, but I don't know if I can."

I look up at him, my heart pounding with excitement and anticipation. "I don't want slow," I whisper, barely audible. "I just want you."

Walt's eyes flash with desire, his jaw flexing. He leans down, his mouth claiming mine. As he kisses me, his hands roam, exploring my body, his touch rough and eager.

He breaks away, his lips trailing kisses down my neck and my collarbone, his hands cupping my breasts. He squeezes gently, his thumbs brushing over my nipples, making me gasp with pleasure.

His mouth finds one peak, his tongue circling, his lips sucking, as his hand continues to tease the other. I arch into his touch, my body responding to his every caress.

Walt moves lower, his lips trailing kisses down my stomach, his hands gripping my hips. He hooks his fingers into the waistband of my pants, tugging them down, revealing my most intimate place.

He looks up at me, his eyes burning with desire. "You're so beautiful," he says, his voice low and husky. "I want to taste every inch of you."

With that, he lays me down in his bed. He forces my thighs apart and kisses along my inner thigh, making me shiver with anticipation. Then, his mouth finds my center, his tongue darting out to taste me.

I gasp, my hips bucking off the bed as Walt's mouth explores me, his tongue delving, his lips sucking. He groans, the sound vibrating through me, sending waves of pleasure coursing through my body.

His hands grip my hips, holding me in place as he devours me, his mouth and tongue working me into a frenzy. Tension builds, my body coiling tight, ready to explode.

Just as I'm about to reach the peak, Walt pulls away, his mouth trailing kisses back up my body. Suddenly, he grabs my hands, pulling them above my head. He pins them there, his grip firm and unyielding, effectively immobilizing me.

I gasp, my eyes widening as I look up at him, my body thrilling at his dominance.

"Don't move your hands," he growls, his voice low and commanding. "Keep them right there."

I nod, my heart pounding. He explores my body with deliberate, possessive touches. His lips glide down my neck, his tongue darting out to taste my skin. I squirm beneath him, needing more, needing it all.

His hands move to my breasts, cupping them, squeezing gently, his thumbs brushing over my nipples. My hands instinctively lower, my fingers threading through Walt's hair as I'm overcome with sensation.

Walt's reaction is instantaneous and shocking. He flips me onto my belly with a swift, fluid motion, his hand coming down on my ass with a sharp smack that leaves me gasping.

"What did I tell you?" he growls, his voice low and dangerous. "Keep your hands above your head."

Just as quickly, he flips me back over. His body covers mine, and his mouth claims mine in a fierce, passionate kiss. He pins my hands above my head again, his grip firm and unyielding.

His words hit all my buttons, flip all the switches in my head, nearly making me come right there. The tone in his voice, the way he didn't hesitate, how he's feeding every depraved fantasy I've ever had—it's overwhelming.

Swoon-worthy.

"I want to feel you come around me," he says, his voice low and growly. "But first, we do this right."

He reaches over to the nightstand, pulling out a condom. He rips the packet open with his teeth, his eyes never leaving mine as he rolls it on. He positions himself at my entrance, the tip of his length notched at my opening.

With that, he pushes into me, his hips moving slowly, his eyes locked on mine. I feel a sharp pain, my body tensing slightly, my nails digging into my palms as I struggle to keep my hands above my head.

Walt stills, his eyes searching mine. "Are you okay?" he asks, his voice filled with concern.

I nod, my heart pounding with emotion. "I'm okay," I whisper, my voice barely audible. "Don't stop."

Walt's eyes widen slightly, a feral gleam sparking in their depths. His lips curl into a savage smile, and his eyes flash with primal hunger. He captures my mouth in a searing, brutal kiss, and he grips my hips, his fingers digging into my flesh as he surges forward, sheathing himself fully inside me.

I gasp into his mouth, my back arching, my body stretching to accommodate his invasion.

He breaks the kiss, his breath coming in ragged pants. "You're mine now," he growls, his voice low and possessive.

With that, he moves. His hips thrust with wild, unrestrained abandon.

My hands fly to his back, my nails digging into his skin, holding on tightly as he rides me hard and wild. His mouth finds my neck, his teeth nipping, his lips sucking, marking me as his.

His hands roam my body, rough and possessive, squeezing my breasts, pinching my nipples, making me cry out with pleasure and pain. I wrap my legs around his waist, my ankles locking behind his back, meeting his thrusts with eager desperation.

Walt's body slicks with sweat, his muscles taut with exertion, his breath coming in ragged gasps. He pounds into me, his hips moving like a piston, his body claiming mine with each savage thrust.

"I want to feel you come around my cock."

Pleasure coils tight in my belly, my body trembling with the force of my impending orgasm.

"That's it, baby," Walt rasps, his voice hoarse with exertion. "Come for me. Let me feel you explode around my cock."

As if on command, my body detonates, waves of pleasure coursing through me, my inner muscles clenching around Walt's cock. He growls, his body tensing, his hips thrusting one last time before he stills, his head thrown back, his body shuddering with release.

We lie there for a long moment, our bodies entwined, our hearts pounding in sync, our breaths coming in ragged gasps. Walt's body is heavy on mine, his weight pressing me into the mattress, and I revel in the feel of him, the scent of him, the sheer masculinity of him.

Finally, he rolls to the side, pulling me into his arms. His body curls around mine. His mouth finds my neck, and his lips trail soft, gentle kisses down my skin.

"You're incredible," he whispers, his voice soft and tender. "You're everything I've ever wanted."

I snuggle into his embrace, my heart filled with contentment and love. I've found my home, my safe haven, my everything.

And I never want to let it go.

THIRTY-SEVEN

Malia

AS WE LIE THERE, our bodies entwined, our hearts beating as one, I know this is just the beginning of our journey together. I can't wait to see where it takes us.

After some time, Walt's hands begin to roam again, his lips trailing kisses down my neck and my shoulder, his desire growing, his body hardening against mine.

"Again?" I ask, my voice soft and teasing.

"Again." Walt's eyes flash with desire, his mouth curving into a wicked grin. "And again and again, until you're screaming my name, begging for mercy, and until you're mine completely and utterly."

He pins my hands above my head, his body covering mine, his mouth claiming mine in a passionate kiss. Walt suddenly sits up as our lips part, his body straddling mine. His eyes narrow, his jaw flexing as he looks down at me.

"Now, since you seem to have a problem doing as you're told, I'm going to have to tie your hands."

He reaches over to the bedside table, retrieving a length of soft rope. He takes my wrists, wrapping the rope around them and binding them tightly together before securing the rope to the headboard. My arms stretch taut above my head, and a gasp escapes my lips at the sensation of being restrained.

Walt's gaze roams over my body, his eyes burning with desire and dominance. "You're fucking gorgeous when you're tied to my bed, and you're all mine," he says, his voice low and possessive. "I'm the first and last man you're ever going to be with. You understand that?"

A moan slips from my lips, my body arching beneath him. The tight bindings around my wrists send a thrill through my every nerve ending. He leans down, his mouth capturing mine. His tongue explores, claims, and possesses. The taste of him, the hunger in his kiss, fuels my desperate need. My body aches for him, yearns for him, craves him.

He rolls on a condom, then surges forward, filling me with one powerful but controlled thrust. This time, there's no sting, just instant heat and pleasure. A cry of pleasure escapes my lips. My inner muscles clench around him, holding him tight.

Walt's body moves against mine, his hips thrusting with a rhythm that's both controlled and intense. The rope around my wrists heightens each movement, each touch, and each sensation. The sting on my ass, and the sheer primal need coursing through my veins, intensifies everything.

My body coils tight, every muscle tensing, every nerve ending alight with sensation. Walt's body tenses, his hips thrusting one last time before he stills, his head thrown back, his body shuddering with release. I follow him over the edge, my body convulsing with pleasure, my inner muscles clenching around him, claiming him as he claims me.

The rest of the day passes in a blur of passion and discovery. Walt takes me repeatedly, each time more intense and exhila-rating than the last. I find myself marveling at this side of him—

the dominant, controlling, and fierce lover who knows exactly what he wants and isn't afraid to take it.

In the dimly lit bedroom, Walt's strong hands guide me to my knees, positioning me on all fours. His fingers trace the curve of my spine, sending shivers down my back. He leans over me, his breath hot against my ear. "You love this, don't you?" he murmurs, his voice low and knowing. "Being taken."

Before I can answer, he enters me from behind, his hips slamming against mine. I gasp, my back arching, my body stretching to accommodate him. His hands grip my hips, holding me in place as he thrusts with wild, unrestrained abandon.

Later, in the shower, Walt's strength is more than enough to hold me against the wall. The hot water cascades over us, steam filling the air as he lifts me effortlessly, my legs wrapping around his waist. He presses me against the cool tiles, his body pinning mine, his mouth claiming me.

His hands grip my ass, holding me steady as he thrusts into me, his body filling mine completely. I cling to him, my nails digging into his back, my breath coming in ragged gasps. The sensation of being claimed, in this raw, primal way, sends waves of pleasure coursing through my body.

We stumble out of the shower, dripping wet, our bodies slick and flushed. Walt leads me to the kitchen, his hands roaming over my body, his touch possessive and demanding. He lifts me onto the counter, his eyes burning with desire as he steps between my thighs. Instead of taking me right then, he drops to his knees, looping my legs over his shoulders.

His mouth finds my center, his tongue darting out to taste me. I gasp, my hips bucking, my hands gripping the edge of the counter for support. Walt's mouth explores me, his tongue delving, his lips sucking, working me into a frenzy. I can feel the tension building, my body coiling tight, ready to explode.

Walt recognizes my love of being dominated, my desire to be

taken roughly. He ties my hands behind my back, the rope biting into my skin. The sensation of being restrained and at his mercy sends a rush of adrenaline through my veins.

As the day turns into night, Walt's dominance becomes a rhythm, a dance that we both fall into naturally. Each time he takes me, it's fierce, controlling, and utterly intoxicating. I find myself marveling at how his dominance makes the sex that much better, how it heightens every sensation, every touch, every feeling.

For two blissful days, we are ensconced in our private haven, the world outside forgotten. We fuck like bunnies, like newlyweds who can't get enough of each other.

And we can't.

Every touch, every kiss, every moment is filled with an insatiable hunger for each other.

Walt is a growly, dominant beast in and out of bed, taking me with a fierce passion that leaves me breathless and begging for more. He claims me in every room, against every surface, in every position imaginable. The couch, the kitchen counter, the shower, the bed—every inch of the house becomes a playground for our desires.

But in the moments between our passionate encounters, Walt is the tenderest man I've ever known. He holds me close, his arms wrapped around me, his body curled protectively around mine. He whispers sweet nothings in my ear, his voice soft and tender, his words filled with love and adoration.

He draws me a bath, the warm water soothing my sore muscles. His strong hands gently massage my shoulders, back, and thighs. He washes me tenderly, his touch gentle and caring, his eyes filled with love.

When we lie in bed, his fingers trace lazy patterns on my skin, his touch gentle and soothing. He kisses me softly, his lips lingering on mine, his eyes searching mine, filled with a love so deep that it takes my breath away.

"You're incredible," he whispers, his voice soft and tender. "You're everything I've ever wanted, everything I've ever needed. I love you so much."

I snuggle into his embrace, my heart filled with contentment and love. "I love you too," I whisper, my voice soft and emotional. You're everything to me."

But our tender moments never last long. Soon, Walt's growly dominant side reemerges, and he takes me again. He ties me to the bed, his rope biting into my skin, his body covering mine, his mouth capturing.

He fucks me with wild, unrestrained abandon, his body claiming mine, his hands exploring, caressing, claiming every inch of me. I meet his thrusts, my body pushing back against his, my breath coming in ragged gasps, my heart pounding with excitement and pleasure.

As the second day turns into night, we finally collapse onto the bed. We're both sated, exhausted, and utterly content. Walt pulls me into his arms, his body curling protectively around mine. He kisses me softly, his lips lingering on mine, his eyes filled with love.

I snuggle into his embrace, my heart filled with contentment and love. Always and forever, completely and utterly, I am his, and he is mine.

∾

NEED JUST A LITTLE MORE
of WALT and MALIA?

∾

See what Walt and Malia are up to as they make their new home in California with the rest of the Guardians! Check out the Bonus Epilogue HERE

Did you know I sell my books DIRECT?

Why PreOrder and BUY Direct?

- **Save 10% off Amazon Prices**
- **Enjoy Early Access (Read up to 2 weeks before anyone else)**
- **Keep the Book Forever: No Lending and Returning**
- MOST IMPORTANTLY…
  - **Enjoy Instant Access to Bonus Epilogues!**

WHEN YOU PURCHASE an eBook directly from my store, **all bonus epilogues are already included—no extra downloads, no sign-ups, no hassle.** You'll get the **complete story**, including those exclusive, extra-steamy endings, delivered **straight to your device.** Because you deserve the **full experience**—right from the start.

The next book in the Charlie Team series will be Gabe, Hank, and Ally's story, and…
IT'S GOING TO BE EPIC!!!
Like…you're going to HATE me, and then you're going to LOVE me!!

Click HERE to order your copy of *Rescuing Ally*

Need to catch up with the Guardians?
Need more steamy hot reads?
Check out the Guardian Hostage Rescue Specialists teams:
Alpha Team
Bravo Team
Charlie Team
Delta Team

Looking to branch out from the Guardians?

Craving more high-stakes romance and pulse-pounding thrills? Dive into the world of "The Starling," where art theft meets forbidden passion.

Experience a daring new adventure in the Guardian HRS universe. Vivianne Faulks and Paul de Gaulle's electrifying dance of deception will leave you breathless.

Don't miss this sizzling story of secrets, desire, and danger.

Grab "The Starling" now and let the games begin!

Epilogue

MALIA

The rich aroma of freshly ground coffee beans fills The Guardian Grind as I adjust the espresso machine's settings, letting the familiar routine settle my nerves. After weeks in captivity, the simple act of crafting the perfect brew feels like coming home.

"Double shot of the Charlie Challenge," Walt calls from his usual spot at the counter, a smirk playing across his lips. "Extra hot."

"You just like watching me work," I tease, but my hands are already moving through the practiced motions—dark roast, a hint of ghost pepper, sea salt to finish. Our signature drinks have become even more meaningful since Kazakhstan. Each team survived their part of the mission, and now their drinks tell stories of victory instead of just valor.

"Guilty." His eyes darken as he watches me, and heat floods my cheeks.

The Guardian Grind buzzes with life around us. All four teams—Alpha, Bravo, Charlie, and Delta—occupy various tables. Their usual post-mission energy is amplified by our narrow escape from what they're calling the Kazakhstan Incident.

Ten miles of steppes completely vaporized when the containment fields finally failed. We barely made it behind the shelter of the mountain.

"You're thinking too hard." Jenna bumps my hip as she passes with a tray of scones. Her smile is knowing—she understands better than most what it's like to be rescued by these men. To fall in love with one of them.

"Just grateful," I answer, watching Walt interact with his team. Hank and Gabe are giving him grief about something; their usual dynamic unchanged by our brush with nuclear annihilation. Seeing them all alive, whole, and home fills my chest with warmth.

Ally enters, and I catch the way her attention gravitates to where Hank and Gabe sit. Something changed during our captivity—or maybe during the rescue. She's different now, a wild light in her eyes that wasn't there before. When she catches me watching, she winks.

"Those two helped me process some—tension last night," she whispers as she passes, grabbing her apron. "They're very good at helping a girl work through trauma."

I nearly drop the portafilter I'm cleaning. "Both of them?"

Her grin is wicked. "They like sharing. After everything in Kazakhstan … Life's too short for hesitation."

The bell above the door chimes as more of the teams filter in. Carter makes a beeline for Jenna, pulling her into a kiss that has several operators whistling. His twin Blake follows with Sophia tucked under his arm.

"One Bravo Boldness and a Tech Tempest," Blake orders, sliding onto a barstool. "And whatever fancy concoction you've invented for Delta."

"The Delta Darkness," I announce, already reaching for the

bourbon-aged beans. "Smooth and sophisticated, with an unexpected kick." Just like the team that earned its name.

"You should have seen her in action," Ally tells Hank and Gabe, her voice carrying across the counter. "Malia kept everyone together."

"Our girl's got skills." Hank grins, but his eyes never leave Ally's face. Beside him, Gabe leans forward with that predatory grace they both share. The air between the three of them practically crackles with possibility.

"Speaking of skills," Forest's deep rumble cuts through the chatter as he enters with Doc Summers. "Any word from our intelligence teams about Malfor's unusual silence during this operation?"

The mood shifts slightly—this is the question we've all been avoiding. Why didn't the mastermind behind the Sentinels try to stop us? Why let us rescue valuable assets without interference?

"Nothing concrete," Mitzy calls from her corner table, surrounded by tablets and tech. "But the timing feels wrong. Malfor never stays this quiet unless he's planning something bigger."

"He could have stopped us a dozen different ways," Sam adds, accepting his Alpha Ambition with a nod of thanks. "The fact that he didn't—"

"Means we need to stay sharp," Ethan finishes, his arm draped around Rebel's shoulders. "But maybe not today. Today, we celebrate being alive."

A cheer goes up from the gathered teams. Someone starts music playing—something upbeat and modern that has several couples swaying together between tables.

I watch Walt laugh at something Rigel says, his whole face lighting up in a way that makes my heart stutter. When he catches me staring, his expression shifts to something darker and more heated. A promise for later that makes me glad I'm already leaning against the counter for support.

"Get a room," Jenna teases, but she's practically sitting in Carter's lap as she says it.

"Already did," Walt responds with a wicked grin. "Starting with the plane."

Heat floods my face even as laughter erupts around us. These people have become more than customers, more than friends. They're family—the kind that fights together, survives together, and loves together.

"Don't let them embarrass you," Ally murmurs, appearing at my elbow with empty cups to wash. "You should hear what these two suggested last night." She tilts her head toward Hank and Gabe, who respond with identical wolfish grins.

"Do tell," Sophia chimes in, leaning across the counter with interest.

"A lady never kisses and tells," Ally responds primly, then ruins it with a wicked smirk. "But let's just say quantum physics isn't the only thing I'm studying in depth these days."

More laughter ripples through our corner of the shop. The sound feels like healing—washing away the sterile silence of our captivity, the terror of watching containment fields fail, and the desperate race to escape the facility before everything went critical.

"Your brother would have a stroke," Walt comments, sliding behind the counter to pull me against his chest. His warmth surrounds me, grounding me in the present.

"Kai's too busy revolutionizing fusion theory to worry about my love life," I reply, relaxing into his embrace. "Besides, after everything that happened, he owes me some happiness."

The memory of those final moments in Kazakhstan flashes through my mind—the facility alarms blaring as Mitzy triggered the evacuation systems remotely, guards rushing us through corridors as power fluctuations made the lights strobe.

"Hey." Walt's voice is soft in my ear. "You're thinking too hard again."

"Just grateful," I whisper back, turning to face him. "For you. For them. For being alive."

His gentle kiss carries undercurrents of the passion we've discovered together. When he pulls back, his eyes hold promises that weaken my knees.

"Get back to work, lovebirds!" Hank calls out. "Some of us are dying of thirst over here."

"You seemed pretty well-hydrated last night," Ally quips, and both men choke on their drinks.

I return to crafting drinks, letting the familiar rhythm soothe my racing thoughts. Each signature blend represents the team it's named after and the bonds between us all. The Alpha Ambition with its pure adrenaline kick. The Bravo Boldness aged in bourbon barrels, bold and uncompromising. The Charlie Challenge for Walt, Hank, Gabe, Blake, and Rigel—dark and dangerous with that ghost pepper kick. The Delta Dawn for their shadow operations.

"You've got that look," Jenna observes, restocking pastries beside me. "The one that means you're planning something."

"Maybe," I admit. "I've been thinking about new blends. Something that captures what we all went through. What we survived."

"The Kazakhstan Knockout?" Carter suggests with a grin.

"The Quantum Quencher," Blake adds.

"The Fusion Fireball," Rigel calls from his table with Mia.

"The Sentinel Silence," Forest rumbles, and the playful mood shifts slightly.

"Speaking of," Sam says from his position near the window,

"we need to talk about Malfor's unusual absence during this operation."

"He had to know we were coming," Ethan adds, leaning forward. "The moment we deployed teams to Kazakhstan. But no interference, no countermoves?"

"It's not like him," Forest agrees, his ice-blue eyes scanning the room. "Malfor never passes up a chance to demonstrate his reach."

Walt tenses behind me, his arms tightening protectively. "Unless this was exactly what he wanted," he growls. "Get us focused on Kazakhstan while he moves pieces somewhere else."

"The Third Sentinel's quantum research facility is completely destroyed," Mitzy points out, her fingers flying over her tablet. "Ten-mile radius of complete devastation. That had to hurt their operation."

"Unless they got what they needed first," Ally speaks up, her voice carrying an edge of expertise. "The containment field calculations, the quantum tunneling breakthrough—all that data could have been transmitted before the facility went critical."

Hank and Gabe shift closer to her unconsciously, their protective instincts obvious to anyone watching. She leans into their space like she belongs there, drawing strength from their presence.

"Guardian Grind was compromised once," I remind them, thinking of Sophia's ordeal. "Malfor had eyes and ears right here on HQ grounds."

"And now we're what—waiting for his next move?" Jenna asks, her hand finding Carter's.

"No." Sam's voice carries quiet authority. "Now we get ahead of him. Mitzy's team is analyzing every scrap of data we recovered. The quantum research, the facility specs, everything. We find his pattern, we find him."

"In the meantime," Walt says, pressing a kiss to my temple,

"we celebrate being alive. Being home." His voice drops lower, meant just for me. "Being together."

The tension breaks again as conversations shift to lighter topics. Ally tells a story about quantum physics that has Hank and Gabe hanging on her every word, their usual swagger replaced by genuine fascination. Blake pulls Sophia onto a makeshift dance floor while Carter spins Jenna past them, both couples lost in their own worlds.

"One more round," I announce, already reaching for fresh beans. "On the house."

"Make mine a double," Ethan calls, earning a laugh from Rebel.

I move through the familiar motions of crafting each team's signature drink, adding personal touches—extra ghost pepper in Walt's Charlie Challenge, a twist of citrus in Ally's Tech Tempest. The routine grounds me, reminding me that this is real. We survived. We're home.

"So," Ally sidles up beside me while I steam milk for another round of lattes, "are we going to talk about how Walt looks at you now?" Her eyes sparkle with mischief. "That whole *'I've thoroughly claimed my woman'* vibe he's radiating?"

Heat floods my cheeks even as a smile tugs at my lips. "Like you're one to talk. I saw how you left with Hank and Gabe last night."

"Best decision I've ever made." She grins, but there's something deeper in her expression. "After Kazakhstan; after feeling so helpless … Being with them makes me feel powerful again. In control."

I understand completely. Every touch from Walt since the plane feels like reclaiming something that was taken from us. Each kiss erases another memory of fear and replaces it with heat and hope.

"Plus," Ally adds wickedly, "they're very—creative. Did you know they have this thing they do where—"

"TMI!" I laugh, bumping her with my hip. "Some things should stay private."

"Speaking of private," Walt's voice rumbles behind me, making me jump. "I remember something about properly christening your office once we got home."

"Subtle," Ethan calls from nearby. "Real subtle, brother."

The teams laugh, but there's warmth in it rather than mockery. They understand—we all do—how precious these moments are. How easily they can be snatched away.

"The search parameters you requested are complete," Mitzy announces suddenly, her voice cutting through the chatter. "Cross-referencing quantum research facilities with power consumption patterns similar to Kazakhstan."

Sam moves to her table, Forest and Doc Summers following. The easy mood shifts slightly as they examine her findings, heads bent together in discussion.

"Should we be worried?" I ask Walt softly.

"Not today." He pulls me closer, his chest solid against my back. "Today we celebrate. Tomorrow, we hunt."

"Here's to that," Hank raises his mug.

"To surviving another clusterfuck." Gabe echoes the gesture while Ally watches them both with hungry eyes.

"To family," Carter adds, his arm around Jenna.

"To love." Blake raises his cup, smiling at Sophia.

"To coming home," Walt murmurs against my ear.

The Guardian Grind fills with voices and laughter, coffee and connection. Outside these walls, Malfor plots his next move.

The afternoon sun slants through The Guardian Grind's windows, turning everything golden. Hank tells some outrageous story about a past mission while Gabe adds color and commentary, both preening when Ally laughs.

"I need to head back to the lab soon," she says reluctantly, gathering her things. "My quantum calculations won't solve themselves."

"Need an escort?" Hank offers immediately.

"Or two?" Gabe adds with a wolfish grin.

She pretends to consider it, though I can see the decision's already made in her eyes. "Well, if you insist. For security purposes, of course."

"Of course," they echo in perfect sync, already rising to follow her out.

I catch Jenna's knowing look as she watches them leave. "Never thought I'd see the day those two settled down."

"Who says we're settling?" Ally calls back with a wink before the door closes behind them.

Walt's hands settle on my hips, turning me to face him. "Speaking of settling ..." His voice drops lower, private despite our audience. "I seem to remember something about making up for lost time."

"You two are impossible." Rigel groans, but he's smiling as Mia curls into his side.

The teams begin dispersing—some to training, others to tactical meetings to dissect the Kazakhstan mission and plan for whatever comes next.

Sam heads to his office with Forest and Doc Summers, already discussing Mitzy's findings. The hunt for Malfor continues, but that's tomorrow's battle.

"Go," Jenna nudges me toward the back office, "I've got this covered."

I should protest—I'm technically on shift for another hour, but Walt's eyes hold promises that make my pulse race.

"Ready to go home?" he asks, though we both know he doesn't mean my apartment.

I reach up to trace the scar on his chest where the bullet

nearly took him from me. His hand covers mine, pressing it flat against his heartbeat.

"I am home," I tell him, and pull him down for a kiss that tastes like coffee, redemption, and the promise of forever.

The kiss deepens until someone—probably Blake—whistles appreciatively. Walt pulls back just enough to rest his forehead against mine, his breath warm against my lips.

"My place will be quiet."

The promise in his voice makes heat pool low in my belly.

As we head for the door, I catch one last glimpse of our family—Jenna expertly crafting drinks while Carter watches her with pure adoration. Blake and Sophia swaying together by the window. Rigel and Mia's heads are bent over some technical discussion with Mitzy. Through the window, I spot Ally walking between Hank and Gabe, her laughter carrying across the courtyard.

Tonight belongs to us—to stolen kisses and whispered promises, to hands that map scars and hearts that beat in sync. To the kind of love worth fighting for, worth dying for, and worth living for.

Walt's fingers lace with mine as we step into the golden afternoon light.

Behind us, The Guardian Grind hums with life and laughter, coffee and connection, hope and healing. And as Walt and I step outside, I realize—home isn't a place; it's the hand you hold through the darkness—and the love that always pulls you back into the light.

The next book in the Charlie Team series will be Gabe, Hank, and Ally's story, and…
IT'S GOING TO BE EPIC!!!

Click HERE to order your copy of Rescuing Ally DIRECT from Ellie Masters' store.

Click HERE to order your copy of Rescuing Ally FROM AMAZON.
(Rescuing Ally will be available to read for FREE in KindleUnlimited TWO WEEKS after released on Ellie Masters' Store.)

When You PreOrder and BUY Direct You can…

- **Save 10% off Amazon Prices**
- **Enjoy Early Access**
  - **(Read up to 2 weeks before anyone else)**
- **Keep the Book Forever: No Lending and Returning**
- MOST IMPORTANTLY…
  - **Enjoy Instant Access to Bonus Epilogues!**

When you purchase an eBook directly from my store, **all bonus epilogues are already included—no extra downloads, no sign-ups, no hassle.** You'll get the **complete story**, including those exclusive, extra-steamy endings, delivered **straight to your device.** Because you deserve the **full experience**—right from the start.

Grab the First Book in The Guardian Hostage Rescue Specialists Series for Free

https://elliemasters.com/RescuingMelissa

Please consider leaving a review

I HOPE you enjoyed this book as much as I enjoyed writing it. If you like this book, please leave a review. I love reviews. I love reading your reviews, and they help other readers decide if this book is worth their time and money. I hope you think it is and decide to share this story with others. A sentence is all it takes. Thank you in advance!

ELLZ BELLZ

ELLIE'S FACEBOOK READER GROUP

If you are interested in joining the ELLZ BELLZ, Ellie's Facebook reader group, we'd love to have you.

Join Ellie's ELLZ BELLZ.
The ELLZ BELLZ Facebook Reader Group

Sign up for Ellie's Newsletter.
Elliemasters.com/newslettersignup

CONTINUE HERE...

Military Romance

Guardian Hostage Rescue Specialists

Rescuing Melissa

(Get a FREE copy of Rescuing Melissa

when you join Ellie's Newsletter)

Alpha Team

Rescuing Zoe

Rescuing Moira

Rescuing Eve

Rescuing Lily

Rescuing Jinx

Rescuing Maria

Bravo Team

Rescuing Angie

Rescuing Isabelle

Rescuing Carmen

Rescuing Rosalie

Rescuing Kaye

Cara's Protector

Rescuing Barbi

Charlie Team

Rescuing Rebel

Rescuing Stitch

Rescuing Mia

Jenna's Protector

Rescuing Sophia

Rescuing Malia

Rescuing Ally

Delta Team (Coming Soon)

Rescuing Ember

Rescuing Aria

STANDALONES IN THE GUARDIAN HOSTAGE RESCUE SERIES YOU CAN READ ANYTIME

Military Romance

Guardian Personal Protection Specialists

Sybil's Protector

Lyra's Protector

The One I Want Series

(Small Town, Military Heroes)

By Jet & Ellie Masters

EACH BOOK IN THIS SERIES CAN BE READ AS A STANDALONE AND IS ABOUT A DIFFERENT COUPLE WITH AN HEA.

Saving Abby

Saving Ariel

Saving Brie

Saving Cate

Saving Dani

Saving Jen

The LaRouge Triplets

Asher

Brody

Cage

Billionaire Romance

Billionaire Boys Club

Hawke

Richard

Contemporary Romance

Cocky Captain

Romantic Suspense

EACH BOOK IS A STANDALONE NOVEL.

The Starling

The Swan

~AND~

Science Fiction

Ellie Masters writing as L.A. Warren

Vendel Rising: a Science Fiction Serialized Novel

If you enjoyed this book by Ellie Masters, the LIGHTER SIDE of the Jet & Ellie writing duo, and aren't afraid of edgier writing, you might enjoy reading BDSM themed books written by Jet, the DARKER SIDE of the Masters' Writing Team.

The DARKER SIDE

Jet Masters is the darker side of the Jet & Ellie writing duo!

Romantic Suspense

Changing Roles Series:

THIS SERIES MUST BE READ IN ORDER.

Command Me

Control Me

Collar Me

Embracing FATE

Seizing FATE

Accepting FATE

HOT READS

A STANDALONE NOVEL.

Down the Rabbit Hole

Light BDSM Romance

The Ties that Bind

EACH BOOK IN THIS SERIES CAN BE READ AS A STANDALONE AND IS ABOUT A DIFFERENT COUPLE WITH AN HEA.

Alexa

Penny

Michelle

Ivy

HOT READS

Becoming His Series

THIS SERIES MUST BE READ IN ORDER.

The Ballet

Learning to Breathe

Becoming His

Dark Captive Romance

A standalone novel.

She's MINE

Books by Jet Masters

If you enjoyed this book by Ellie Masters, the LIGHTER SIDE of the Jet & Ellie writing duo, and aren't afraid of edgier writing, you might enjoy reading BDSM themed books written by Jet, the DARKER SIDE of the Masters' Writing Team.

The DARKER SIDE
Jet Masters is the darker side of the Jet & Ellie writing duo!

Romantic Suspense
Changing Roles Series:
THIS SERIES MUST BE READ IN ORDER.
Command Me
Control Me
Collar Me
Embracing FATE
Seizing FATE
Accepting FATE

HOT READS

A STANDALONE NOVEL.
Down the Rabbit Hole

Light BDSM Romance
The Ties that Bind

EACH BOOK IN THIS SERIES CAN BE READ AS A STANDALONE AND IS ABOUT A DIFFERENT COUPLE WITH AN HEA.

Alexa

Penny

Michelle

Ivy

HOT READS
Becoming His Series

THIS SERIES MUST BE READ IN ORDER.

The Ballet

Learning to Breathe

Becoming His

Dark Captive Romance

A STANDALONE NOVEL.

She's MINE

About the Author

Ellie Masters is a USA Today Bestselling author and Amazon Top 15 Author who writes Angsty, Steamy, Heart-Stopping, Pulse-Pounding, Can't-Stop-Reading Romantic Suspense. In addition, she's a wife, military mom, doctor, and retired Colonel. She writes romantic suspense filled with all your sexy, swoon-worthy alpha men. Her writing will tug at your heartstrings and leave your heart racing.

Born in the South, raised under the Hawaiian sun, Ellie has traveled the globe while in service to her country. The love of her life, her amazing husband, is her number one fan and biggest supporter. And yes! He's read every word she's written.

She has lived all over the United States—east, west, north, south and central—but grew up under the Hawaiian sun. She's also been privileged to have lived overseas, experiencing other cultures and making lifelong friends. Now, Ellie is proud to call herself a Southern transplant, learning to say y'all and "bless her heart" with the best of them.

Ellie's favorite way to spend an evening is curled up on a couch, laptop in place, watching a fire, drinking a good wine, and bringing forth all the characters from her mind to the page and hopefully into the hearts of her readers.

FOR MORE INFORMATION
elliemasters.com

facebook.com/elliemastersromance
x.com/Ellie__Masters
instagram.com/ellie_masters
bookbub.com/authors/ellie-masters
goodreads.com/Ellie_Masters

Connect with Ellie Masters

Website:
elliemasters.com
Purchase Direct:
elliemasters.com/shopify
Amazon Author Page:
elliemasters.com/amazon
Facebook:
elliemasters.com/Facebook
Goodreads:
elliemasters.com/Goodreads
Bookbub:
elliemasters.com/Bookbub
Instagram:
elliemasters.com/Instagram

Final Thoughts

I hope you enjoyed this book as much as I enjoyed writing it. If you enjoyed reading this story, please consider leaving a review on Amazon and Goodreads, and please let other people know. A sentence is all it takes. Friend recommendations are the strongest catalyst for readers' purchase decisions! And I'd love to be able to continue bringing the characters and stories from My-Mind-to-the-Page.

Second, call or e-mail a friend and tell them about this book. If you really want them to read it, gift it to them. If you prefer digital friends, please use the "Recommend" feature of Goodreads to spread the word.

Or visit my blog https://elliemasters.com, where you can find out more about my writing process and personal life.

Come visit The EDGE: Dark Discussions where we'll have a chance to talk about my works, their creation, and maybe what the future has in store for my writing.

Facebook Reader Group: Ellz Bellz

Thank you so much for your support!

Love,
Ellie

Dedication

This book is dedicated to you, my reader. Thank you for spending a few hours of your time with me. I wouldn't be able to write without you to cheer me on. Your wonderful words, your support, and your willingness to join me on this journey is a gift beyond measure.

Whether this is the first book of mine you've read, or if you've been with me since the very beginning, thank you for believing in me as I bring these characters 'from my mind to the page and into your hearts.'

Love,
Ellie

THE END